ONCE UPON A SONG

ONCE UPON A SONG

NADINE BELLS

Once Upon A Song
by Nadine Bells
Published by Quill & Crow Publishing House

This book is a work of fiction. All incidents, dialogue, and characters, except for some well-known historical and public figures, are either products of the author's imagination or used in a fictitious manner. Any resemblance to actual persons, living or dead, or actual events is purely coincidental.

Cover Design by Fay Lane

Edited by Tiffany Putenis, Lisa Morris

Printed in the United States of America

ISBN: 978-1-967911-10-3

ISBN: 978-1-967911-09-7 (ebook)

Publisher's Website: www.quillandcrowpublishinghouse.com

Für meine Oma Anni

For my grandma Anni

THE CASTLE IN THE SNOW

Ana's fairytale ended before it began, on the empty road to an address that didn't exist. She took a deep drag from her cigarette and exhaled the smoke into the air, gray as the fog that lay ahead. The taxi idled next to her, the sputtering and coughing of its motor the only sounds disturbing the quiet forest.

The driver leaned out of the window and shuddered as the cold wind hit his face. "If it doesn't start, it doesn't start."

"I have somewhere to be," Ana said, her hopes melting away like the snowflakes landing on the windshield.

"You don't say. Listen, I tried calling roadside assistance, but there's no phone service here. We have to wait until the next car comes along."

Ana shook her head. "If we wait for another car, we might be on this damn road all day. I'm already late."

"Well, you have a good excuse."

"I'd much rather be on time than have a good excuse." Ana flicked her cigarette to the ground and stomped it out with the tip of her boot. "Forget it. I'll walk."

The driver's bushy eyebrows snapped together. "In this weather? You don't even know where it is."

"I know where it is. I have the directions. It shouldn't be much farther."

What did it matter that no one she asked had ever heard of the place or its address? She had traveled all this way; she would overcome this last hurdle.

He snorted. "Look around. There's nothing here for miles. You'll get yourself killed."

"I'll take my chances."

The driver looked as though he wanted to say more, but he just shrugged.

Ana shoved her stiff fingers into her coat pockets. "Good luck with the car," she said as she started to walk.

"Good luck with the audition," the driver called after her. She glanced back at him, but by then the fog had swallowed the cab altogether.

Snow drifted through the air as Ana trudged between the frosted road and the tall pines. The ground beneath the newly fallen snow was muddy and slippery, so she had to tread with care. She cursed the winter and her luck.

Perhaps she ought to give up and turn back. From the job advertisement, Ana knew it was not the sort of place women like her tended to work. In the few pictures she'd found, the hotel looked like a castle from a storybook where tales of glamor and magic unfolded. She had more experience with shabby motels that offered bitter coffee and stained sheets and anonymity. There was a part of her that dreamed of a Cinderella story, but she had no fairy godmother, no glass slippers, and only a broken-down taxi for a pumpkin carriage. Still, she clung to the hope that one day her chance would come, that she wouldn't spend the rest of her life in a greasy diner serving greasy customers.

Dark clouds crowded the sky, and Ana pulled her coat tighter as the wind picked up. Something rustled in the forest. She whipped around, but she couldn't see further than an arm's length through the thick fog. She stood still and listened for another noise, but none came. Her mind was playing tricks on her, prompted by the cab driver's warning.

Ana sped up, although there was no sign that anything other than concrete and trees lay ahead. The temptation to head back to the taxi gnawed at her. Then something broke through the wall of fog. Another path diverged from the winding road, snaking deep into the forest. Ana sucked in a sharp breath; as the crisp air filled her lungs, hope flowed back into her body. Without another thought of the driver's words, she left the main road and hurried along the narrow street.

Branches, bare and thin like the fingers of a skeleton, hung in her way. One of them scratched her cheek. Ana flinched but persisted, focusing on what awaited her at the end of the road.

All at once, the fog lifted. Despite the icy gusts of wind biting into her skin, Ana stood motionless as shivers crawled up her spine. Like a palace of ice and snow, the Hôtel de Neige rose in the distance, nestled amongst the snow-capped pines. The grand building's vast shadow spread before it, the majestic hotel blocking the few rays of sun that dared to poke through the late November sky.

The hotel seemed to belong to a different time altogether. High towers and battlements, like those of a medieval fortress, reached up to the cloud-darkened sky. The stones making up its walls were of the purest white, sparkling as though polished to match the color of fresh, unblemished snow.

Ana felt her heartbeat in her throat. She approached the massive doors, and they swung open for her, drawn by two porters. They faced straight ahead like statues, but she could feel their eyes following her. Did they think her an intruder, some beggar planning to impose on their illustrious guests?

The lobby of the Hôtel de Neige glittered with delicate snow crystals decorating every surface. A grand silver chandelier hung from the high ceiling, and rugs of white and pale blue spread across the stone floor. Lush sofas and velvety armchairs, accompanied by crystal tables, adorned the grand hall. A wide staircase unfurled at the far end of the lobby, leading to a gallery lined with an ornate balustrade.

A black grandfather clock towered over the reception desk, reminding Ana how late she was. A lean man with deep creases on his forehead and between his low brows stood beside the desk, his dark eyes fixated on her. She pulled her attention from the wonders surrounding her and made her way towards him.

"Welcome to the Hôtel de Neige," he said in a posh British accent. "How may we help you today?"

"I'm here for the auditions. For the new singer," Ana responded, resisting the urge to fidget with her clothes.

"The auditions began almost an hour ago." He pointed to the clock.

"I know, I'm very sorry. The weather and then my cab—"

The concierge held up a hand to stop her. "The weather is always terrible and never an excuse."

Ana gritted her teeth but clung to a polite tone and a cordial smile. "As I was about to say, my cab broke down. I had to walk the rest of the way. And, might I add, this place is not easy to find."

The receptionist's gaze wandered up and down her body, causing Ana to cringe. "The Hôtel de Neige," he said, "looks for certain qualities in its employees. Tardiness is not one of them."

Ana sensed that he faulted her for more than the late arrival. "Please, just tell me where the auditions are taking place. I came all the way from New York City."

"That is unfortunate. The Hôtel de Neige wishes you better luck in the future."

Heat twitched through her. "Are you serious?"

"I am afraid so. Goodbye, miss."

By the time he finished his infuriating farewell, Ana was halfway to the doors, trying to restrain the tears of anger and shame while scrambling for her phone. It seemed the day was not yet done mistreating her, as the purse slipped from her grasp and dropped to the floor, spilling its contents onto the cold stone.

"Fuck."

In her peripheral vision, Ana saw the man behind the reception desk watching her with oozing condescension. Her chest tightened.

She yearned to storm out of the hotel, but had no choice but to drop to her knees and scoop up her belongings.

"May I help you?"

Ana's gaze fluttered upward to the man towering over her. He was clad in all black, though the light coming in through one of the stained glass windows bathed him in shades of emerald and sapphire. Before Ana could decline his offer, the stranger squatted down beside her and began gathering her belongings.

"I don't need help, thank you."

"I am sure you don't. Still, I am a gentleman who enjoys playing the knight in shining armor." His words were laced with a faint trace of a Russian accent. He handed Ana the last item, a box of tampons.

She grabbed it, her cheeks heating from embarrassment, and shoved it in her purse.

They got back to their feet, and Ana surveyed the man who had come to her aid. He looked to be in his late twenties and stood a few inches taller than her. Given her height, this was not a feat many accomplished. A perfectly tailored suit hugged his body. One stray strand of dark hair hung between his deep blue eyes, and a lazy smile curled the corners of his lips. Ana knew she should thank him, but she'd had it with the hotel and the embarrassment. Before she could turn away and escape, he extended his hand towards her.

"Pleased to meet you," he said. "I'm Dimitri Morozov."

Ana didn't take his hand.

"And your name is?"

"Listen, I don't mean to be rude, but I would like to leave now," she said.

"You are here for the auditions, aren't you?" Dimitri asked, and Ana stilled.

"Yes, I am. Though I believe I missed my chance."

"That is unfortunate," he said, echoing the receptionist's words with a cheeky smile.

"Thank you for reminding me, Mr. Morozov."

"Please, call me Dimitri."

Ana could tell he thought himself utterly charming.

"So," he continued, "why would a girl from New York City want to work at a hotel in the middle of nowhere?"

So he had eavesdropped on the entirety of her humiliating conversation with the concierge. "Well, I'm broke, and I heard this place pays well."

"It certainly does."

Ana cocked her head to the side. "Are you a guest here?"

When he shook his head, she perked up. "You don't happen to know where the auditions take place?"

His smile grew. "I know about everything that goes on in the Hôtel de Neige."

"Tell me."

Dimitri laughed. "And if I tell you, how do you plan to get past our guard dog?" He nodded towards the concierge, who watched them like a hawk, ready to strike. Ana wouldn't be surprised if he were prepared to call security if she stayed much longer.

"I guess you will need to distract him," Ana said. She had nothing to lose, other than her mangled dignity.

The glint in Dimitri's eyes reassured her. She knew this type of man—enough confidence to believe himself irresistible and enough boredom to use that confidence unwisely.

"What do I get out of it?" he asked.

"You get to play the knight in shining armor."

Dimitri pulled a small, golden box from his pocket and extracted a slim cigarette which he placed in the corner of his mouth. "Walk down the hallway to the right of the reception desk," he said as he produced a lighter from his pocket. "When you reach the glass statue, turn right, then straight ahead until you come to the black door on your right. That will be it."

While Ana scrambled to memorize the directions, Dimitri lit the cigarette. "One more thing," he said. "You still haven't told me your name."

Nor did she want to, but she supposed it was only fair. "Ana. Angelica Greene." In the corner of her eye, she saw the concierge coming their way.

"Greene," Dimitri echoed. "Like your eyes."

Just like my eyes. The social workers had named her for them when they had failed to discover her true last name.

The concierge approached them, flustered. "Mr. Morozov," he exclaimed.

The amusement of mischief glinted in Dimitri's eyes. "Yes, Charles? How may I help you?"

"The cigarette, Mr. Morozov."

"Would you like one?"

The concierge's reddening visage told Ana it was time to go. "Goodbye, Mr. Morozov," she said and backed away.

"Oh, we're not allowed to smoke here?" She heard Dimitri say behind her. "But I do it all the time."

"Mr. Morozov, smoking inside will—"

Ana spun around on her heels and rushed down the hallway as Dimitri had instructed. Once she was safely out of their sight, a feeling of victory filled her. She had found the hotel and would make it to the auditions after all. But the hardest part still lay ahead, so she denied herself the full feeling of triumph. With quick steps, she made her way down the long corridor, wishing she could stop and marvel at its beauty—the pointed windows, oil paintings, and marble sculptures.

Ana halted when she came upon the glass statue Dimitri had mentioned. With its bluish hues, it looked like ice rather than glass. The statue stood before her, depicting a man who gazed into the distance with longing in his lifelike eyes; he seemed so familiar that she felt a momentary ache in her chest. She squinted, sure she had seen him before, perhaps in the colorful strokes of a painting or as a stranger glimpsed in passing.

Ana scurried on until she arrived at the large door, its raven color breaking through the shades of white and blue. She took a deep breath to steady herself, then pushed open the heavy door.

She stepped backstage, the area decked with mirrors, technology, and a wide array of props. Painted canvases depicting wintery scenes and mannequins draped in extravagant, glittering costumes caught

Ana's attention as she approached the chairs freckling the hall, occupied by more than a dozen men and women. The auditions were still ongoing, and quiet singing could be heard in the distance. She slipped into the closest unoccupied chair, exhausted even though she had yet to audition. She despised waiting. It brought out all the ugly doubts she tried so hard to suppress.

A few minutes later, a bald man in a brown suit exited from stage right. "Next," he called.

PHANTOM IN WHITE

$\mathcal{A}$na looked at the other applicants, but nobody moved. Her chest tightened as she realized she was the only one left to audition. If not for the people surrounding her, she might have jumped up and fled. But with them around, she couldn't run off, and after all the trouble, she owed it to herself to take the chance.

Ana got to her feet and wriggled out of her jacket, dropping it and her purse on the chair. Straightening her burgundy dress, she approached the stage. She ran her fingers through her wild blonde curls, hoping to fix what snow and stress had likely ruined beyond repair.

The spotlight momentarily disoriented her as she walked toward the microphone. She blinked until her eyes adjusted. Beyond the stage, a grand hall filled with round tables and countless chairs spread before her, with fanciful box seats in a ring around the top of the massive theater.

Ana could only guess how many spectators the theater held during a performance—likely hundreds. Just five people occupied the vast room for the auditions. She stood alone on the stage while four judges sat at the foremost table, two men and two women, their full attention on Ana. She swallowed down the rising wave of fear and grasped the old-fashioned microphone in the spotlight.

"What's your name?" one of the men asked. He was not much older than Ana herself, perhaps twenty-five years old. He wore an elegant navy-colored suit, which flattered his dark complexion and granted him an air of distinction.

"Angelica Greene," she responded after clearing her throat.

"A pleasure to have you, Ms. Greene. I'm Everett Shaw." He smiled as he spoke, as though hoping to relieve her nervousness.

"Let's start, shall we?"

The voice came from the woman seated in the midst of the panel. She leaned back in her chair, an idle kind of readiness in her composure. Thick, shining waves of chestnut colored hair framed her face, reaching down to her narrow hips. Pale fingers with neatly manicured nails tapped on the surface of the polished wooden table before them.

"Sing, please," she said, her voice musical in its own way.

Ana's hands shook around the microphone as she studied her audience, their focused expressions like stone. She dared not meet their eyes.

In the foremost of the high boxes, something shifted, grabbing Ana's gaze. For a moment, she suspected the concierge was there to expel her, or Dimitri Morozov had arrived to watch the fruits of his labor. She caught a glimpse of a silhouette, clad in white, bright and pure like a blanket of fresh snow in sunlight. Her grip tightened on the microphone. She could not see the figure's veiled face, but she sensed it watching her, honed in with more intensity than the panel of judges. A gust of cold swept through her, like sharp icicles beneath her skin. She repressed a gasp at the sudden sensation.

She tore one of her trembling hands from the microphone to place it on her chest in some hope of steadying herself. Her anxiety was playing some cruel trick on her.

"Is something the matter?" the woman from the committee asked in clipped tones.

"No, no, I'm sorry," Ana responded, trying to keep her teeth from chattering. She wished she had not left her coat behind. When she looked up to the boxes again, she spotted one more glimpse of the ghastly appearance before it vanished, swallowed up by the darkness like it was never there at all.

Ana rubbed her chest, feeling the rapid thumping of her heart. *Be still,* she commanded it. *It was nothing, just nervousness.* She closed her eyes and sang.

The world inside of her grew calm. Chaotic noise transformed into a sweet melody as she let herself get lost in the delicate notes. Singing was what brought her back to the home she'd never had, the one she imagined in her music.

The song began as a gentle tune. It was fuzzy blankets, a crackling fireplace, the soft footfalls of running children. Outside the make-believe home, snowflakes glided towards the ground, but inside it was warm and smelled of freshly baked Christmas cookies, of chocolate and cinnamon and nutmeg.

When the melody grew deeper, the scenery in her imagination changed. She found herself standing on a grand stage before a crowd of smiling faces, draped in a flowing dress of emerald green. Her voice filled the hall, rising and falling like the waves in the ocean, yet still echoing the touch of fresh snow and the pleasure of chocolate melting on one's tongue. It wrapped a warm hug around Ana in the midst of the cold night. Nothing bad could happen to her as long as she sang. Her wounds mended beneath the touch of the notes, and old scars faded away.

"Alright."

Ana's eyes flew open, meeting those of the woman who interrupted her. She watched Ana with a grave expression. In the background, the music continued, leaving Ana behind.

"Is there a problem?" Ana asked. "The song isn't over."

"I think we've heard enough," the woman said. "Please call in the next person."

Ana stared at her. None of the others chimed in, simply exchanging glances unreadable to Ana.

"I think I was the last one," Ana said.

"We will make our decision and announce it shortly," the man in the navy suit said, gesturing to the exit.

Ana stood rooted in place in the spotlight, which was no longer meant for her. She had to pull herself away from the microphone. To her, it was an act of great determination. To the panel of judges, it was a nod and some rapid steps, leaving the stage.

When Ana reappeared backstage among her competition, some heads turned her way, though most remained occupied with themselves. Ana melted into her chair. It stung that they disrupted her performance so soon. She wanted to bury her head in a pillow and scream, overcome by the desire to be back in her dingy room in New York City.

Time dragged by. Ana examined her competition. Most were older than her and more in accordance with the Hôtel de Neige's character. They wore suits and heels and blazers. In their hands, they held resumes and portfolios, although the job advertisement had asked for neither.

Noises surrounded her—long sighs, the clicking of heels, the faint melody of someone playing a game on their phone. With every minute, the volume and weight of it all seemed to grow. She could no longer hear her own thoughts.

"I need to go to the bathroom," she said, more to herself rather than anyone around her. She scrambled out into the corridor, setting out to find the closest bathroom, where she promptly locked herself in one of the stalls. At last, there was silence.

Ana leaned against the side of the stall. She thought about smoking a cigarette, but she had gotten herself in enough trouble for the day. Plus, she really needed to quit for good this time. She resorted to long, slow breaths in hopes of calming herself, then closed her eyes and began to hum. She still had her voice. It might be unwanted, but it was hers.

The lights above her flickered, grabbing her attention. She heard the door to the bathroom open, followed by low footfalls and soft rustling sounds. Ana raised her brows. The bathroom had no windows, but it felt as though a cold breeze swept through the room. She hugged herself and felt the goosebumps on her arms.

The unsteady lights blinked out entirely, and Ana stiffened. "Hello? Did you just turn the lights off?"

She had to bite her lip to keep it from quivering, though she blamed her sudden shudders on the cold rather than the blackout. The other woman in the bathroom was utterly quiet. Was she still there at all?

Ana squatted down to get a glimpse beneath the stall's door. In the darkness, it was nearly impossible to distinguish anything. She squinted until her eyes adjusted. A few feet away, by the sinks, the hem of a long, white skirt touched upon the ground. As the fabric swayed, it glittered like fresh snow. *A bride, perhaps,* Ana thought. The Hôtel de Neige certainly made for an enchanting wedding venue. She chided herself for prying and was about to straighten when she saw the skirts sway. The figure turned, coming toward her stall.

Ana stumbled backward. Her fingers dug into the flesh of her arms as she shivered, staring at the closed door before her. All grew quiet—so quiet that Ana feared her heartbeat was audible.

Sound broke through like claws scratching against a chalkboard. Ana pressed a hand over her mouth to suppress a gasp. She saw a sliver of the white skirt on the floor, inches away from her feet. The other woman stood right outside, running her sharp nails along the door separating them.

Ana froze, unable to will her body to move, as though the frightful cold turned her to ice. Her eyes widened as her breath formed white clouds in the air. As quickly as it had begun, the horrific noise stopped, and the bathroom door creaked as it opened. The moment it shut again, the lights returned, and some of the warmth seeped back into her body.

Filled by a sudden and powerful urge to escape, Ana hesitated not a moment longer. She stormed back into the hallway, expecting to see the woman in white. But the corridor was empty. Had she somehow imagined it?

Ana focused on steadying herself, taking deep gulps of air until her breathing calmed. Perhaps someone had played a cruel trick on her. Despite the weakness in her knees, she hurried back to the theater. Out of breath and slightly dizzy, she reentered the backstage area. She returned just in time to see the members of the committee shaking hands with the man in the brown suit while everyone else packed up their things.

A wave of nausea rolled through Ana's body. *This can't be. Not like this.* The first people left while she stood frozen to the spot. It took her a moment to break through the ice coursing through her veins, then, with her eyes downcast, she grabbed her belongings and fled the room.

The beautiful hallways flew past her unnoticed. Her lower lip trembled as she tried to hold back tears of anger, frustration, and grief. She cursed herself for being such a naïve fool.

Moving as quickly as possible without breaking into a run, Ana made her way back to the lobby. She readied herself to see the concierge and Dimitri Morozov once more, but neither of them was there. All the better for it.

Despite the weather, she decided not to wait inside. She needed fresh air and a cigarette. When she approached the doors, the porters opened them in unison. Cold wind gushed in, though she hardly felt it. She tried to wipe away the tears, but they fell too fast for her to combat.

How many more times could she endure it? How many more rejections could she take until the starry-eyed girl who had run off to New York four years ago would give up at last? Back in the city, nothing awaited her but a job at a rundown diner and a drafty apartment shared with three other vagabonds.

Ana looked skyward to keep the tears from running down her cheeks. The bright clouds blinded her while snowflakes landed on her cheeks, catching in her lashes. For a moment, as she stood there in the shade of the grand Hôtel de Neige, she felt at peace, despite the turmoil that had raged within her seconds earlier.

"Angelica Greene!"

Even though the voice rang out loud and clear, Ana hesitated to turn, unsure whether she had misheard. The doors of the Hôtel de Neige stood open, framing the man from the committee—Everett Shaw.

"What?" she asked, lacking the energy to conceal her bewilderment. "Did I leave something backstage?"

"I thought you'd already left," Shaw said with a smile, though he appeared slightly out of breath. "Let's go inside. Would that be okay?" He shifted from one foot to the other, shivering already. He was ill-dressed to be standing outside in the snow, wearing no jacket or gloves.

"I'm waiting for my taxi," Ana replied.

Shaw rubbed his hands together for warmth. "I guess I'm telling you out here, then," he said, his words forming clouds in the air. "You got the job."

Anger flared through Ana's body. She felt like slapping him for making fun of her. "What do you mean?" she asked. "That man who auditioned before me got the job."

"No. Well, technically, yes. But no. Let me explain," he said and stepped back into the comfortable warmth of the hotel. When he beckoned her to do the same, she followed.

"So, what is it?" Ana asked, her tone harsher than intended. "Did you change your minds?"

"Not quite," he responded. "It was an order from the top." He didn't meet her eyes, gazing instead at the balustrade.

Ana squinted at him. "An order from the top?"

He nodded. "We are very sorry for the confusion. Are you still interested in the job?"

"Of course," she said, her voice trembling.

Shaw gave a small, wavering smile. "This is not a joke, I promise," he said, as though he could read her mind. "The Hôtel de Neige would like to take you on as a performer. We would be delighted to have you join us as our new singer." With that, he extended his hand towards her.

His words rippled through Ana as though winter suddenly turned into spring. She had to avert her gaze so he would not see the tears in her eyes. She had dreamed of an opportunity such as this her entire life. When she took his hand, it pulled her back into the moment, and suddenly, it was real. Warmth blossomed in her chest.

"Welcome to the Hôtel de Neige, Ms. Greene."

WELCOME TO HÔTEL DE NEIGE

Three days later, after another long journey by foot and by train and by taxi, the towers of the Hôtel de Neige crested the edge of the horizon, filling Ana with a childlike awe once more. With the snow drifting around the building, it seemed even more brilliant than the last time she had beheld it. It was like stepping into a snowglobe—and not one of the gaudy ones littering the souvenir shops in the city. A beautiful, handcrafted snowglobe, equipped with delicate snowflakes that glittered like jewels in the sunlight. The taxi came to a halt, and Ana paid before clamoring out of the car.

The few feet to the doors of the Hôtel de Neige were the final stretch after a long, tiresome journey. When she departed from her apartment in the city a few hours earlier, Ana had cried tears of joy but also tears of exhaustion. She had spent so many years alone and desperate for a chance. Now it was here, the moment she had been dreaming of.

Something appeared in the corner of her vision. She turned her head and squinted. Amongst the brilliant white covering the world around the hotel, she spotted a small figure, sunken into the snow. She blinked to make sure she was not mistaken.

Immobile in the wintry landscape, somewhat obscured by the wind which swirled snow through the air, stood a child.

"Hey," Ana called out. "You over there, can you hear me?"

The child didn't stir. He wore no coat, no hat, no gloves. "Come here," Ana shouted. "You'll freeze to death out there."

She received no response. The cold crept into Ana, chilling her to her core, and she glanced at the hotel doors, which promised warmth and comfort. She knew she couldn't leave the boy where he was; he was sure to catch his death.

Ana cursed under her breath. The snow was higher than expected, and as she took the first step in, the cold pricked into her skin like tiny needles. She gritted her teeth and forced herself to push on.

By the time she reached the boy, her jeans were soaked up to the thigh. The wind blew snow crystals into her face, where they melted, running down her cheeks like tears. Ana grabbed the boy by the shoulder and, without much gentleness, whipped him around so he'd look at her.

"What the hell are you doing out here on your own?"

There was no one else in sight. The walls of the hotel lay just a few steps away, but Ana didn't see a door. Either he'd waltzed out of the main entrance nearby, or he'd come from elsewhere and traveled some way through the cold.

The child faced her, an expression of utter confusion on his face. Ana guessed he was around six years old. Despite all the foster siblings she'd had throughout her life, she knew little about children. A mess of blond hair sat on the boy's little head, and he gazed up at her with wide hazel eyes.

"Where are your parents?" Ana asked. They had to be guests at the hotel, perhaps somewhere inside, desperately looking for their wandering child. She cursed them for their neglect.

"My parents are dead."

Ana startled, instinctively taking a step back from the boy, almost losing her balance in the high snow. "I'm sorry?"

"It's okay, they've been dead for a long time."

Ana stared at him, recalling suddenly why she had avoided children for the past few years. "Well," she said after a pause, "I'm sure they're rolling around in their graves, seeing you out here in the freezing cold without a jacket."

The boy cocked his head to the side, making her wonder if she had been too harsh. The weather was getting to her, and she wanted to rush back inside before they both suffered from hypothermia. It had happened to her once, and she was not eager to invite such misery again.

"It's not so cold right here," the boy said. Before him was a line drawn in the snow, and he nodded toward it. *"That's* where it gets cold."

"What are you even doing out here?" Ana asked. The beauty of winter enthralled her, too, but she preferred to admire it from inside with a cup of hot chocolate in her hand and a blanket around her shoulders.

"I'm always out here," the boy argued.

"I highly doubt that. Who is taking care of you?"

The boy contemplated for longer than he should, then shrugged, too nonchalant for someone so young. "Everyone."

"Everyone?"

The boy nodded like it was the most obvious answer. Ana glanced back at the hotel, wondering if she should head inside and leave the child to his own folly, deservedly so. In the end, she sighed, sending a puff of vapor into the air. "Well, you can't be out here in the snow, alone. Let's go back inside and find, I don't know, your legal guardian."

The boy frowned, but when she stretched out her hand to him, he took it, and they trudged back to the entrance of the Hôtel de Neige. Ana readjusted her duffel bag on her shoulder, and they stepped through the doors into the lobby.

The lobby's glamour dazzled her just as much as it had the first time, and she paused to let it enact its magic on her. Faint music played from somewhere, though Ana failed to locate its source. It sounded strangely like a lullaby. She rubbed her hands together to shake off the chill, grateful for the hotel's blissful warmth, but the boy stood still.

"Aren't you cold?" Ana asked him.

Again, he considered this, then shook his head.

"You should probably see a doctor."

"Why?"

Exasperated, she didn't bother to respond. She gazed around, unsure of what or whom she was looking for. She'd hoped someone would meet her in the lobby to show her where to go from there.

"Come along," Ana told the boy as she headed to the reception desk.

To Ana's relief, the concierge was not the uppity man who tried to expel her on the day of her audition. A kindly woman stood behind the desk, preoccupied with a couple of guests.

"The Hôtel de Neige has a rich history," she said. "Built during the Gothic Revival period, its architecture was inspired by Strawberry Hill House, the estate of Horace Walpole who—"

Waiting, Ana turned to study the lobby once more. In the gallery, she saw something moving and narrowed her eyes at the white fabric swaying amongst the white surroundings. She inhaled sharply as it materialized into a lithe silhouette, seeming to flow over the ground, its face veiled by shadow. She thought back to her audition, to the moment on the stage when she saw something in one of the boxes. And she remembered the encounter in the bathroom. She had tried to convince herself she imagined it, but she was starting to doubt it. Once more, the feeling of someone watching her crept up her spine.

Ana wished the guests in front of her would move on soon, but the concierge continued speaking to them animatedly about the hotel's first owner, some Danish aristocrat.

Ana regarded the boy again. "Do you happen to remember which room you're staying in?" she asked him.

"I'm not a guest," he responded at once as though she had insulted him. "I live here."

"You live here?"

"Yes," he said, sounding impatient.

Ana had half a mind to chide him for the attitude, but she had never chided a child in her life and was unsure how to go about it. Her gaze flickered back to the balustrade. The silhouette in white had vanished, but she still felt like someone was lurking, breathing down her neck.

"Let's take you back to your room," Ana said to the boy.

His brows drew together. "Who even are you?" he asked in a critical tone.

"I'm Ana Greene, I'm—"

"You're the new singer."

She startled and frowned at him. "Yes."

News of her coming had traveled, and still, nobody bothered to receive her. This time, she had arrived punctually at the agreed-upon time. A thought struck Ana. "Do you happen to know where I might find Mr. Shaw?"

The boy looked at the clock next to the reception. "Everett's probably in the music room now. I'll take you there."

Before Ana could reply, he grabbed her hand and began walking. Unsure how else to react, she followed along, hoping it didn't look as though she was abducting a child.

"Do you have a name?" Ana asked as they walked.

"Yes, of course."

Ana considered abandoning him right then and there. "And what is your name?"

"It's Mikkel. But you can call me Mike."

Ana had more questions, but before she could ask them, her attention shifted. They left the lobby, turning a corner into an embellished hallway. Tall stained-glass windows lined the side, scenes of white clouds, doves, and swans adorning them. One showed a silvery sleigh pulled through the snowy sky by great white horses. Another depicted a dancing couple, the colors so vivid in the sunlight, it seemed as though they were truly moving, spinning around before the backdrop of the wintry world outside.

They passed by a small restaurant, the Danish Pavilion, and a ballroom which was closed, though a large placard announced the upcoming Christmas Eve Ball. Ana felt as though she had stumbled into a fairytale; even though she would not become a princess at the Hôtel de Neige, it felt like a Cinderella story, nonetheless.

Quietly at first, the sweet tunes of a piano reached them. Mike's stride grew more purposeful as they approached a door opened by a slit. The boy entered first while Ana followed with lighter, more cautious steps, lest she disturb the musician. A grand room expanded before her. Mirrors covered an entire wall, giving it the appearance of a ballet studio, save for the large piano occupying one corner. Ana stopped. Everett Shaw was hunched over the keys, eliciting a gentle melody, oblivious to their presence.

She could see the passion pouring into the piano and through the music, his emotions transferred to her. Deep notes filled the room; interwoven with every heartfelt sound was a kind of pain that struck her in the gut. She meant to close her eyes and take in the song, but Mike strutted ahead to the entranced pianist.

Ana reached out to keep him from interrupting, but she wasn't quick enough. He approached Shaw and tapped him on the shoulder. The music ceased, and the magic vanished.

Shaw looked up, a dazed look in his eyes. "Oh, Mike," he said and gave the boy a smile. "What is it?"

Mike turned and pointed at Ana. Heat rushed into her cheeks. "Hello," she said, wishing she had been able to stop Mike from disturbing his focus.

A look of realization hit Shaw, and he shot to his feet, toppling over the piano stool. "Oh, dear," he said. From his pocket, he pulled a golden pocket watch, then he cursed under his breath. "I'm so sorry, I meant to be there when you arrived, but it seems I lost track of time."

"It's no problem," Ana said. "*I'm* sorry that we interrupted you."

"No, no, it's good that you did." He waved her toward him.

Ana stepped further into the room, watching as Mike began to wander. "I found him outside in the snow," she said with a nod towards the boy. "No coat or anything."

"Yes, he does that."

Ana raised her brows; it was not the reaction she had anticipated. "He was alone out there. Who's taking care of him?"

Shaw sighed. "To be honest, we all are. I'm not sure whether he told you, but he's an orphan. He has no family left, so the employees of the hotel took over."

Ana blinked. As someone who grew up in the foster system, this arrangement sounded odd to her, and hardly legal. She glanced at the boy again, who looked as though he had not a care in the world.

"I have some paperwork for you to sign," Shaw said. He pulled a white folder and a key from his leather bag.

Ana took both with great care as though they were fragile things, ready to crumble in her hands. She was aware she held a treasure, a new beginning. "Thank you, Mr. Shaw."

"Please, call me Everett. We all call each other by our first names, with some exceptions, but I will warn you about those."

He handed her a pen, and with no hesitation, she signed where he indicated. She fought a growing smile as her heart pumped faster.

"We're very happy to have you here," Everett said. "About time this hotel had a singer again."

"I'm very happy to be here, too," Ana echoed. She had yet to fully realize it, everything was still a blur, a dream.

"Let me show you to your room."

When they departed the music room, Mike tagged along like a loyal pup. Once more, they wound their way through the hotel. Ana wondered how she would ever learn to navigate the twisting corridors. At last, they came to a narrow hallway which featured no painted ceilings or lace-trimmed curtains. The off-white rug and the yellowy light from the minimalistic lamps lining the corridor gave it a warmer feel than the rest of the castle.

"These are the staff quarters," Everett said. "Down the corridor is the staff kitchen and the common room." He came to a halt at one of the doors. "This is your room."

Ana looked down at the key in her hand. She'd clutched it tight all the way through the halls, afraid it might otherwise slip from her grasp and be lost forever. The room beyond the door would be her home from now on. She had no reason to be nervous, yet she could hardly breathe. It felt like the portal to a new realm.

Warmth greeted her when she opened the door. She tiptoed inside, her eyes growing wide. Though it was not a large room, it held more space than the one she had inhabited in New York City. A bed dressed in white sheets and clouded with fluffy pillows stood in one corner beside a grand window framed by pale blue curtains. The soft light of winter filtered into the room.

A wardrobe stretched across the wall, with mirrors serving as its doors. Ana doubted her clothes would fill more than a quarter of it. Next to it was another door. With hesitant steps, she opened the door and suppressed a gasp. It led her into a small bathroom with beautiful marble flooring, a bathtub, and soft lighting. She'd never had a bathroom that belonged only to her.

Dazed, Ana stumbled back to the bedroom to Everett and Mike.

"To your liking?" the pianist asked, a smile flickering across his lips. "I remember when I first moved to the Hôtel de Neige," he said. "Its beauty draws one in like a spell." For a moment, Everett gazed into space before rolling his shoulders as though to physically shake off some unwanted thought.

"Some more things," he said. "The internet and telephone connection here can be quite spotty. Same goes for the electricity, though that is more stable."

Ana frowned. She had lived in places where power outages had occurred from time to time, but she had not expected it from a luxury hotel. Perhaps it was due to the age of the building or its remote location.

"I'll let you get settled now," Everett said. Then he added, "The staff is having a little party up on the roof tonight. Would you like to join us?"

A party on the roof in November? Ana shuddered at the thought of it, but couldn't decline such an invitation on her first day. "Yes, of course."

Everett smiled. "Wonderful. We will come and get you later. Let's say at 9?"

Ana nodded, and they said their goodbyes. As Everett and Mike left, she shut the door behind them. It was yet another new sensation to be alone in her room. She had adjusted the image in her head, shrinking the size of the room and dulling its colors to make it more realistic. As she looked upon it again, she found herself struggling for breath and squirming like a child on a sugar high. At last, she allowed herself to truly believe it was not a dream destined to fade away. It was real.

IN THE MAGIC GARDENS

As the hour of the party drew near, nervousness crept into Ana. She wondered what such an occasion at the Hôtel de Neige entailed. Even if it didn't include the illustrious guests themselves, Ana still pictured glittering dresses, sparkling champagne, and intellectual discussions. The first she had never owned, the second never tasted, and the third rarely partaken in. The only parties Ana was familiar with meant skimpy clothes, cheap tequila, and momentary distractions.

Ana decided on the burgundy dress and black tights she wore for her auditions, hoping they would again grant her good luck. She tied a black sweater around her shoulders, wary of the cold awaiting her on the roof.

Around 9 pm, when the world beyond her window had descended into a deep black, a knock sounded on Ana's door. It was Everett, accompanied by a young woman with warm brown skin and chin-length black waves framing her heart-shaped face.

Ana straightened. "Hey."

"Ana," Everett responded with a smile, then nodded to the woman by his side. "This is Bahar Yilmaz. She works as a maid here at the hotel. Bahar, this is Ana, our new singer."

Bahar received Ana with a wide smile. "A pleasure to meet you."

Much to Ana's relief, Bahar wore a black skirt and a deep violet sweater similar to her own outfit. Everett sported an elegant suit, but Ana assumed it was his regular attire; he didn't seem like the type for jeans and sneakers.

"Are you ready?" Bahar asked and held up a bottle—cheap tequila.

"Let me get my coat," Ana said, turning back.

"You won't need one," Everett told her. When she lifted her brows, he added, "I promise."

They headed to the elevators—not the stately ones used by the hotel guests, but those intended for the staff. A couple more people joined them, so five of them squeezed in together. The metal creaked, and it took a good minute until they reached the uppermost floor.

They found themselves at one end of a long hallway, its stone walls ornately carved and adorned with silver. Magnificent paintings of wintery landscapes decorated the corridor. Ana yearned to stop and revel in it, but Bahar waved her along.

They arrived at a small set of stairs in some distant, far less opulent corner. It led to a heavy door of dark wood which opened to the hotel's roof. Ana tensed, expecting a blast of cold air. Instead, warm light met them. Passing through the door, Ana found herself embraced by flowers, colors swirling around her. Clear glass walled them in, shielding them from the icy night. Plants blossomed around them, the stars twinkling above them beyond the glass. Snowflakes drifted onto the ceiling where their crystalline shapes dissolved.

"It's beautiful," Ana whispered. The vibrant colors on the rooftop contrasted with the interior of the hotel's pale splendor.

"The winter gardens," Everett said. "It used to be a terrace for the staff members to smoke. A few years ago, some of us decided to turn it into this."

Ana lacked words, so she silently followed Everett and Bahar as they wandered further into the gardens, marveling at the splendor surrounding her. Every few feet, they stopped to greet other employees of the hotel. Ana was introduced to so many of them that she doubted she would remember a fraction of their names by morning.

Vines and flowers hung in their path, and they pushed them aside carefully. Ana inhaled their comforting scents with deep breaths, at times running her fingers over the colorful blossoms. Yellows, purples, pinks, and reds contrasted with her fair skin. She felt as though it was the first day of spring.

They reached the bar, which sat nestled in a clearing furnished with mismatched chairs and tables. Miraculously, they found three unoccupied seats and settled down together. Bahar presented them with some paper cups and poured three generous shots of tequila mixed with orange juice.

"Here you go," she said, handing Ana her drink. In her words, Ana detected a soft accent she couldn't quite place. "So tell me about yourself. Everett says you're from New York City."

"Yes," Ana said. "Not originally, though. I grew up in Montana, but I've lived in New York for the past four years."

"I've always wanted to visit the city."

"You haven't been?" Ana asked. "It's not so far from here."

Bahar gave a slight shrug. "I suppose my work schedule always prevented it."

"May I ask where your accent is from?" Ana asked Bahar.

For a moment, Ana feared she had said something tactless as Bahar's jaw tensed before she put on a smile again.

"I'm Austrian," Bahar told her. "My family is originally from Turkey, but I was born and raised in Austria."

Ana raised her brows. "You came all the way from Austria to the Hôtel de Neige? Why?"

Bahar exhaled a long breath. "Circumstance, I guess."

Ana was familiar enough with the power of circumstance. It had thrown her into unexpected places at times. Yet for someone from Austria to end up in a hotel in upstate New York seemed stranger to her still.

Everett cleared his throat. "Look who's here," he said, nodding toward a little group that had just arrived at the bar.

Ana recognized them at once—the three other people from the committee who presided over her audition. Seeing them at the party seemed wrong. She surveyed the dark-haired woman who had interrupted her performance. Her porcelain complexion would have made her look like a child's beloved doll were it not for the distant look in her eyes. She was slight, though she carried herself with her shoulders high and curved her spine in a way that accentuated her hips and bosom.

As she studied the other two, Ana's forehead creased into a frown. One of them was a woman, though she looked like a teenager still, a dainty thing with olive skin and black hair who appeared like she had yet to outgrow her adolescent years. Next to her, so close their bodies melted into one another, was a curly-haired boy who also seemed far too young to be employed by the Hôtel de Neige.

"They are the other performers, our ballet dancers," Everett explained as he perhaps noticed Ana's perplexed expression. "They are Palmira and Saverio Fiore," he said, nodding at the teenagers.

"Are they siblings?" Ana asked.

"They're married," Bahar responded.

Ana's eyes narrowed. "Married?"

Bahar chuckled. "Yes, that's everyone's first reaction." She shrugged. "They are a bit strange, I must admit. I can't remember ever seeing them apart."

"Who is the other woman?" Ana then asked.

"Hedwig Sternberg," Everett answered. "She is our prima ballerina."

Hedwig's posture was clearly that of a dancer. It took effort to look away from her—her presence alone commanded attention. The thought of potentially sharing a stage with her made Ana shrink back.

The three ballet dancers disappeared into the crowd, and Ana turned to Everett and Bahar again.

"Who wants another drink?" Bahar asked.

Since Bahar had finished hers already, Ana downed the rest of hers. Bahar threw her a look of approval, then prepared the second round. They sipped and talked for a while before Ana rose.

"I think I'll look around a bit," she said. The allure of the gardens drew her in, and she needed a break from the masses around her.

"Don't get lost," Bahar said. "It can be quite the labyrinth up here."

It seemed to be a theme for the entire hotel. "I'll be careful."

Bahar soon proved to be correct. The gardens stretched out far beyond what Ana anticipated, expanding over the greater part of the hotel's roof. It took her a while to leave behind the music and chattering, but at last both faded into the background. She inched ahead, across a path winding beneath low-hanging branches and vines that brought Ana to a dead end. While the path concluded at a glass wall, the world unfolded beyond it.

Ana looked upon the nightly forest. Frost covered the tall pine trees framing the Hôtel de Neige. She laid a hand on the glass. Despite the warmth radiating within the gardens, her breath formed tiny clouds. Above, the stars sparkled like distant diamonds, snowflakes floating beneath them. They fell straight onto the glass and rested there. Soon, they would cover the ceiling and transform the gardens into a jungle within an igloo. Behind her, leaves rustled.

She turned, torn away from the intimate moment. She had thought herself alone with the tranquil beauty. Amongst the greens and vibrant colors, she spotted a touch of white. An icy touch scraped across the nape of her neck.

With small steps, she approached the quiet noise. For a moment, she believed she had lost sight of it, then something shifted in the distance. Cold air filled her lungs at the sight of the apparition from the theater lurking among the plants. The faceless, eyeless creature that watched her like a predator.

The phantom in white.

Ana followed. Part of her felt mad for chasing what might well be an optical illusion, a ghost conjured by her own anxiety. The foreign white figure stayed ahead of her, teasing her just enough to keep her moving. What if it were real? What if it were dangerous?

Ana's steps grew faster, although her mind rebelled against it. She flexed her fingers to keep them from growing stiff with the cold. The figure, always just beyond her reach, lured her deeper into the gardens. She pushed aside thorny vines and climbed across wild bushes until she reached a crossing of paths.

Greens, pinks, purples, yellows, oranges, and reds. The startling white silhouette was gone. What had she expected, a confrontation with a ghost?

Yet some primal instinct told her the threat had not yet passed. She rubbed her hands. The air had changed, the temperature dropping significantly. By her feet, the flowers hung wilted, drooping towards the ground. Something had sucked all life out of them. The knot in her stomach grew so tight that it made her nauseated. The drinks had been stronger than expected, she thought, blaming her tipsiness.

With goosebumps still covering her arms, Ana broke into motion again. All this would feel like a ridiculous frenzy once she returned to the others. She scurried ahead, afraid that if she let herself be still, the frost would get her. The paths around her had become unfamiliar and evermore. Bahar's prediction rang true—she was lost. She slowed and listened for voices or music, but neither reached her ears.

She believed herself utterly alone until she turned around another corner and collided with someone.

Ana froze—*the phantom.*

Though when she looked up to see the person looking down on her, there was none of that unnatural white to blind her.

Hedwig Sternberg, the ballerina, stood before her. Ana had to hold back the sigh of relief. "Sorry," she muttered.

"Ana Greene," the ballerina said.

Ana frowned upon hearing the cold tone. "Yes," she responded. "Hedwig Sternberg, right?"

Hedwig gave a curt nod. She surveyed Ana, her gaze wandering over her body in a way that made Ana wish to withdraw. She straightened her shoulders.

"I would like to say, I am very grateful for this opportunity," Ana said, mustering a smile. "Working at the Hôtel de Neige is a dream come true for me."

"We shouldn't have hired you."

"Excuse me?"

"We wanted a different singer," Hedwig said, her demeanor so cold it sent a chill up Ana's spine.

She did her best to stand upright and to keep the irritation from her expression. "I'm sorry you're not happy I was chosen. But obviously someone wanted to hire me."

An order from the top, Everett had said.

"Yes, someone," Hedwig echoed. "Someone who didn't partake in the hiring process and who knows little about music chose you on a whim. There's little pride to be taken in that."

"I'm sorry, what's your problem?"

Hedwig released a long breath as if to say she didn't even know where to begin. "Look around. The Hôtel de Neige is for a certain class of people. You're a decent singer, I suppose. For a bar or... Well, I don't know, some kid's birthday party. But not for this place."

A knot tied in Ana's throat that she failed to swallow down. "You have no right to judge me before I have the chance to prove myself," she said, choosing cold politeness over the red-hot anger flaring within her.

"I think I do. After all, you had your chance at the auditions, didn't you?" the ballerina responded. "Tell me, have you ever received any professional training? Do you have any experience? Any previous employers who will praise your hard work, your commitment, your portrayal on stage?"

Ana remained quiet, and Hedwig nodded.

"I didn't think so."

Throughout the years, Ana had dealt with more than her fair share of bullies. She suppressed the urge to slap the ballerina across her arrogant face. The satisfaction of it would be temporary. This was no run-down high school, no trashy bar, no scrappy diner.

"I look forward to proving you wrong," Ana said.

Hedwig mumbled something in a language Ana didn't understand. Then she eyed Ana again, brown irises aflame. "You should leave," she said. "For your own good. Otherwise, you might meet the same fate as our last singer." Then she spun on her heels and strutted away, leaving

Ana staring after her. All that remained was the sweet scent of lily perfume and the rapid beating of her heart.

With a bitter taste still in her mouth, Ana set out again. She managed her way back to the party by following the scent of lilies back to the makeshift clearing. The crowd near the bar had grown, and she had to squeeze through to get back to the others. Despite the anger pulsing within her chest, she was determined to keep it hidden.

From a distance, Ana heard boisterous laughter. As she came closer, she realized it belonged to Bahar. "Angie," she cried out as Ana reached them. "I can call you Angie, right? We thought you'd gotten lost."

Ana took a deep breath, then plastered a smile on her face as she sat down. "I kind of did, actually."

"You did?" Bahar burst into another bout of laughter. She grabbed the tequila bottle next to her, now much emptier, and poured two more drinks—one for herself and one for Ana.

"*Prost*," she exclaimed, raising her cup skyward before downing it like water.

Ana watched her, holding back a grimace. She knew this sort of drinker all too well. Often enough, she belonged to their lot. Exchanging a glance with Everett, Ana could tell he was none too happy about Bahar's state.

"Let's play a drinking game," Bahar suggested. "Never have I ever—"

"Let's not," Everett chimed in.

"Do you want me to grab you some water?" Ana asked. How long had she been away for Bahar to be this far gone already? Though she did feel some gratitude, for her drunken state was helping distract her from the unsettling encounter with Hedwig.

"Stop acting like I'm wasted," Bahar snarled. She sank from her chair to the ground and propped herself up against Everett's legs.

"I'm sorry," Everett said to Ana. "Did you enjoy looking around the winter gardens?"

"Yes," Ana responded, too quick for it to sound natural, but Everett didn't notice.

Ana scanned their surroundings, afraid Hedwig might appear, but she and the other dancers had vanished. Did they share the same opinion as her? And what about Everett? Did he consider Ana the right choice for the Hôtel de Neige? She had hoped to leave all those doubts in New York City, but it seemed they had followed her to the Hôtel de Neige, where they flared up with a novel force.

"Everett," she said, trying and failing to muster a casual tone. "I was wondering—"

His attention shifted from Ana to Bahar, who was trying to refill her drink once more. Like an exasperated parent, he fished the cup out of her hands. "I'm getting you some water," he declared, then rose and disappeared into the crowd.

"Are you okay?" Ana asked Bahar.

"Yes, I am," she answered immediately, though her words were slurred.

"Bahar, maybe you know this," Ana said. "Everett mentioned how nice it was to have a singer again. Has it been a while since the hotel had a singer?"

Hedwig had told her to leave—*otherwise, you might meet the same fate as our last singer.* Ana didn't like threats.

Bahar grew still, her forehead creasing. "Oh, well," she said and hiccupped. "It's...it's been a while. Before I was hired."

Ana nodded. "Why isn't that person working here anymore?"

Before Ana could stop her, Bahar grasped the tequila bottle and drank a large gulp straight from it.

"You know," Bahar then said, stabbing her finger into the air in Ana's direction, "one day, I'll move to a place where it never gets cold. I'm so fucking sick of the cold." She met Ana's confused stare. "That's what you get for working at a place called the Hôtel de Neige. Do you speak any French? Hôtel de Neige means 'Hotel of Snow.' And it is. Always. Fucking. Cold." Bahar moved to take another sip straight from the bottle.

"That's enough," Ana said and reached out for the tequila bottle.

Bahar screeched and pulled it away. It slipped from her grasp, bursting into a thousand tiny pieces at her feet. She drew her brows together, clearly not sure what had happened.

"Alright," Ana said, as she stood and held her hands out to Bahar. "Come on, let's get you up."

Bahar's face contorted with hysterical laughter. Then, just as quickly as the bottle had shattered, Bahar broke apart, her laughter transforming into choked sobs.

Ana stared, part of her wanting to flee the scene like she would if this were one of the parties in New York City. But she was far from home. Leaving Bahar there, drunk and crying, would be poor etiquette on her first day.

Ana squatted down beside her, mindful of the devious shards. "Are you alright?" she asked again.

Bahar only continued to wail, her cheeks stained black by her mascara.

"What happened here?"

Ana looked up and was relieved to see Everett returning with a water bottle in his hand and a look of shock on his face.

"The bottle broke," Ana said. "Then she started crying."

Everett groaned. Together, they pulled Bahar back into her chair. He leaned toward her and whispered gently. "It will be okay."

When he handed her a linen handkerchief, Bahar made an effort to wipe away the tears of mascara and glittering eyeshadow, though she mostly smudged them across her face. "You always say that," she mumbled. "I can't hear it anymore. How can you still believe that bullshit?"

"Because I must."

"You're lying to yourself."

Ana awkwardly retreated into her own seat, wondering if she should leave altogether. She felt she was intruding upon something not meant for her ears. But before she could take the chance and sneak off without saying good night, Bahar turned to her again.

"I'm sorry, Angie," she said, pressing the words out in between the sobs. "I'm so sorry."

"It's okay. We've all broken something before."

"No, no, not for that. For everything. For—"

"Bahar," Everett cut her off, and Ana squinted at him.

Bahar blinked, spilling more tears. She gazed at Ana. "You will always be cold. You may be warm, but you will be cold inside. Forever."

Ana stared at Bahar, dumbstruck by the ominous, drunken speech. Before she could attempt to decipher it, Everett rose.

"Alright," he said, taking Bahar by the arm. "That's enough. Let's get you to your room."

Everett pulled Bahar to her feet. Ana stood up as well, unsure what to do, where to put her hands. Bahar leaned against Everett, putting most of her weight onto him. He started dragging her ahead, the crowd parting for the two of them. They were almost out of Ana's line of sight when Bahar dug her heels into the ground and stopped them. She looked back at Ana and waved her to their side.

Tentatively, Ana approached until she reached them. There, Bahar leaned in and whispered, "He died."

The words struck into Ana's core like a prick of ice, even before she fully comprehended them. "What are you talking about?"

"The last singer," Bahar responded, almost drowned out by the noise all around them. Not even Everett seemed to hear. "He died."

For a moment, the gardens spun around her, nausea roiling up to her throat. She had no time to reply, not that she knew what to say. The ballerina's words weren't hollow bullying. They had been a warning.

Everett dragged Bahar along. "I need to get her to bed," he told Ana without looking at her. "We will see each other tomorrow at rehearsals. I'm so sorry about this."

Then they were gone, leaving Ana with an empty feeling in her chest. She had thought her new life at Hôtel de Neige would alleviate her sorrows, and it was true—she had what she'd long dreamed of. A true home, a job as a singer, a steady income. Yet her first day had left her confused, out of breath. Between strange orphans, drunk speeches, and not-so-subtle threats, it was exhaustion rather than thrill that clutched at her.

THE PORTRAIT BEHIND THE BLACK VEIL

An empty corridor stretched out before Ana, and for a moment, she believed someone had torn away the ceiling. Blindingly white snow covered the hallway, and shivers crept into her limbs. She raised her stiff arms, expecting her skin to be shades of blue and purple, her fingers ready to break like a porcelain doll's, but she found herself intact. When she looked up, she saw a dozen shimmering chandeliers like ice crystals glittering beneath an unobscured full moon.

Where am I?

Ana walked ahead, though she had forgotten where she meant to go. She vaguely recalled wanting to meet with someone, but she couldn't remember who. She inched ahead, each step through the snow cutting into her legs like knives. She reached out to the wall beside her, and her hand met ice. She pulled it away at once, but the cold barrelled through her. She stepped closer to the wall and let her fingers run across the frost, despite its sting. Motion by painful motion, she wiped the snow away until it revealed a window.

Outside lay a frozen lake beneath a bright white sky. It glowed in deep blue and shining silver, framed by tall pine trees, their emerald branches covered with fresh white snow.

Distant voices in her head screeched at her to get out, but her body moved of its own volition. Ana found and freed the next window, uncovering a vast landscape of mountains reaching up to the cloudy sky. She went on, discovering scene by scene, all beautiful and blanketed in snow, until she reached the end of the long hallway.

Like a prisoner in her own body, she started laboring on the wall, even though her hands had gone blue from cold. She scraped off the remaining snow until her skin turned raw and bloody. Beneath its layer, Ana found a wall of ice so thick she could not see through to the other side. When she placed her hand on it, it cracked. She imagined breaking bones made that same noise.

Ana jumped back as frost swirled through the air in an opaque fog. The voices in her mind grew louder, commanding her to flee. Before she could will her numb legs into obedience, a woman stepped from the mist.

All remaining warmth fled. The woman who towered over Ana looked part human, part statue, made of ice and snow. She lacked all color, except for one eye with a brown iris. Ana stumbled backwards, each gasp for air piercing her lungs.

"I have been expecting you," the woman said, her melodic voice echoing through the hallway. "I am glad you finally decided to come home."

Fear gripped like a noose.

Get out. Now.

Her body snapped into action. She spun around and ran.

Thousands of tiny ice crystals whipped into her face. Snow blocked the corridor, reaching up to her knees. Every step was a struggle, but she did not stop. Ana clawed and shoved and pushed until the snow walled her in. She looked back, expecting to see the woman before her, reaching for Ana with claw-like hands.

She was gone.

Ana could grasp only one clear thought: she needed to get as far away as possible. She turned back around to find the woman of white standing mere inches away. The scream froze in Ana's throat. She scrambled backward and lost her footing on the ice beneath. Her body crashed to the ground.

Ana could not see anything through the snow whirling around her. *Was she safe? Was the woman in white gone?*

Among the dancing ice crystals, something shifted.

Adrenaline pulsed through Ana, but not enough to push her to her feet in time. Long fingers reached for her from the snow, grasping hold of her throat. She gasped as sharp nails pressed into her skin.

Ana's eyes opened a second before the claws pierced her flesh.

A dream.

Tension ebbed from her bones. Just a dream. She was safe. But her stomach turned when her gaze adjusted to the darkness around her.

This wasn't her bed.

This wasn't her room.

Ana clasped a hand over her mouth to rein in a choked yelp. She did not recognize her surroundings. She scrambled to her feet, but her limbs remained stiff from the imaginary cold, barely following her commands. A draft rippled across her body. She had felt the cold of her nightmare, too, though not like this. She closed and opened her eyes repeatedly, yet she could not wake.

"No," she whispered. "No, no, no."

This wasn't real. Ana shook her head as though it would take her somewhere else, yet this dark and strange place did not surrender its hold. Tears blurred her vision, making it harder to see anything beyond arm's length. Something creaked and squeaked.

Ana spun around. *Was someone else close by?* The thought did nothing to reassure her.

Ana placed her hands on her chest as she took quivering breaths. She forced herself not to run around like a panicked animal while her eyes adjusted. She was in an empty corridor. Chandeliers hung above her, one flickering on and off.

Was she still in the Hôtel de Neige at all? She had to be; leaving the hotel in this weather would have killed her. She had sleepwalked for a while as a child, but she had shaken that habit long ago, after many reluctant sessions with a psychologist.

Ana rubbed her hands, hoping for a touch of warmth. She couldn't tell whether the hallway itself was cold or if she was suffering from the aftereffects of the nightmare. She shuddered. It was only a dream. She was awake now, or so she hoped.

With unsteady motions, Ana tiptoed ahead, as quiet as possible. Unlike the rest of the hotel, this corridor was neglected—certainly not meant for the guests. There were no windows, no indicators as to where she was. Ana considered calling out, but she held back. She didn't want anyone to find her there. She couldn't tell what made her more uneasy—the location itself or the person who would hear her there, in this abandoned wing of the hotel.

One lone door stood on the side of the hallway, and she swore she heard the faintest tunes of a piano beyond. Her mind had to be playing tricks on her. This was all a figment of her imagination. Nobody was beyond that door; nobody would roam this dark part of the hotel. Nobody except a panicked, sleepwalking fool.

Although the corridor itself was not a display of beauty, dozens of paintings hung on its walls. Ana knew she should find a way out, but by some unwanted instinct, she stepped towards the nearest one. Dust covered the image, and she coughed as she swept it away.

Her heart clenched. Part of her had expected it, but that did not lessen the blow.

The painting showed a frozen lake, surrounded by tall, snow-crested pine trees.

Ana stared for another moment, then reeled to the next painting. The picture, created with fine strokes, revealed high mountains, their peaks obscured by puffy gray clouds. She distinguished only one difference from her dream: in it, the clouds had moved, slowly traveling across the horizon. Her lips parted to laugh, but a pitiful rasp escaped her. Something was happening to her—something was wrong with her.

She ran on to the next image, then the next. With each one, the knot in her chest tightened, making it more difficult to breathe. The paintings were nearly indistinguishable from the windows she had looked through in her dream. It couldn't be a coincidence. Had she somehow seen them when sleepwalking? Was she losing her mind altogether?

In the nightmare, a wall of ice stood at the end of the corridor, and from it came the woman in white. Ana turned from the paintings and looked down the corridor. She was still some distance from its end, yet she could see the outline of a frame, covered by a swath of black.

Get away from it, commanded the rational part of her mind. But it was as though something, someone, watched her from beneath that sheath, and she needed to know. She needed to see that there was nothing to fear. A strange nightmare, nothing more. The alcohol had caused it, just as it had led her to sleepwalk again after all these years.

Ana passed the door and ignored the sound of the piano. It was another distortion, another manifestation of anxiety and exhaustion.

The dark sheath obscured the painting like a Victorian widow's veil, but she could see the outlines beneath. A portrait. Was she allowed to touch it? Ana feared she would somehow taint it, but she couldn't rein herself in. *Only a peek, only to make sure there is nothing to be afraid of,* she told herself, and reached out to lift up the silky fabric. The moment she touched it, the veil fell, descending to the ground as light as a feather.

"Fuck," Ana whispered and looked around. Again, she felt someone watching her. She scrambled to pick up the sheath, then her gaze climbed to the painting. A lump formed in her throat. She knew the woman in the portrait.

It was the woman Ana had seen in her dream. Or some rendition of her, at least. A beautiful girl with golden blonde curls, pinned up in an elaborate hairdo, was centered in the portrait. A small smile adorned her full lips, rosy as her plump cheeks. She wore a pink, ruffled period dress, perhaps from the mid-19th century. Her brown eyes sparkled as she gazed down at Ana. This girl looked different, yet so similar to the woman from Ana's nightmare. She was a younger, softer, more colorful version of the beastly, snowlike creature Ana encountered in her sleep.

How could she have seen the woman in her dreams, along with all the other pictures? She had to be sleeping, even though her entire body felt wide awake.

With trembling hands, she threw the veil over the portrait again. She wanted to forget it, or at least never lay eyes on it again. Once she left this corridor, all of this would make sense again.

Ana turned from the painting, but still felt its eyes on her. She took a few fast steps, then broke into a run, not caring where she was headed.

She was almost at the end of the corridor when a soft noise sounded behind her. She stopped in her tracks. Every fiber of her being told her not to look back, but a powerful urge forced her to turn. The hallway lay still, soundless. It was unchanged, except for the portrait at its end. The veil had fallen again, and the painted woman watched her more intently than ever. The music from the piano ceased.

Ana hesitated, then spun around and bolted.

She tumbled through the halls without direction, driven by the desire to put distance between herself and that ghastly portrait. Her steps were uncoordinated, as if she were intoxicated. After a series of sharp turns, she came to a set of winding stairs leading downward. It felt as though they went on forever, and Ana was dizzy by the time she reached the end. They brought her back to a well-lit corridor on the ground level with large windows. Beyond them lay the night and the glittering snow.

Only then did she—and her heartbeat—slow down. Ana laid a hand on her chest to steady herself. She tried to reassure herself that it had been a dream, nothing more. Even as she tried to rationalize it all away, her body quivered with fear.

When Ana heard chattering and soft music nearby, she slowed. She was a mess, still in the clothes from the party with her curls ruffled and tangled, and shock sticking to her features. She would startle anyone taking more than a passing look at her—especially one of the hotel guests.

Once more, Ana quickened her pace. She kept her head low and scurried around a corner and passed by a bar, still busy despite the late hour. She prayed nobody would notice her.

Yet much to her dismay, somebody did.

"Ana Greene."

She turned around slowly, reluctantly meeting the gaze of Dimitri Morozov.

He wore a smirk, though it vanished a few seconds later, replaced by a stern expression. "Are you alright?" he asked.

Ana took her first steady breath since the nightmare began. At last, she believed she had made it to safety. "I'm fine. Thank you, Mr. Morozov."

"Don't be so formal," he responded. The smile tugged at the corner of his mouth again, though in his eyes, Ana saw the skepticism. "Call me Dimitri."

Ana sensed that calling him by his first name was the first step down a dangerous road, but she was too drained to protest. "I'm fine, *Dimitri*," she said, surrendering.

"Are you sure? You look… Well, either you had too much to drink or are in desperate need of a drink."

Ana sighed. "A bit of both, I guess."

"Why don't you sit down with me, and I'll get you something to drink," he said, gesturing to the bar behind him.

"I don't think that's a good idea. I should go to bed," she said, though she doubted she could fall asleep anytime soon. The nightmare and memories of the portrait clung to her like her own dark shadow.

"Alright," he said, still studying her. Ana could tell unspoken words lay on his tongue, but all he added was, "Good night."

Ana gave a nod and stepped past him. She made it no more than a few steps before she came to an abrupt realization. "Mr. Morozov."

He paused.

Ana bit back a groan and corrected herself. "Dimitri."

With that same disarming smile, he turned to face her. "Yes?"

Ana swallowed her pride. "You don't happen to have a universal key? I left mine in my room."

Dimitri raised his brows, then pulled a set of keys from his pocket and jingled them. "Take the lead," he told her.

Ana pulled herself ahead, and he caught up with her quickly. She expected him to be pleased to be the knight-in-shining-armor to her damsel-in-distress once again, but when she glanced at him, she saw concern rather than smugness.

"What happened?" he asked.

Ana sighed, capitulating to the softness of his tone. "I was sleepwalking."

"Sleepwalking?"

"Yes, and I ended up in some creepy corridor." She attempted a smile, managing a grimace instead. With a sigh, she continued, "I used to sleepwalk a lot when I was a child. I had horrible nightmares back then. I thought I had shaken it off."

"Perhaps it is the flair of these Gothic halls," Dimitri mused. "There are parts of the Hôtel de Neige that can make for dreary nightmares."

Ana lifted a brow. "Is that so? Does it give you nightmares?"

"Sometimes it does," he said, a distant look on his face.

They reached the staff corridor and came to a halt by her door. Much to Ana's relief, nobody else was around this late at night. All lay silent.

Dimitri got out his keys again and unlocked the door. Once more, Ana was ready to be alone, but as she stood in the doorway, he spoke.

"I quite forgot—congratulations on joining the Hôtel de Neige as our new singer," Dimitri said.

Ana's stomach turned queasy. She had hoped to tiptoe around that matter. "Thank you for helping me get it," she responded after a pause.

Dimitri smirked. "I quite enjoyed that, I must admit. I rarely get to be mischievous these days. I'm glad you made it to the auditions in time."

Ana bit her lip. "That's not what I meant." When Dimitri raised his brows, she added, "Thank you for *getting* me the job."

"I don't understand."

Ana met his blue eyes, which lay intently on her. "Please don't act like you don't know what I'm talking about."

Only then did she recognize the surprised look on his face. "I'm afraid I honestly don't know," Dimitri said. "What makes you think I got you the job?"

The events of that day replayed in Ana's head like a movie. Recounting the initial rejection nearly pained her as much as it had back then. "The committee wanted someone else, but they changed their minds," she told Dimitri. "They got 'an order from the top.' I assumed it was from you."

Dimitri shook his head. "I had nothing to do with it, I promise you."

"Now I don't understand," Ana admitted. She had been so sure she owed her spot at the Hôtel de Neige to Dimitri Morozov and their chance encounter.

A small smirk played around Dimitri's lips. "I never even heard you sing, so why would I have given you the job? No offense."

Ana swallowed hard. In the past, men had offered her career opportunities in exchange for certain favors. Perhaps she had thought Dimitri was one of their lot. She was glad that the hallway was barely lit; it concealed the flush on her cheeks.

Ana was still scrambling for words when Dimitri spoke again. "I am glad you are here, though. I think you will breathe fresh life into the hotel."

"Wait," Ana said. "If you didn't get me the job, who did?"

Dimitri didn't respond.

Ana squinted at him. "You know, don't you?"

"Yes." So much self-satisfaction charged into a single syllable.

"Will you tell me?"

"Oh, no, of course not."

Oh, fuck off. Ana took a deep breath to make sure those words didn't leave her mouth by chance. "And why not?" She yearned for an answer, just one answer on this day that had aroused so many questions within her. Who had decided to grant her this chance, supposedly without ever hearing her sing?

"You'll find out soon enough."

Ana pressed her lips together. "Fine," she snapped back. "Since you won't tell me, I'm going to bed now."

Slowly, hoping he would stop her, she stepped into her room. She kept her eyes on him, on his smirk, which had yet to waver.

"That is rather impolite," Dimitri said as she was about to close her door.

Ana peeked outside. "I can live with that," she replied. "I was mainly being polite to you because I thought you'd gotten me this job."

"Hurtful but valid," Dimitri said. "Then again, I am still the hotel manager."

She opened her mouth to ask whether he was serious, but he understood the question before it crossed her lips.

"Yes, I really am," he said.

Ana grimaced. If she had spoken to her previous boss in such a way, she would have been in for substantial pay cuts and begging for forgiveness.

"Don't worry," Dimitri said, apparently reading her expression. "I appreciate someone who speaks their mind. Besides, considering who hired you, I doubt I could fire you even if I wanted to."

Ana raised a brow, wondering if he would reveal what he knew after all, but Dimitri only chuckled and shook his head.

"Still," Ana said after a few moments, "I should go. I'm quite tired."

Dimitri's smile softened. "Better lock the door for the rest of the night," he said. "Who knows where else your nightmares might take you."

A chill ran down Ana's spine. "Good night, Dimitri," she said, suddenly even more eager to shut the door.

"Good night, Angel," he responded.

Ana scowled at him. "Please don't call me that."

"What else then?"

"Ms. Greene will do," she responded, hoping he meant his earlier words about not being able to fire her. "Good night."

Dimitri responded as the door shut. "It was a pleasure, Angel."

LOVE SONGS AND OTHER LIES

$\mathcal{A}$na woke, her eyes immediately roaming her surroundings, driven by fear of the dark, eerie corridor, and the veiled portrait. She found herself in her bed, coddled by soft pillows and warm blankets. The gentle light of morning slipped past her curtains into the room.

Ana blamed the alcohol for the vividness of the nightmare. The woman's face lingered in her mind with such clarity, as though she stood right before her. Ana shuddered, hoping to shake off the haunting image of the woman's mismatched eyes, one ice blue and the other warm brown.

She was determined to start the day afresh, not weighed down by the strange events of the party or her nocturnal exploration. Her first rehearsals awaited, and her excitement grew anew. Her chance had come, and she would not let it slip from her grasp.

After a long, steaming shower, Ana headed to the staff kitchen at the end of the corridor. The kitchen, rather than emulating the Hôtel de Neige's characteristic glamor, had a warmth the rest of the hotel lacked. Ana spotted Everett and Bahar at one of the tables, who waved her over, smiling when she joined them. She couldn't remember the last time she had eaten breakfast with someone else.

"Good morning," Ana said, scrutinizing Bahar.

"Good morning," Bahar responded, with a grin, her voice as chipper as ever. "How are you? You look a bit sleepy."

Ana squinted. It was true—an unrelenting tiredness hung in her bones. She was used to working twelve-hour shifts as a waitress, which should make her more accustomed to sleep deprivation. Yet it felt as though the dream, the running and trudging through the high snow, had drained her before she even opened her eyes.

"I'm good," Ana said. "What about you? I honestly thought you'd be lying in bed with a terrible hangover."

Bahar shrugged. "I don't really get hungover."

"Maybe you should," Everett commented, taking a sip from his black coffee. "Then you'd finally learn your lesson."

"Was it so bad last night?" Bahar turned to Ana, a mischievous smile on her lips. "I remember nothing."

Everett grimaced. "Unfortunately, we remember."

At his grave tone, Bahar's smile vanished, her shoulders slumping. "I'm sorry, Angie. I didn't mean to ruin your first night at the Hôtel de Neige."

"Oh, no, don't worry," Ana responded hastily. "You didn't." Hedwig Sternberg had taken care of that. The threat—*otherwise you might meet the same fate as our last singer*—haunted Ana now that she knew Hôtel de Neige's last singer had died. She didn't know the circumstances, but she was determined to find out. The more she understood about it, the less power Hedwig's threat would hold over her—or so she told herself.

"I'm getting another coffee," Everett said and got up. "Ana, do you want one too?"

"Yes, thank you."

Everett set out, and Bahar released a low groan. "He didn't even ask me," she said. "I think he's really angry with me this time."

Ana found that hard to argue with. "You were pretty upset about something last night," she told Bahar. "I was worried about you."

"Were you?" Bahar chuckled mirthlessly. She found her fingernails suddenly intriguing, eyeing them instead of Ana. "I'm just that kind of drunk."

"You apologized to me for something. I'm not sure what you meant by it. You said I'd be cold forever."

Bahar flinched and wrapped herself tighter in her thick cardigan. Her purple nails tapped in an uneven rhythm against the table as though she was waiting for the conversation to end. "What a weird thing to say."

"Yes," Ana responded, scrutinizing her. Bahar refused to meet her gaze. "You also mentioned something about Hôtel de Neige's last singer." A twinge of guilt ran through her for lying so blatantly, but she couldn't let this rest, and telling Bahar and Everett about Hedwig's words was out of the question. It would only make the ballerina a fiercer enemy.

Bahar's face paled. "I did?"

"You did," Ana responded, adamant. "You told me that—"

"Oh no," Bahar exclaimed abruptly, her voice high-pitched.

"What?"

"Will you look at the time?" Bahar said. "I have a shift starting in a couple of minutes. I need to go." She jumped up as though her life depended on it, nearly knocking over her empty coffee cup. Ana stared at her.

"I'm sorry, Angie," Bahar said, pulling her mouth into a thin smile. "Let's talk later, okay?"

With that, she took off, scurrying out of the staff kitchen and pulling the door shut behind with such force that the walls shook.

Ana glanced at the large clock on the wall behind her—9:04 am. Gaping at the empty chair, Ana was unsure what bewildered her more —why Bahar lied, or how anyone could be such a terrible liar.

When Everett returned with two cups of steaming coffee, a look of surprise rippled across his features. "Where did Bahar go?"

"She said she had a shift starting in a couple of minutes," Ana replied, holding back an exasperated sigh.

Everett frowned but didn't comment. They finished their breakfast in silence. After they had eaten, they headed to one of the few spots of the Hôtel de Neige Ana was familiar with—backstage. It was strange to return. Despite everything, a childlike giddiness rushed through her chest. After all her distress the night before, she had nearly forgotten—her dream extended before her. To be reminded was to be reawakened, recharged.

Everett nodded toward the stage. "In two weeks, with your debut, we begin our Christmas shows. We perform three nights a week, leading up to the grand finale on Christmas Day. The whole set tells a story—my original compositions." A mixture of awkwardness and pride crept into his voice as he spoke.

"What is it about?" Ana asked, expecting a Christmas tale.

Everett fidgeted with the chain of his gold pocket watch. "At its core, it's a love story," he explained. "It tells the tale of a young couple, deeply enamored. So the first songs are soft and light. Then one of the lovers is stolen away, cursed by the kiss of a witch. The other sets out on a quest to rescue her lost love." His voice grew more animated as he spoke. "The lovers are played by Palmira and Saverio Fiore," he continued. "Hedwig Sternberg plays our witch."

Ana bit back the smile. The casting was certainly suitable. "How does it end?"

"The lovers reunite, but are discovered by the witch," he responded. "The final song ends with their deaths."

"An interesting choice for a holiday show," Ana said.

Everett didn't respond, apparently so lost in thought that he didn't catch her remark. The pianist presented her with a heap of sheet music, but assured her they had plenty of time to rehearse. She studied the pages. In the margins, he had scribbled additional comments.

"Have you performed in front of a larger audience before?" he asked.

She pursed her lips. She had hoped to steer clear of her previous experiences as a singer. When she moved to New York City, it seemed to brim with opportunity. Then, four years passed, and although she had worked a few gigs, none of which had earned her much money, let alone valuable experience. The stages she had dreamed of remained far from reach.

"No," she admitted. "But don't worry, I—"

Everett shook his head. "I'm not worried. I was only curious." He paused. "Are *you* worried?"

Instinctively, Ana meant to deny it—to him and to herself. Her nervousness, her fear—they could be ugly emotions, so she considered it best to stash them away whenever she could.

"Just a little bit," she finally admitted.

"There's nothing to worry about," Everett responded, his tone gentle. "We chose you for a reason."

Ana swallowed down the taste of bile rising in her throat at his words. He meant them as encouragement, but they served as a reminder that they hadn't truly chosen her. Someone else had made the decision.

"Should we get out there and practice?" Everett asked, leaving her little time to contemplate.

Ana nodded, and they headed onstage. Like a magnet, some force pulled Ana's gaze to the theater box where she first noticed the ghastly silhouette. There was nothing there now, but she shuddered nonetheless.

Ana looked down the hall, filled with cushioned chairs and large tables. She believed them all empty until she saw a lone figure sitting in one corner.

"Is that Mikkel?" she asked.

Everett squinted, then nodded. "Yes, it is." Not a sliver of surprise rang in his voice. "Hello, Mike," he called out. The boy looked up from the book in his lap and waved at them.

Everett leaned toward Ana. "He isn't allowed to be here during the performances, so he likes watching the rehearsals. I hope that's alright with you."

Once again, it baffled Ana that a young child roamed the colossal hotel without any supervision, like a stray cat that had picked its temporary caretakers rather than the other way around. Before she could voice any concerns, Everett beckoned her to the grand piano at the front corner of the stage. She followed him.

"This first song tells the story of our lovers seeing each other for the first time," Everett told her as he sat down by the piano. "I will play it for you, and you can join in whenever you feel ready."

The melody began, and Ana remembered why she had yearned to be at Hôtel de Neige, why she had pursued her dream of becoming a singer for so long, even when it seemed hopeless. Everett's passion vibrated in the air and fluttered through her chest as his fingers danced over the keys.

It was a song of first love, simultaneously innocent and fiery. She painted vivid scenes in her head as she sang, creating the atmosphere and the emotions demanded by the music. This song, however, intimidated Ana with its difficulty.

When Everett played the piece for the second time, she joined him.

Ana thought of scenes from movies and stories. She pictured Cinderella's first dance with the prince, the way they regarded each other with silent understanding as they waltzed through the ballroom. Then, she imagined Beauty, holding the limp and dying body of Beast in her arms as she confessed her love to him. Tales such as those had touched her all throughout her life.

And yet, it was not the feeling of love which stirred within her. Rather, as she played out those romances, a touch of envy invaded her song, paired with a longing in her chest.

After the melody drew to its close, Everett turned to her. "That was good," he said tentatively. "Though I think it needs more emotion. Let's do it from the top." With a gentle smile, he added, "Think of a time when you fell in love."

Over the years, Ana had gone through a handful of boyfriends and girlfriends, though none had lasted longer than a few months. She doubted she had ever truly been in love with anyone.

A time when she had fallen in love. It didn't have to be with a person, did it? She recalled that overwhelming sensation that had grasped her when she first saw Hôtel de Neige. It had trembled through her bones, raising the hair on her skin. Along with it had come the warmth of hope, of possibility.

The lovers' gazes first met, the fog lifted, and the Hôtel de Neige rose into sight. Time stood still, and heartbeats quickened. Ana closed her eyes to see it before her. Electricity twisted through her body as all at once, the song made sense, its pieces falling together.

When the music stopped, it left her shaken, and she swayed, regaining steady footing.

Everett looked up at her, a look of wonder on his face. "That's more like it."

After that first song, half a dozen more followed until the world around Ana was more music than matter. When Everett rose and stepped away from the piano hours later, she had to reaccustom herself to the silence.

"Drink lots of tea with honey," Everett told her. "We start from the top tomorrow."

In that moment, Ana decided she would brave any threat or nightmare, for nothing could outweigh the bliss of her dream coming true.

They headed backstage, and Ana stayed behind a little longer after Everett had left. When she had waited for her audition, she had rushed through. Now she wanted to seize the chance to take a closer look at the delicate props and the fine costumes.

As Ana tried to match each set to its corresponding song, a melody arose from the theater once more. At first, she believed it to be only in her head, an echo from her rehearsals, but then it grew, and she realized someone else had taken over the stage. With Everett gone, the music came from the speakers, a faint semblance of the magic he had produced.

Ana approached, ignoring the fear urging her to stay back. She craned her neck, catching a glimpse of the woman who now occupied the stage. Ana was captivated, unable to turn back around.

Hedwig Sternberg stood where Ana sang just a short while ago.

She was tiny compared to the theater, yet she seemed to be its center, forceful enough to fill it to the brim with her presence.

Hedwig began to dance, and it appeared as though her feet hardly touched the ground beneath her. She floated, weightless, but when Ana focused, she could see the strain on Hedwig's muscles. How much effort did it cost her to make it look so effortless?

"You know, it is impolite to spy on others."

Ana whipped around. Behind her, a few feet away, stood Palmira Fiore. She had approached without Ana hearing even the faintest sound. Like Hedwig, Palmira wore her costume for the ballet, a blush tutu which flattered her dark eyes.

"I wasn't spying," Ana responded once she had gathered herself. She was only watching her fellow performer dance. They would soon be sharing a stage, although the thought of it churned within Ana's stomach.

Palmira fell silent as she surveyed Ana, her arms crossed and her eyes narrowed. "You'd do best to listen to Hedwig," she said, her sharp tone softened at the edges.

So the aversion Hedwig held towards Ana extended to the other dancers. "And what if I refuse to listen?" Ana responded. "Will I die like the last singer?"

"Watch your mouth," Palmira shot back. Then, in a more mellow tone, she added, "How do you know what happened to the last singer?"

Ana gritted her teeth and moved closer to Palmira, towering over the girl's petite frame. "Tell Hedwig to save the empty threats," Ana said. "I am here to stay." With that, Ana pushed past Palmira and made her way out of the theater.

THE LADY OF ICE AND SNOW

The following two weeks rushed by like the landscape observed from a train's window, a blur of colors and impressions. Ana spent nearly all her time in the theater or the music room. The strange events that marked her first days faded into the distance; she decided to leave them there. Ana kept her door locked at night, though, determined not to wander the dark corridors again.

The night of her debut, Ana met Everett backstage an hour before the show. Nausea rolled through her empty stomach—she hadn't managed a single bite of her dinner.

Everett greeted her with a bright smile. "Ana," he said, his voice softer than usual.

"Everett," she responded, wrapping her arms around herself.

"Come on," he said, studying her for a moment. "I want to show you something."

He guided her ahead until they came upon Bahar, standing in front of one of the dressing rooms. A wide grin broke across her features when she spotted Ana and Everett. Mike was there as well, though some ornate prop had captured his attention and he barely acknowledged their arrival.

"What is it?" Ana asked, eyeing Everett and Bahar and their exaggerated smiles. *They're going to kill me,* she thought. *I hope they kill me.*

"Your dress is ready," Bahar said.

Ana paused. She hadn't given it any thought before. Warmth tingled through her, momentarily driving out all her anxiety.

Bahar stepped aside and opened the door, revealing her costume. The sight of it traveled through Ana like a wave of electricity.

Wide skirts of a light, crisp blue cascaded to the floor, glittering like fresh snow in the evening sun. Shades of white and silver softly caught and reflected the light, and it set the dress aglow. The skirts led up to a tight, sleeveless bodice of white and sparkling blue with a swooping neckline. Ana had to take a step back to appreciate it in its entirety. It stretched out before her like a frozen lake, shining in the colors of deepest winter.

"It's gorgeous," Ana whispered, unable to stop staring. It reminded her of a piece of art, a painting in a museum hanging far away from the visitors, never to be touched.

"Let's get you into this," Bahar said with determination.

Everett slipped away, taking Mike with him. Ana stripped off her own clothes, which had lost all color next to the enchanting gown.

It quickly became clear that Ana needed Bahar's help; it would be impossible to get into the dress on her own. It was heavier than expected, but fit her like a second skin.

"Look at you," Bahar said and clapped her hands.

Ana gazed at the stranger in the mirror. She looked taller, older, more sure of herself. Her wild curls were pinned back, revealing more of the sharp structure of her cheekbones and jawline. She looked elegant, unrecognizable from her former self.

"Can we come back and look?" Mike called.

"Yes," Ana said. "You can come back in."

The boy ambled back into the dressing room, stopping to assess Ana. His head leaned to the side, his arms crossed.

Everett regarded Ana with a soft smile. "You look beautiful."

She cringed at all the attention she was receiving. To think she would be on stage before hundreds of spectators in less than an hour.

"I don't like the color," Mike said.

Ana couldn't help but chuckle at his judgment, spoken with utter seriousness. "You don't?" She responded. "What color do you think it should be?"

Again, he gave the question considerable thought. "Orange," he finally answered. "That's my favorite color."

"Orange," Ana echoed. She glanced at Everett and Bahar, who observed the boy, amused. "Well, perhaps the next one will be orange."

Mike shrugged. "I doubt it."

"Okay, Mike," Bahar said. "How about we get out of here and let Everett and Angie prepare for their performance?"

Ana looked at the clock, realizing the show was rapidly drawing closer. Her stomach churned, and her hands began to tremble.

"How are you feeling?" Everett asked.

Ana forced her shaking hands to still. "I'm nervous, to be honest." She'd feared speaking it aloud would worsen her anxiety, but admitting to it had a calming effect.

"I know. I still remember how nervous I was before I played my first show." He gave her a gentle smile. "You love to sing, don't you?"

Ana nodded. Singing had always been her escape. When her foster homes suffocated her, when classmates pushed her around, when her bosses treated her like scum, she had always turned to music.

"Well," Everett said, "that's all you need to do. You only need to stand there and sing."

"Yes, I know. That's the terrifying part."

"But it's also what you love the most, isn't it?"

Ana's chest fluttered as she thought of it. So long she had dreamed of this day; the hope of it had kept her persistent even on the darkest days. "It is."

"You took this job to do what you're passionate about. To sing. The audience—they don't matter. Don't sing for them today. Sing for yourself, and enjoy it."

Ana remembered how she'd pictured it all in her dreams. In those beautiful images, the audience applauded her, though she had heard only its echoes. In the center, it was always only her, losing herself to the music, proving it to herself rather than to those watching her.

She looked at Everett and gave him a timid smile. "Thank you."

Soon after, Ana stood behind the curtain and listened to the distant clinging of silverware as the guests finished their desserts. The time to the show drew closer, the seconds ticking away seemingly faster than usual.

Distant chattering rose as the clinging ceased. Ana imagined waiters swooping in to clear out the tables. A few moments later, Everett turned to her.

"Are you ready?"

Ana nodded, hoping it was true. Everett gave her one more smile of encouragement, then he headed to the microphone at the heart of the stage. Her dress seemed to compress around her body, threatening to choke off all the air from her lungs.

The curtain drew open, and the audience received him with soft clapping.

"Good evening." His voice boomed. "We welcome you to the first show of our Christmas concerts. Tonight, we welcome the new singer of the Hôtel de Neige, Ms. Ana Greene."

Everett gestured towards Ana, and, more marionette than woman, she walked onto the stage. The spotlights held her in their grasp and blinded her for a few steps, drowning her in their brilliant white.

Ana reached Everett, and he moved away from the microphone for her, taking his seat by the piano. For a moment, time stood still as Ana's gaze wandered through the audience. She believed there to be nearly three hundred people in attendance, though the theater might as well have been filled with thousands of spectators, watching her with intensity.

Ana spotted a familiar face among them. In the first box sat Dimitri Morozov, looking at her as though nothing else in the room mattered to him. Their eyes met, and he smiled, giving her a slow nod as though he, too, meant to encourage her. Ana's gaze lingered on him before moving on to the woman who sat to his left.

Ana's breath hitched in her throat, and she caught herself before she could stumble. That face—she had seen it before. She blinked, once, twice, thrice—she did not trust her own eyes. She looked around, to Everett, then to Dimitri. Did they not see the woman? If they did, how could they be so calm? Every impulse in her body screamed for her to run, but hundreds of people were focused on her. The spotlight had transformed into a cage.

All the incidents she had blamed on her imagination came back to her. She had seen the woman before, up in that box the day of her auditions, up on the balustrade in the lobby, and out in the winter gardens. She had seen her in her nightmares.

The phantom in white.

Now there she sat, in the midst of the audience, commanding an air of elegance and authority. Long, pure white hair flowed down to frame her tall body. Her pale skin had the same shade as did her dress, decorated with silver stones and white embroidery. She looked like a character from some long-forgotten fairytale Ana had read as a child.

Ana couldn't move or breathe, let alone sing. She thought it could be an illusion once more, but the woman didn't vanish, not this time.

"Ana," Everett whispered, drawing her back into her body.

She forced herself to cease staring. It demanded a great effort from her to glance away from the woman and at Everett.

"It's time," the pianist whispered as his fingers touched upon the keys of the piano. The house lights dimmed, and the melody of the first song flooded the hall with its sweet beauty.

Ana was still half frozen, half in shock. She took a deep breath and turned away from the woman in white, but the image lingered in her mind. She wanted to gasp for air, but she had to sing. Magnified by the microphone, her voice rose. And it trembled.

The wrongness almost made her stop. She clung to the microphone, her gaze traveling to Everett for rescue. Ana felt the woman in white watching her, her gaze like a tightening corset.

"Focus on the music," he mouthed as his fingers danced across the keys.

Focus on the music. All she needed was to sing, to do the part she loved the most. Ana closed her eyes. *Focus.*

Ana captured the next note, and the world around her disappeared. She traveled back to the day she had first seen the Hôtel de Neige. Its grandiose image rose before her, along with the emotions it evoked within her. The bliss and the butterflies of falling in love sang their duet. Ana poured herself into the song, leaving no part of herself untapped, surrendering herself to the music. She trembled with the strength it took to give herself up so entirely.

Ana knew Everett, Palmira, and Saverio were on the stage with her, but she paid them no thought. It was only her and the melody.

Upon the third song, her body felt strained, and she feared she might collapse. She swept across high, pure pitches to low, melancholy notes. The love story continued, its passion and intensity growing. Before her inner eye, Ana saw the halls and corridors of the hotel. She even pictured herself there on stage, in the spotlight. Her heart pounded, threatening to jump out of her chest.

The end of the last song approached without her ever opening her eyes. Her hand lay on her chest, which rose and fell along with the melody. They climbed towards the end of the song, and Ana felt like a shooting star, aflame with her own force.

She grasped the last note and held onto it, opening her eyes as she sang. Through tears, she saw her captivated audience. The moment she finished, applause rang through the hall.

Ana stared down, out of breath yet with a smile on her lips. "Thank you," she whispered into the microphone as the house lights came back on, and her voice came out loud and clear, the spoken words themselves still melodic. She looked over to Everett, whose entire face had lit up with joy and what she believed to be pride. Up in the first box, Dimitri smiled down at Ana and clapped.

Then Ana's eyes found the woman in white again. She wasn't clapping, but when their eyes interlocked, she gave Ana a subtle nod and smile of approval. Her long, thin fingers wrapped around the stem of her wine glass, which she raised in Ana's honor. Despite the heat of the moment, a chill rushed through Ana's body. She blamed it on the cold sweat.

Ana met at center stage with Everett, Palmira, and Saverio, and together they bowed, receiving another round of applause. Everett then offered Ana his arm, and they set off together, following the ballet dancers. She felt overcome with the thrill of it, tears of bliss in her eyes. Once they had left the stage, Everett offered her a handkerchief.

"Stop ruining your makeup," he told her, a sparkle of amusement in his expression.

Ana sniffled and tapped away the teardrops. They found a quiet place to sit down—a great relief for her—as she doubted her feet could support her for much longer. Her gown formed a semicircle of glittering fabric around the chair.

"Congratulations, Ana," Everett said, his eyes and smile bright. "You were wonderful out there."

"It was…" She didn't know how to put the sensation into words. It had left her breathless, speechless. The world before her was a blur of radiant colors.

"This will help."

Someone handed Ana a glass of water. As she opened her mouth to thank whoever had handed her the glass, she saw Dimitri Morozov standing above her, his head cocked to the side. "Angel," he said. "Congratulations. You were astonishing." He reached for Ana's hand and pressed a kiss to it.

"What do you want, Morozov?" Everett asked, his tone icy.

Ana studied the two men before her. Dimitri wore his usual, self-assured smirk, but Everett's jaw had grown tense.

"As you can see," Dimitri responded, "I have come to congratulate our new, extraordinarily talented singer." Dimitri threw her a glance, as though a compliment would draw Ana to his side. She sensed Everett was right—he wanted something.

"Just spit it out, Morozov," Everett said.

"Why? Are we low on time?" When Everett glared at him, Dimitri chuckled. "Alright, I will get to the point since you despise my company so much." He regarded Ana with a lopsided smile, ripe with mischief. "Ms. de Winter sent me. She wants to meet you."

Everett inhaled sharply. Ana didn't need to ask who Ms. de Winter was; she knew instinctively.

Dimitri held his hand out to her. "It is not a request you can deny, Angel."

For once, she sensed a touch of sternness in his tone. Ana glanced at Everett, and he gave a stiff nod.

"He's right."

She rose without taking Dimitri's hand.

"Is the age of gentlemen truly over?" he asked.

Before setting out, Ana turned to Everett. "I will see you in the staff kitchen later?"

"Yes," Everett replied with a hasty, wavering smile.

Ana had no time to contemplate Everett's strange behavior as Dimitri took off, and she followed him, her dress rustling with each step. Once they were out of Everett's earshot, Dimitri turned back to Ana.

"I meant it when I said you were wonderful out there."

The genuine warmth in his voice sent an unexpected tremor through her. "Thank you."

Dimitri led her to the entrance of the theater and up a set of wide stairs. Even from a distance, she could see the ghastly woman sitting with her back to them; nonetheless, Ana felt she sensed their coming.

When they drew near, the woman rose, turning, and Ana came to an abrupt halt. Ms. de Winter looked as though she'd been conjured from ice and snow, crafted into a living, breathing creature. She stood taller than Ana and even a bit above Dimitri. In close proximity, Ana got a true glimpse of her eyes. One was chestnut brown, the other pale blue—just as Ana had dreamed. She clutched the skirts of her dress so hard that she feared the delicate fabric might tear.

"Ms. Greene," the woman said with a voice sweet as honey, tinged with a soft accent. "What a pleasure to meet you. My name is Erica de Winter." After a short, purposeful pause, she added, "I am the owner of Hôtel de Neige."

Ana was unsurprised; part of her had guessed as much already. Erica de Winter suited the role perfectly. She was the human embodiment of the hotel, with all its glamor and beauty, and she had the same air of mystery about her.

"A pleasure to meet you," Ana responded, straightening her shoulders.

"Please, sit down," Erica said and gestured towards the empty chair to her left.

Dimitri pulled it over for Ana, and she saw no choice but to obey, even though the presence of the hotel's owner made her weary and uncomfortable.

"You delivered a breathtaking performance," Erica said, leaning towards Ana. Her pale skin resembled fragile porcelain. "I am glad to know I made the right decision."

Understanding barreled through Ana. "You're the one who chose me for this job," she said, and Erica inclined her head. "Thank you, Ms. de Winter." She scrambled to stitch the words together, still rather shaken from her performance and the encounter with the ghost she'd been seeing.

"Call me Erica, and there is no need to thank me. You are a truly gifted singer. I fell in love with your voice the moment I first heard it. It made me...nostalgic."

Erica smiled. "Honestly, I found it hard to believe my committee did not choose you in the first place. All the other singers were mediocre at best. Perhaps dear Hedwig did not want you to steal the show." She winked at Ana with her pale eye.

"We are glad you had the last word," Dimitri said and raised his glass. "To Ana."

Erica lifted her own glass as well. When she spoke, her voice had lowered, sounding almost melodic. "To Ana," she echoed.

Ana hoped it would conclude their introduction, but with a gesture to her staff, Erica ordered a bottle of champagne and an additional glass for Ana.

"Please, tell us more about yourself, Ana," Erica said in her most enticing voice, and Dimitri, too, perked up. "I know nothing of you except your name. I simply cannot have anyone in this hotel more mysterious than myself."

Ana gave a low chuckle, not entirely sure whether Erica de Winter meant it as a joke. "There's honestly not much to tell," she responded.

A server arrived with the champagne, granting Ana a short grace period as they toasted again and drank the first sips. It sparkled on her tongue. She had never known alcohol could be so delicious.

"Everyone has a story to tell," Erica said after setting her glass down. "What did you do before you joined us at Hôtel de Neige?"

Ana blushed. "I was a waitress in New York City," she confessed. The diner where she had worked seemed a world away. She doubted Erica de Winter would ever set foot near such an establishment.

"How intriguing," the hotel's owner responded. While her tone sounded convincing, Ana detected a sliver of boredom in her eyes. "Have you always lived in New York City?"

Ana shook her head. She decided to stick to safe truths. "Before I moved to New York, I grew up in Montana."

"Does your family still live there?"

Most of Ana's foster families still did, as far as she knew. She kept in touch with none of them. "Yes."

A spark reawakened in Erica's eyes. Ana feared the hotel's mistress knew she wasn't telling the whole truth. "They must miss you."

"We're not close." Ana wagered all her foster families had thanked the lord every time she'd run off, and had pouted whenever social services dragged her back.

Before Erica could ask the next unwelcome question, Ana decided to divert the attention. "What about you?" she dared to ask. "Where are you from?"

Erica straightened, one thin brow lifting. Apparently, she hadn't expected reciprocity. "Copenhagen, Denmark. Though I haven't paid a visit to my home in many years."

"Do you still have family there?"

Erica gave a low laugh and reclined in her chair. She took a sip from her champagne and then shook her head, not as an answer, but rather as an admonition for Ana, warning her not to overstep. She glanced at Dimitri, whose gaze flew back and forth between Erica and her. He wore the faintest smile upon his slightly parted lips.

"Ana," Erica said, "I am sure we will see much more of each other in the future. I am looking forward to your next performance."

Ana understood that was the signal for her to depart. She drank the last sip of her champagne and thanked them for the invitation. "It was a pleasure," she added as she rose.

Erica nodded, her eyes catching each of Ana's movements.

"Until we meet again, Angel," Dimitri said, despite having remained uncharacteristically quiet.

Ana left, turning her back to them. Despite the warmth of the theater, chills crawled across her skin, and she wished for something warm to wrap herself in.

TRUTH OR DARE

After her unsettling encounter with Erica de Winter, Ana changed back into her own clothes, which proved quite the challenge without Bahar's help. Once returned to normalcy, she meant to head straight to the staff kitchen until she saw someone lingering backstage.

Hedwig Sternberg stood a few feet from the exit with Palmira and Saverio Fiore. The ballerina hadn't performed earlier, though she would appear in the upcoming shows. Ana had done her best to steer clear of her after their exchange in the winter gardens. This time, a run-in with her seemed inevitable.

Ana met the ballerina's steely eyes as she crossed her arms, surveying Ana. Neither spoke. After Ana passed the group, she heard low whispers she was determined to ignore. She had no need for their approval—she had proven herself on the stage and earned her applause. Nothing else mattered.

Ana made her way to the staff kitchen, which was abuzz with activity, the air thick with the presence of so many people. Despite her dislike of crowds, she was grateful for the warmth; it drove away the icy cold that clung to her, incited by Erica de Winter, then sharpened by Hedwig Sternberg.

Ana found Everett and Bahar at a table in the back. She wasn't fully accustomed to spending so much time with them. She hadn't been close to other people in a long while—or ever, if she thought about it.

"There you are," Bahar exclaimed as Ana took a seat. "Everett told me you were amazing."

Ana blushed, feeling a sense of pride and warmth upon all the praise she was receiving. "Thank you."

"I think this needs to be celebrated," Bahar said, an impish glint in her eyes.

Everett cleared his throat and tilted his head to the side. He looked at her like a patient, though firm father waiting for his child to do what was expected of them.

Bahar rolled her eyes. "I will be more moderate today, I promise." She turned to Ana. "What do you say?"

"I could use a drink." Her nerves were still somewhat on edge. If the others noticed, they didn't let on.

They fetched the alcohol, and Ana set about mixing cocktails. She had briefly worked as a bartender until the owner realized she was only eighteen and kicked her out. Still, she held onto the useful skills.

"Let's play a drinking game," Bahar suggested once everyone had a full glass in front of them. "How about Truth or Dare?"

Everett grimaced. "What are we, sixteen?"

"Don't be such a snob. I like Truth or Dare." Bahar turned to Ana. "What about you?"

Ana had long held an aversion to games like these—they pried too deep. Still, she had some questions she wanted to ask. "Yeah, let's give it a try," she said.

Bahar clapped her hands in excitement. "Perfect. Then let's start with you." As Bahar grinned at her, Ana began to regret her decision. "Truth or Dare?"

"Truth," Ana responded and prayed for a gentle question.

Bahar thought for a moment, then asked, "When did you lose your virginity?"

"Bahar, really?" Everett said and shook his head. "Ana, you don't have to answer that question."

Ana took a generous drink from her glass. Many would consider the question highly intimate, but for her, it hardly felt personal. If they had asked about her family situation or her childhood, she would have experienced far greater discomfort.

"Fifteen," she said. "In the back of his mom's car. I bumped my head so hard I thought I had a concussion."

Bahar burst into boisterous laughter while Everett chuckled into his fist. Ana pressed her lips together, restraining the smile. With relief, she realized their eyes held no judgment, only shared amusement.

"Everett, your turn," Bahar declared. "Truth, I assume?" When he nodded, she sighed but didn't argue. "Were you ever chased by the police?"

"Bahar, you know the answer to that question."

"Yes, I know everything about you. But Ana doesn't, and it's such a good story."

Everett groaned, then launched into the tale of a drunk escapade during which he had attended an illegal party in a hidden bar. "It was already close to dawn, and the police showed up. I was there with my boyfriend at the time, and we managed to make it out through the back exit, but had to climb up the building next door to evade the officers."

"And they stayed there to watch the sunrise," Bahar added, swooning. "Isn't it romantic?"

Ana smiled, though she noticed the tension in Everett's jaw. Perhaps the relationship had come to an unpleasant end. As far as she knew, he wasn't currently involved with anyone.

A few more rounds of cliché questions and dares passed while they consumed their share of cocktails and occasional shots. The edges of Ana's vision had a soft blur to them, and she could tell Everett and Bahar were intoxicated as well. It was time to ask some of the questions spiraling through her mind.

"Truth or Dare?" Ana asked Everett.

"Truth," he said, making Bahar roll her eyes.

"You're too boring for this game," she told him.

"There's no rule that I can't always choose Truth."

"I'm making one now. Next round, you have to do a dare."

Everett wrinkled his nose in distaste. "Fine. But I still have Truth for this round."

Ana gave a nod, then dared to ask the question. "Why do you dislike Dimitri Morozov?"

Everett stiffened, trying to overplay the reaction with a chuckle. "Now that is a boring question," he said, failing to sound casual. "For one, nobody likes Morozov. He's a jerk."

Ana sensed there was more to it. She raised her brows, beckoning Everett to elaborate. Instead, Bahar jumped in.

"He's a sell-out," she said, her expression turned sour.

"A sell-out? To whom?"

Everett cleared his throat. "Dimitri Morozov is a rich asshole who only cares about himself. Honestly, that's it. There's no personal history or grudge to it. I simply cannot stand the guy."

Ana nodded slowly, though the answer didn't satisfy her. "What about Erica de Winter?"

Their small corner had grown eerily quiet compared to the rest of the kitchen. Had she gone too far? The questions she asked were only natural—unlike Everett and Bahar's reactions to them.

"She's the owner of the hotel," Everett responded, his tone clipped. "What more do you need to know?"

"Well, is she a good boss, for starters?"

Everett shrugged. "She doesn't bother much with the everyday mechanisms of the hotel. For the most part, Mr. Rutherford takes care of the business."

"What about Dimitri? Isn't he the hotel manager?"

"Officially, yes, but I think he grew tired of it years ago."

While he spoke, Bahar narrowed her eyes at Ana. "Are you on a first-name basis with Dimitri Morozov?"

Fuck. Ana bit her lip and clasped her hands around her glass, unsure what else to do with them. She'd prefer to keep her exchanges with Dimitri a secret, especially since Everett and Bahar vehemently disliked him.

"I ran into him a couple of times," Ana admitted. "On the day of my audition and then after the party in the winter gardens."

"I mean, you're pretty, so you're probably his type," Bahar said, making a barfing noise. "How could you even stomach talking to him?"

Ana swallowed hard. How had this exchange turned on her so quickly? "I guess you're right, he's kind of a jerk," she said. "But he was also nice to me."

Bahar frowned. "Which one is it? Is he a jerk or is he nice?"

Ana gritted her teeth and wished she had just kept her curiosity to herself. Irritation itched at her, in part at herself, and in part at them for their odd behavior and their refusal to give her any honest answers.

"Wait," Bahar said after Ana hesitated to respond. She clasped a hand over her mouth. "Did you sleep with Dimitri Morozov?"

Ana stared at her, irritation transforming into outright anger. "No, of course not!"

"I think we should change the topic," Everett said.

"I think I should go to bed," Ana countered. She finished the rest of her drink in one go, hoping the ice in it would cool down the rising heat within her. "I'd say I'm sorry, but honestly, I just asked a few questions."

With that, she stood up and turned on her heels. She wished she could make a dignified exit, but the kitchen still brimmed with people, and she needed to apologize to at least a dozen of them before she squeezed her way out.

Once in the staff corridor, Ana staggered ahead a few steps before leaning against the closest wall. She took a quivering breath, charged with anger. Anger at Everett and Bahar, anger at Hedwig Sternberg and her entourage, anger at Erica de Winter and Dimitri, anger at herself. It tainted the beautiful memory of her first performance.

All her life, Ana had longed for a place for herself, a place to call home. When she'd gotten the job at Hôtel de Neige, she allowed herself to believe she had finally found it. Yet just as quickly, it had begun to slip from her grasp. The hotel remained a maze and a mystery to her, as did its inhabitants. She felt like an intruder still, unable to venture beyond its beautiful surface and see what lay hidden beneath.

Ana pushed herself into motion, cursing the vodka and tequila and whatever else she had consumed. She made it to her room without stumbling or further embarrassing herself.

As she entered, a wave of soberness washed over her. There was something strange about the room. A new scent hung in the air, sickly sweet like summer flowers beginning to rot. The effects of the alcohol wore off as her heart raced.

She scanned her surroundings, positioning her key between her fingers. Utter silence enveloped her. It didn't look like anything had been touched. She allowed her shoulders to relax—maybe she was just paranoid. She approached the bathroom door with cautious steps, unable to shake off her dark premonition. It lay open by a slit. She pushed it further, then pressed the light switch.

The key dropped from Ana's grasp. Her breath caught in her throat as she stared into her bathroom.

PIECES OF A BROKEN MIRROR

Tiny pieces of glass covered the floor, glittering with treacherous beauty. Her mirror was shattered, and a message was scrawled on the wall next to it, letters of crusted blood smeared against the white paint. *Leave while you still can.*

Ana felt both drunk and sober all at once. Her gaze jumped around. Curtains fluttered, her shadow dancing on the walls with the fabric. Someone had broken in, had written that threat. What if they hadn't left?

She darted to the ground to grab her key as if it could protect her. A few inches away, the edges of the broken mirror glinted at her through her tears. Those jagged pieces were sharper than a key. The logical part of her brain screamed a warning, but it was quiet compared to her panic. She grabbed the largest piece of mirror. It dug into the flesh of her palm, but she clasped it tighter. With the adrenaline rushing through her body, she barely felt its sting. Drops of her blood pattered on the floor.

Something rustled behind her.

Ana shot up, raising her makeshift dagger. "Show yourself."

There was no answer, but that scent of rotting flowers still hung in the air. She smelled blood—was it the message on the wall or her own, running down her wrist and soaking her sweater?

Her reflection flashed upon the bloody shard, her bloodshot eyes looking back at her.

There was only one person who could have done this. Another bout of rage flared up in her. She had no idea where Hedwig Sternberg would be, but she knew she'd find her.

Ana stormed out of her desecrated room, nearly colliding with two people. Tangled words stumbled out of her mouth in a semblance of an apology, then she realized who stood before her. Everett and Bahar, slowly coming into focus, gawked at her.

"Angie, are you alright?" Bahar said, then her gaze fell. "Oh my god, you're bleeding."

Ana looked down at her hand, stained red, but still gripping the mirror. She needed to protect herself. "I'm...I'm fine." Even in her daze, she knew she didn't sound convincing.

Everett stared at her hand. "What the hell happened, Ana? We came to apologize, but—"

"Someone...there's..." A sob cut off her words. Unable to speak, she nodded toward her room.

Everett and Bahar exchanged glances of confusion, then the pianist ran inside. For a few moments, silence reigned, then a low gasp sounded, followed by quiet mumbling.

"What is it?" Bahar demanded as soon as Everett returned. Instead of waiting for a response, she darted into the room to see for herself. Her reaction was louder, accompanied by curses as she came back out.

"Everything will be alright," Everett whispered. He gently reached out to Ana, carefully prying her fingers from the shard of mirror until it fell to the ground. Droplets of crimson splattered on the pristine carpet.

"What happened, Ana?" Bahar asked.

It took Ana another moment before she was able to respond. "I came back just a few minutes ago and found it that way."

"Okay, we'll get you away from here," Everett said and took Ana by the arm. "Bahar, we'll go to your room. She can settle down there."

"No, I don't want that," Ana said. "I'm fine, really."

"You don't look fine."

Anger shot through Ana, driving away some of the shock. "I can handle it by myself," she told him, and she meant it.

"I know. But you don't have to. Now come on."

Ana lacked the energy—and perhaps the willpower—to protest. Exhausted, she obliged when Bahar took her by the arm and led her away. They entered Bahar's room, and Ana sank down on the bed.

Everett left, returning with a first aid kit a few minutes later. He sat down beside Ana and took her hand. She felt nothing at all as he cleaned and bandaged her wound. The image of the broken mirror and the bloody message flashed in her mind, as aggressive as stroboscopic light.

Bahar paced, spitting out curses in at least three languages. "I can't believe anyone would do such a thing. Was that…was that real blood, you think?"

"It looked like real blood," Ana said, her tone hollow.

"Why the hell would anyone do that? *Who* the hell would do that?"

Ana wiped away some of her smudged mascara. "I know who did it."

Bahar came to an abrupt halt. She and Everett stared at Ana.

"Who?" Everett asked.

"Hedwig Sternberg."

The room seemed to hold its breath. Everett and Bahar looked at each other, bewildered.

Everett took a seat next to Ana. "Why do you think Hedwig did it?"

Ana had hoped to avoid reliving her first encounter with the ballerina, but saw no way to avoid it. "During the party in the winter gardens, when I went to look around, I ran into Hedwig," she told them. "She told me I don't belong here, that I wasn't good enough for Hôtel de Neige. She made it clear she wanted me gone."

"What the hell?" Bahar exclaimed. "I mean, we know she can be a b—"

Everett held up a hand to stop her. He regarded Ana. "Hedwig truly said that?"

"She did."

Everett leaned back, rubbing his temples. "I can't believe she would say that," he said, more to himself than to Ana. "Let alone do such a thing to your room."

A moment passed before he faced Ana again. Only then did she notice how tired he looked. The deep rings beneath his eyes aged him. "There's something you should know," he said.

Ana raised a brow. In this place where secrets were so carefully guarded, she was eager to jump at any revelation.

"The day of the auditions," Everett began, "we did want to hire you. I thought you were wonderful, and even Palmira and Saverio adored you—and they hardly ever adore anything but themselves and each other." He paused, surveying Ana. "Hedwig, though, remained adamant about not hiring you. Our decision took so long because we had a heated discussion about it. She shut down any argument in your favor without clear reasoning. In the end, she managed to sway Palmira and Saverio, and that was it."

"Until Erica de Winter decided she wanted me as the new singer," Ana added. The discovery should have come as a relief to her, to know she had deservedly landed the job. Instead, it unsettled her.

"There's something else," Ana said. "Hedwig told me that unless I left, I would meet the same fate as the hotel's last singer."

Everett froze while Bahar merely stared, the words knocked out of her.

"What happened to the last singer?" Ana asked. "I know he died, but how, exactly?"

Everett and Bahar exchanged a long look, perhaps silently deciding whether to let her in on the secret. Time stretched until Everett raised his voice again.

He seemed to be in physical discomfort as he spoke. "It was an accident that happened some years ago. He went outside in the winter, and apparently, he fell, knocking himself out. He died of hypothermia."

What a fitting death.

"So there was no foul play involved?"

Everett shook his head. "No. He died of natural causes."

"I can't believe Hedwig would threaten you like that," Bahar said and started pacing again.

"She's a complicated person," Everett responded.

"A complicated person?" Ana breathed out a hollow laugh. "She's cruel. She broke into my room to shatter my mirror and write a threat on my wall. She's not complicated—she's a high school bully."

"I'll go talk to her," Everett said. "Bahar, can Ana stay in your room tonight?"

"Of course."

Ana grew still. She meant to confront Hedwig herself, but the fire that had raged within her earlier had reduced to embers. Yet despite the exhaustion, she doubted she could sleep without knowing what the ballerina had to say for herself.

Everett left, and Ana heaved herself up from Bahar's bed. "I need to smoke a cigarette or two," she announced.

"Do you want me to come along?"

"No, it's fine. I need a few moments alone."

Bahar never asked whether she should fetch Ana's coat from her room or if Ana had any cigarettes with her. All the better for it.

Ana slipped out of the room and spotted Everett at the end of the corridor just as he entered the staff elevators. The doors closed behind him, and he was gone without a sign as to which floor he was headed to. She knew the only way was up, and that, given the notorious slowness of the elevator, she would likely be faster than him.

She hurried up the stairs and reached the second floor hallway where she paused until she heard the low scratching of opening elevator doors. Ana inched ahead, careful to keep out of sight until she heard a knock and came to a sudden halt. She peeked around the corner, seeing Everett just as Hedwig opened the door for him.

Ana pressed her back against the wall and held her breath, afraid even the smallest noise would reveal her presence.

"Everett," Hedwig said. "What gives me the honor of a visit at such a late hour?"

Everett spoke. "Our new singer found a disturbing message written in blood in her room tonight."

Ana yearned to see the ballerina's expression, to watch her mouth twist in the face of accusation. She wondered what she would give, how she would try to twist herself out of it.

"Yes, I'm aware," Hedwig responded, her tone unchanged. "I left the message."

Ana pressed her lips together to rein in her reaction. Had Hedwig truly confessed so readily?

"And there's no need to be so dramatic," Hedwig added. "It was lipstick."

Ana didn't feel relieved. Even if the blood on her wall had not been real, *she* had still bled. Stains of it clotted on the hem of her sweater.

"What?" Everett asked, dumbfounded. "Why would you do such a thing?"

Hedwig released a long, theatrical sigh. "The real question is, why wouldn't you?"

"What is that supposed to mean?"

"Honestly, Everett, this charade you keep up day by day—doesn't it exhaust you?"

Ana could no longer hold herself back. She had to steal a look around the corner. Hedwig leaned against the doorframe, her arms crossed, with that expression of superiority on her delicate features once again. Everett gaped at her. Ana couldn't see much of his face, but his stance showed he was on edge.

"I choose to remain optimistic," he said after a pause. "I'm sorry you cannot do the same."

Hedwig released a cold laugh. "Optimistic? What are you optimistic about? You pore over your piano all day long, trying to create your magnum opus, and for what? So you can play it in front of a dining hall?"

"Just because you're unhappy doesn't mean I am," Everett responded. Ana had never heard his voice infused with such bitterness. Except, perhaps, when he had spoken to Dimitri.

"You're so blind, Everett. You put so much time and energy into your attempt of optimism, you cannot see what is happening around you. Just look at Yilmaz. She's halfway to becoming an alcoholic. Do you truly believe positivity and hope can fix that? You've got coal in your hands, and your optimism will not turn it into diamonds, no matter how hard you cling to it."

"You have no right to make such judgments," Everett said. "Choose to be bitter, I don't care, but leave other people out of it. Ana deserves better than this."

Hedwig laughed. "You're right. Ana does deserve better than this. Which is why I'm trying to protect her. You ought to do the same rather than sell her a beautiful illusion because you're afraid of the truth."

Ana held her breath. Was the ballerina truly claiming she only meant to protect her? And if so, from what?

"What good does your acceptance of the truth do you, Hedwig?" Ana flinched upon the low rumbling of Everett's voice, which grew more adamant with each word. It didn't suit the gentle pianist she knew. "You are still in the same place as the rest of us, except you think you will change something by smearing lipstick on walls and breaking mirrors. Even if you succeeded in chasing Ana away, then what? We'd hire the next person, and the next, and one will stick eventually."

When Hedwig laughed again, it no longer sounded humorless. She chuckled as though she genuinely found his words amusing. "You're blind and you're deaf, Everett."

"What are you talking about?"

Ana held herself as still as she could, fighting the urge to scream that same question at her. She feared that if she moved the slightest bit, she would lose control and storm to the door to demand the answer herself.

"You have listened to her sing so many times, Everett. If you don't understand by now, I cannot help you. I will only pray that everyone else remains as oblivious as you."

"Hedwig, what—"

The ballerina stopped him. "Everett, it is late, and you're wasting our time. Listen to me or forget my words—it makes no difference to me. I tried to help, but I believe it is time to surrender. Maybe I shall try your battle plan and hope a little."

With this, she shut the door, leaving both Everett and Ana frozen and speechless. By a stroke of luck, Ana quickly regained her senses and slipped away before he headed back to the elevator. She remained by the stairs, letting herself sink to the floor. For every answer she had gotten, she had a thousand more questions pressing down on her.

The conversation played over and over in her head like a broken record. Hedwig had confessed without hesitation, yet she sounded as though she had tried to do Ana a favor, as though the scarlet warning was an attempt to protect her. She knew something. Something about Ana that Everett was too blind and deaf to grasp. Ana leaned her head against the wall and wished she had taken cigarettes with her after all.

YOU ARE CORDIALLY INVITED

Through the next couple of weeks, some form of normality returned to Hôtel de Neige and to Ana's life. The mirror in her bathroom was replaced, the wall scrubbed clean. When she moved back in, no signs of Hedwig's presence remained except the soft tinge of lily perfume in the air. It refused to fade, no matter how many times Ana aired out the room.

Preparations for the Christmas concert monopolized her days. The final show would be the conclusion of the tragedy—the death of the lovers. "It's generally the highlight of the winter," Everett had told Ana at rehearsal as the day drew closer.

He never spoke about his conversation with Hedwig. Whenever Ana tried to pry it from him, he'd pretend he hadn't talked to the ballerina since the incident. After a while, Ana acquiesced, realizing her efforts led nowhere. The frustration slowly wore off, and once some time had passed, Ana almost fooled herself into believing it all lay in the past. Despite that, the suspicion that more was yet to come haunted her.

On the day before Christmas, after dress rehearsal, Dimitri waited for her outside her room. He leaned against the doorframe, wearing his signature smirk.

"Dimitri," she said, not bothering with a polite greeting. Outside, the world grew dark, and she was tired after another long day.

"Angel." His voice dripped like thick, sweet honey. "Aren't you happy to see me? It's been a while."

Ana crossed her arms. "What do you want, Dimitri?"

He clutched his chest in mock outrage as though she had offended him. Ana glared at him, and he quit the charade.

"Erica sent me," he said. A chill ran over Ana's arms. "You are invited to her annual Christmas Eve ball tonight."

He handed her a card. Handwritten, elegant letters swirled across light blue paper. *You are cordially invited.* Ana grimaced as she read on, and her gaze traveled on to the theme. "A Victorian masquerade?"

"Doesn't it sound glamorous?"

To Ana, it sounded like a world where she didn't belong. "I don't own a mask or anything to wear to a Victorian ball," she told him.

"I suggest you consult that loud little friend of yours. Bahar Yilmaz, right? I wager she has some ideas." He studied her for a few moments, then added, "It is an honor to be invited."

Ana couldn't imagine why Erica de Winter wanted her at the party, nor could she think of any compelling reasons to attend. "I'm exhausted, Dimitri," she told him. "I've been rehearsing all day, all week."

"Then it sounds like you need a break."

When Ana groaned, Dimitri replaced his smirk with a smile that almost seemed genuine. He laid a hand on Ana's arm, his touch unexpectedly soft.

"Why does she want me to attend?" Ana asked. "Are any of the other staff members invited?"

Dimitri hesitated. "Well, this is probably not helpful, but Hedwig and the Fiores are invited."

Ana's stomach churned. He evidently knew what had happened to her room, what Hedwig had done. She scrutinized him, wondering whether he also knew why the ballerina had done it. Though she doubted he'd be any more forthcoming than the other people at the hotel.

"I will be there," Dimitri added with a wink.

Ana sighed. "Fine, I will come. I can't say no anyway, can I?"

Dimitri shook his head, more somber. "No, you can't."

"Then I will see you tonight."

Shortly after Dimitri left, a knock sounded on Ana's door. Momentarily, she wondered whether he had returned to pick her up for the party, though it was still too early for that. When she opened the door, she found Everett and Bahar standing out in the hallway.

"We came to ask you if you wanted to come eat with us," Bahar said. "No fancy Christmas Eve dinner or anything, though Everett offered to cook up something for us. And we can have eggnog and mulled wine."

Ana bit her lip. "I can't come."

They frowned at her.

As a wordless explanation, she handed them the invitation Dimitri had delivered, and she watched as Everett's face fell. Ana didn't waste her time asking what was wrong. She no longer hoped for answers from him.

"Oh," Bahar said, her mouth remaining slightly open even when no more sound sprang from it. She glanced at Everett, who busied himself by inspecting his shoes.

"Have you ever been?" Ana asked.

Bahar gave a slow nod. "Erica only ever invites brand new staff and some of her favorites… It's pretty elitist, if you ask me."

"I'd much rather eat with you two," Ana said. "But she'd probably fire me if I did." She chuckled, though nobody else joined her. "Bahar, I was wondering," she continued. "Could you help me find something to wear? I don't really have any Victorian ballgowns hanging in my closet. I know you probably don't either, but maybe—"

Upon this, the somber expression on Bahar's face changed and brightened. "Of course." She glanced at Everett. "Dinner can wait a while longer, right?"

He gave a stiff nod without ever looking at her. His gaze remained on the invitation like it was some type of puzzle to decipher. It seemed to take him a great deal of effort to hand the piece of paper back to her. He gave her a thin smile. "I will see you tomorrow, Ana."

Before she could try to figure out what went on within him, Bahar took her by the arm.

"Come," she said. "There's a place I'd like to show you."

Ana obediently followed as Bahar led her behind the staff corridor and through the halls. As they walked, Ana realized how little she knew of Hôtel de Neige. They ventured into parts of the hotel she had never laid eyes on until they reached a small, hidden set of stairs, bringing them down into the cellar.

Ana hugged herself, overcome by the sudden cold. It was so dark she lost sight of Bahar until the lights flickered on. Before her lay a vast room, filled to the brim with clothes.

"Where are we?"

Bahar grinned at her. "This is one of the hotel's storage rooms. Hôtel de Neige keeps quite the collection."

Ana passed by racks upon racks of clothing items, ranging from lacey blouses and glittery dresses to fine suits.

"Why does the hotel keep all of this?" Ana estimated that it held enough to wear for hundreds of people.

Bahar hesitated, then shrugged her shoulders. "I suppose I'd find it difficult to part with such beautiful things, too," she said.

Ana ran her fingers over the sumptuous fabrics, from old-fashioned petticoats and ballooning skirts to blue jeans and leather jackets. Some clothes were well-worn, while others seemed as though they had hardly ever been touched.

"The Victorian gowns are further back," Bahar said and waved Ana along.

They wound their way ahead, at times climbing over trunks or slipping through curtains of dresses, until they entered what felt like a different time altogether. She found herself encircled by the most marvelous gowns she had ever laid eyes upon.

"Do you have any preferences?" Bahar asked.

Ana shook her head, overwhelmed by the selection. "I trust your judgment," she said.

Bahar smiled. "Good decision. I will make sure you are the belle of the ball."

As they began rummaging through the collection, the sparkle in Bahar's eyes grew brighter. She muttered to herself as she examined the pieces, lost in contemplation.

"Are you here often?" Ana asked.

"Usually only every few months," Bahar responded. "Though I could live down here." She released a sigh. "I used to dream of becoming a fashion designer, so a place like this is paradise to me."

Ana lay aside the corset she was studying and turned to Bahar. "What happened?"

"It's a long story."

"We have time, don't we?"

Bahar clicked her tongue and glanced at Ana with a smile that didn't reach her eyes. "If you insist," she said while handing Ana a pair of black gloves. "Try these on."

As Ana obeyed and slipped the soft satin over her hands, Bahar began her story.

"I come from a rather strict family," she said, looking through the gowns before her. "We were often at odds. The idea of my pursuing such a risky career was out of the question for my parents. As were a lot of other things. Sometimes I tried to live by their ideals, but more often, I rebelled against them." She pulled a pair of old-fashioned black heels from a shelf and pressed them into Ana's hands.

"There was one day when we got into another big fight. I was still living with them, and I felt suffocated by all their rules and tirades. So that night, after they had gone to sleep, I packed my things and left. I was angry, impulsive. I didn't know where I would go, but I knew I could no longer stay. I ran away." Bahar's gaze grew distant. "That was when I came upon Hôtel de Neige."

"Didn't you say you were from Austria?"

Bahar gave a low chuckle. "I suppose I ran quite far," she responded, averting her gaze.

Ana raised her brows. Something didn't add up. She had more experience running than most, and she had been happy to make it to the next town without getting caught or running out of cash. And the Hôtel de Neige was not a place to simply stumble upon. "How did you–"

"When I entered the hotel," Bahar continued, not acknowledging Ana's words, "all I wanted was to warm up and get a drink. As I sat pouting at the bar, Erica de Winter took the seat next to mine. To say I was fascinated by her would be an understatement. Erica was the epitome of elegance and class. She wore this magnificent satin gown I still think about to this day. And, much to my surprise, she seemed to take an interest in me. We talked, and I told her about my situation."

When Ana attempted to picture it, her imagination fell short. She had believed Erica was always one step away, at a distance. Though Ana recalled her exchange with the hotel's owner and Erica's curiosity.

"She offered me a job," Bahar said. "To work here at the hotel as a maid. I was broke and homeless. I told myself it would be temporary." Bahar smiled, though Ana could see the glint of tears in her eyes.

Even for a place as eccentric as Hôtel de Neige, this hiring process was strange.

"Why didn't you leave?" Ana asked.

It took Bahar a while to answer. "It was a slow death, I suppose," she said then. "I was just working here at the hotel, and I guess I grew accustomed to it while my dreams slipped away." She lifted her shoulders like it was something she had long accepted.

Ana watched, her brows knitted together, as Bahar devoted herself to searching for a gown again. She felt a sting within her chest. Bahar's tale reminded her of her own life's story. Like Bahar, she had gone off to follow her dreams. She had run away from home more than a dozen times, although she'd never truly considered any of her foster families her home. At seventeen, she had escaped once more, and at last, they hadn't found her—or maybe they stopped trying.

As much as Bahar's story touched her, Ana didn't believe it. Not all of it. The hotel lay so far from anything else, hidden within deep forest and deeper snow. Nobody could simply stumble upon it. Least of all, a girl from the other side of the world.

"Bahar, can you explain how—"

Bahar gasped.

"What is it?" Ana asked.

Bahar looked at her, beaming. "I found the perfect dress."

Ana couldn't look at the gown. Bahar refused to look at anything else. Something was wrong—it itched Ana like a wool sweater. Something was wrong with Bahar's story; something was wrong with this cellar. Something was wrong with every stone and crystal of this hotel.

A VICTORIAN MASQUERADE

Christmas songs played in the distance, echoing through the empty halls as Ana set out for the Victorian Masquerade. She didn't see a single soul on her way there—everyone was either at the ball already or in the staff kitchen, celebrating Christmas Eve. The heels of her 19th-century shoes clicked against the stone floor, the classical music rising in volume as she came closer to the ballroom.

Mr. Rutherford stood at the doors, guarding the entrance, ready to chase away any unwelcome guests. He inclined his head when she approached, eyes narrowing as she drew closer.

"Ms. Greene. I almost failed to recognize you," he said.

Ana did not doubt it, though the black, lacy mask she wore was not what truly disguised her. She felt like a new woman altogether, from a different era, a different life. Bahar had chosen a magnificent gown. Her shoulders lay bare, and the neckline plunged. A tight corset accentuated her curves, and wide, flowing skirts adorned with lace trimming matched her mask.

Ana pulled her invitation from the beaded reticule Bahar found and presented it to Mr. Rutherford. He examined it, then allowed her to step through the doors.

Ana had thought she was used to the glamor of Hôtel de Neige, but when she laid eyes upon the ballroom, her breath caught in her throat. The vast hall sparkled like fresh ice beneath a full moon. Chandeliers shone above her, their fine crystals like falling snowflakes. Ice statues stood by the tall, frosted windows, silently surveying the scene. White and blue roses adorned their pedestals.

Just as Ana entered, a new melody arose, growing as she stepped into the ballroom. Dozens of couples danced on the silver floor, waltzing to the sweet rhythm. Glittering skirts swayed about, adding to the illusion that she looked upon snow-crested land rather than upon a ball.

Yet as she observed the magical scene before her, she began to feel tense, out of place. All was swathed in the colors of winter. The elegant suits, ballooning dresses, and delicate masks of the guests were in shades of snow and ice—white and blue and silver.

The grand gown Ana wore was deep red. She stood out as an orb of color, like fresh blood upon the otherwise unblemished snow.

"Angel?"

Ana turned and saw Dimitri, who gazed at her with his lips parted. He wore a dark suit, perfectly tailored for him. A black mask adorned his face, though Ana recognized him at once, the blue of his eyes even more noticeable than usual.

"Dimitri," she replied.

"You look…" He said no more but kept staring at her.

"Thank you." A smile tugged at the corner of her lips.

Ana looked around. So far, Dimitri was the only familiar face in the ballroom. All other attendees were guests of the Hôtel de Neige, and Erica de Winter was nowhere to be seen. Neither were Hedwig Sternberg and the Fiores, much to Ana's relief.

"Welcome to the Victorian masquerade," Dimitri said. He bowed his head and offered her his hand. "May I be your guide?"

Ana hesitated. It would be inappropriate to spend the evening with the hotel's manager, but she knew no one else and felt lost in the grand ballroom.

Cautiously, Ana laid her gloved hand into his. His thumb brushed over her fingertips, sending a jolt through her body.

Dimitri led them to a corner of the ballroom where they could watch the dancers. They settled down on a plush sofa, Ana's crimson skirts billowing around her, leaving hardly any space for him. A waiter appeared and delivered two glasses of champagne.

"I must give my compliments to Ms. Yilmaz," he said. "She chose well for you."

"I feel like I missed some details about the dress code," Ana responded, unable to untether her gaze from the spinning couples. "Though perhaps I should've known everybody else would adhere to the hotel's colors."

"I think you made the perfect choice by wearing red," Dimitri said, his gaze once more flying across her body. "You are stunning."

Ana felt herself blushing and momentarily turned away before meeting his eyes again.

"Please don't make that face," Dimitri said. "People will think you don't want to be here."

"I don't want to be here."

Dimitri laughed. "I do admire your forwardness, Angel." After a short pause, he added, "I hate these parties, too."

Ana lifted her brows. "Do you? You seem pretty comfortable here."

"Well, I'm pretty and comfortable everywhere."

"I said 'pretty comfortable.'"

"Ah, my English again." He grinned at Ana, inviting her to continue teasing him, but instead, she rolled her eyes and took a sip from her champagne. She was tempted to look up how much each sip cost.

"So, Angel," Dimitri said and leaned back, crossing an ankle on his knee, his arms lazily draped across the back of the sofa. "What have you been up to since we last spoke? I watched your performances, of course, whenever I could."

Ana had seen him nearly every night she performed, sometimes accompanied by Erica, though often alone. Always in the first box, always with his eyes on her like there was nobody else in the room. In the beginning, it had made her nervous, but then it became comforting in a way. Not that she'd ever admit it.

"My life would bore you," Ana responded.

A spark of curiosity glinted in Dimitri's eyes. He knew about the incident, about Hedwig. Ana hoped he wouldn't ask about it.

"Well," Dimitri said after a moment, "if your life is boring, perhaps you should spend more time with me."

"Is your life so much more interesting?" she asked, relieved that he kept the conversation light.

"It would be with you in it," he said and laughed, then shook his head. "No, I must admit my life at the moment is not particularly interesting. *I* am interesting, though."

"Are you now? Tell me something interesting about yourself then."

Before Dimitri could start bragging, something shifted in the crowd. The music faded away; the dancing ceased. Chattering transformed into low muttering. Ana turned her head and watched as Erica de Winter made her ceremonious entrance.

She held the entire ballroom in the palm of her hand. A white taffeta gown with a slim silhouette hugged her body, and with it, she wore a white mask, adorned with a thousand tiny crystals, glittering as though covered in snow and ice.

"Welcome, my dear guests," Erica said. Her voice reached into every corner of the room and into every corner of Ana's body.

Ana surveyed the guests, who all looked to Erica de Winter in awe, reveling in the performance of her appearance. Amid the eager spectators, Ana spotted Hedwig Sternberg. The ballerina wore a modest midnight blue dress. Their gazes met, and Ana resisted the urge to look away. A strange expression crossed Hedwig's delicate features—a touch of sadness in her dark eyes in place of her usual glare.

"I am elated to see all of you here tonight," Erica said. "Hôtel de Neige prides itself on its distinguished guests and its ability to offer them an extraordinary stay. These Christmas Eve balls have become a tradition and a celebration of who we are." She smiled widely. "Without further ado, I wish you all a delightful night." With a wink, she added, "And please make sure to enjoy our open bar."

The short speech earned her a round of applause, then the guests returned to chatting, drinking, and dancing. Ana stiffened as she realized the hotel's owner was headed in her direction.

"Ana Greene," Erica said when she reached Ana, her voice as enchanting as ever. "A pleasure to have you here." She glanced at Dimitri and her eyes momentarily reduced to slits. Yet when she regarded Ana again, the sweet expression returned. "I am highly anticipating your performance at the Christmas concert tomorrow."

As she said it, a couple of guests approached, demanding Erica's attention. "Ms. de Winter," the woman said, and gave a large smile. She was perhaps in her early twenties, with the looks of a French runway model and the accent of a country bumpkin. "What a marvelous party. It is an honor to be among such illustrious guests—and such illustrious hosts."

Erica gave a gracious smile. "Thank you. We are glad to know you are enjoying it."

"I cannot believe I'd never heard of this hotel until a few weeks ago," the woman added. "It is truly astonishing."

"We prefer to remain a bit of a mystery. It is how we ensure our exclusivity."

The woman's smile widened, clearly taking the remark as a compliment. "We truly could not be more pleased with our stay so far." She nodded to the man in her company who looked to be at least twice her age. "Michael and I are in the honeymoon suite, and it is just as we had hoped. We—" The woman rambled on merrily while Ana zoned out.

Dimitri gently elbowed her. "Angel," he said. "May I have a dance with you?"

Ana gaped at him, then laughed and shook her head. "No, thank you."

It seemed he had anticipated the response. His smile never wavered as he replied, "Why not? I will teach you the steps. I happen to be an expert dancer."

"I'm sure you are. However, I'd prefer to stay on this very comfortable couch."

"Angel, you cannot attend a ball and never dance. Indulge me, just one time."

Ana glanced at the waltzing couples. Something in the way they floated through the ballroom incited a spark within her. She knew she would likely never get an opportunity to live out a scene from a fairy-tale again.

"Fine," she said to Dimitri. "One dance."

Dimitri rose and offered her his arm. As she took it, she questioned her decision. Looking back over her shoulder, Ana saw Erica watching them.

Dimitri led her to an unoccupied spot to the side of the ballroom and came to face her. "Put your hand on my shoulder," he said, and she obeyed. "I will put my hand here." He placed his palm on the small of her back, and slowly, he pulled her closer to him. His fingers brushed against the curve of her spine. "Then," he continued, "You start with your right leg and you go backward, while I go forward."

Dimitri took the first step, his body moving forward, gently nudging her backward.

"Next, we go—"

Before he finished speaking, Ana swayed left and drew him along with her. They fell into the rhythm of the dance.

Dimitri stared at her. "Angel, do you know how to waltz?"

Ana smirked. "As an aspiring singer with hopes to make it to Broadway, I thought it would make sense to take some dance classes—including ballroom."

While they spoke, their bodies descended into dance. Some time had passed since Ana had last practiced the steps, but in his arms, they became instinctual.

"You could have told me," Dimitri responded, eyeing her with a mock glare.

"Perhaps so."

"Though it seems you did not always pay attention during your classes," Dimitri said. "Otherwise, you would know that the man is supposed to lead."

"I wasn't sure whether I trusted you with such a weighty task."

Dimitri chuckled. "Be careful, Angel, or I might start accidentally stepping on your toes."

She pressed her lips together to hold back her growing smile. "Fine," she capitulated. "Take the lead."

For a while longer, they danced the basic box step at the side of the ballroom until their motions became more natural, attuned to each other. Then they dared to protrude deeper into the hall.

By then, the first song, the first dance she granted him, had long passed, yet neither of them pulled away. Ana let herself be held both by the melody and by him. Dimitri spun her around, and in that moment, she felt as though she was floating rather than dancing.

"I feel like I'm in a fairytale," Ana whispered, momentarily forgetting Dimitri could hear her words. She gave herself to the beautiful illusion as the edges between her and Cinderella from the storybooks blurred. She was the poor little girl who had at last made it to the ball. Her childhood dreams bloomed with each note.

Lost in thought, Ana almost didn't notice that Dimitri's gaze had fixated on her. When their eyes met, something stirred within her. She looked away quickly. On her back, one of his fingers drew circles. She felt his breath on her face and neck and bosom. If she were Cinderella, what did it make him?

"I could dance with you all night," Dimitri said.

To her own surprise, Ana felt the same wish stirring in her chest. The music had caught her. She would dance until it ceased or the sun had risen upon the horizon.

Ana had feared the watchful gazes of those around them, but as they danced, all else fell away. It felt as though they had the grand ballroom to themselves. The flutes and clarinets, the horns and trumpets, the cellos and violins—all played solely for them. She closed her eyes, and in her mind, the walls disappeared so they danced beneath the moonlight. Their gliding steps and her swaying skirts whirled the snow into the air.

When she opened her eyes again, Ana looked into the deep blue of Dimitri's irises. He watched her with the hint of a smile. Heat shot into her cheeks.

One waltz ended, and the next melody began to the backdrop of a bell chiming.

"Midnight," Dimitri whispered upon the twelfth stroke, a smirk upon his lips. "If you are thinking of fleeing in a pumpkin carriage, I advise against it. I had the stairs smeared with pitch."

"It is midnight already? How long have we danced?" Ana felt as though awakening from a delirium, albeit a most exquisite one.

"A long time," Dimitri replied.

"I think it is time to take a break," she said. Only then did she begin to feel the weight of her body again. "My feet are beginning to hurt."

In response, Dimitri laid his hands on her waist, lifting her and then spinning her through the air before setting her down softly.

"Anything you wish," he told her, smiling.

AFTER MIDNIGHT

They left the dance floor and returned to the side of the ballroom. Ana realized she was out of breath, something she hadn't noticed while enraptured by the music.

"Shall we get some fresh air?" Dimitri suggested.

All her dread about the ball had fled by then. She enjoyed watching the other couples, drinking the delicate champagne, and pretending to be one of them rather than a one-time guest. Still, she nodded, ready for a break from the crowd.

Once more, he took the lead, and they made their way through the hall until they reached a door hidden behind blue curtains, which brought them out to a frosted terrace. Before they even stepped outside, Dimitri handed her his jacket, as though it was only natural for him to do so. Ana meant to protest, but decided against it when she felt the cold breeze that greeted them.

"Thank you."

They walked out to the balustrade encircling the terrace. Beyond it lay the forest surrounding the hotel. A soft wind ruffled through Dimitri's hair and deposited little snowflakes in it. He looked younger, the darkness smoothing out his features. He turned to Ana, their eyes meeting. One of his brows lifted.

"What are you looking at, Angel? Are you staring at me?"

Before Ana could deny it, smugness rippled across his face. He laughed, pleased with himself.

"I wasn't staring at you. I was enjoying the view," she replied.

"Yes, and I was your view."

Ana gritted her teeth. "I should have known you'd twist my words."

"Don't be embarrassed," Dimitri added with a smirk. "I stare at you all the time."

An unwelcome heat rushed into Ana's cheeks, and she hoped the night concealed her blush.

"You are beautiful, Angel," Dimitri said. "And unlike me, you are exceedingly interesting. I still know nothing about you, which I find quite vexing."

Studying him, Ana realized the opportunity his remark held. "I will trade you an answer for an answer," she responded. "I tell you something about myself, and you tell me something about yourself in turn."

Dimitri cocked his head to the side. "Intriguing." He straightened, the distance between them diminishing. In the freezing cold, she could feel his warmth beside her. "I will start," he declared. "Why are you so secretive about your family?"

Ana swallowed hard. Some time had passed since the conversation with Erica, when she had done her best to evade all questions about her family. She hadn't anticipated that Dimitri would remember. While she'd prefer to keep it to herself, she could no longer back out. "It's hard to be close to your family when you don't have one," she responded.

"You don't have a family?" he asked, a note of bewilderment in his voice.

"My turn," Ana said, deflecting. "Are you close to your family?"

"No. How come you don't have a family?"

Ana was starting to dislike her own game. "I might have one, but I don't know them." She paused, struggling to find the right words. Years had passed since she had last told anyone this story. "When I was six years old or so, some people found me lost by some road, on the brink of death. Nobody came looking for me, so they dumped me into the foster system. I don't remember anything before that."

Dimitri's brows drew together, but he stayed quiet.

"Why aren't you close to your family?" Ana asked, turning his own question on him, and grateful he hadn't expressed pity for her circumstances.

Dimitri seemed equally displeased about having to answer. "My father wanted me to uphold the family legacy, but I was young and not interested in old names and older traditions. Eventually, he banished me from our home and told me to make it on my own. I tried but failed, so I had to come crawling back. I was foolish enough to think he'd allow me to return."

"He didn't let you come home?" Ana knew how much she would give to have a family. It baffled her that someone could toss it aside so carelessly.

Dimitri shook his head. His usual, carefree behavior had vanished. "No, he didn't. I stood at the doorstep. Inside, I saw the warm light and silhouettes of my mother and my sisters. I hadn't seen them in two years at that point. All I wanted was to go inside and embrace them again. But he never let me in, never told them I was out there in the cold."

Ana felt the urge to express how sorry she was for him, but she caught herself. "Your dad's a dick," she said instead.

Dimitri looked at her, then chuckled.

"I mean it," Ana said. "All my life, I dreamed of a family. I looked through other people's windows and envied what they had. Your father is an idiot for throwing it away."

Their eyes met, and Dimitri smiled at her. "So what was it like for you growing up? It must have been difficult." After a short pause, he added, "You don't have to talk about it if you don't want to."

"No, it's okay," Ana said. Was it still part of the game? She didn't know. "Lonely most of the time. I was a difficult child, guarded and distant. In the first few years, I hardly spoke. I also changed foster families a lot, which didn't help. There was never a time when I felt truly at home anywhere. Not all of them were bad, of course, but I found myself always out of place, yearning for something I had lost and could not even remember." She shifted, drawing his coat tighter around her.

"As I grew older, I became rather rebellious. Just as I hadn't fit in with the foster families, I didn't fit in at school. When I was eleven, I tried running away for the first time. They found me two days later, hiding out in someone's shed. It took me six more years of trying before they stopped looking for me. It was then that I headed to New York City."

"It sounds like a turbulent life," Dimitri remarked.

Ana nodded. "So when did you end up at Hôtel de Neige?" she asked him, hoping for a more pleasant tale.

"I came upon the hotel just after I tried to return to my family. I had nowhere else to go. Erica offered me a job, and I jumped at the chance."

"How charitable of her," Ana responded.

A hollow smile crossed Dimitri's lips. "I doubt charity was her intention. I think she saw qualities she appreciated in me—a good ally, so to speak."

"Did you and Erica ever…?" Ana trailed off.

It took Dimitri a moment to understand the question, then he laughed and shook his head. "God, no."

Ana hesitated to believe him. "Why not? She's a beautiful woman."

"She certainly is," Dimitri responded. "But I'm not an idiot. I wouldn't want to be among the men who have been with her. Besides, she's not my type."

From the way he looked at her, Ana could tell he wanted her to ask who his type was. She refrained.

"Should we go back inside?" Dimitri asked. "You're shivering."

She'd barely noticed the cold throughout their conversation, but now that he'd said something, it gripped her, and she hugged herself.

"That suffices as an answer," Dimitri said.

Together, they headed back to the doors off the terrace. There, Ana stopped to take off his jacket and handed it back to him.

"Angel," Dimitri said before they could return to the warmth of the ballroom. A smirk played around his lips. "I feel obliged to tell you that you—*we*—are standing beneath the mistletoe."

Ana looked up, and there it hung, just before the closed door. She met Dimitri's blue eyes, aglow with the moonlight reflected in the snow and the soft light coming from inside. They stood so close to each other that Ana felt his warm breath on her skin. He laid a gentle hand on her neck, his fingers reaching up to her face.

"May I?" Dimitri asked, his gaze jumping back and forth between her eyes and her lips.

Ana knew the answer should be no. She knew it would be utterly foolish to let him kiss her—he was the manager of the hotel, after all. But his touch tingled on her skin, filling her with heat in the midst of the cold night.

"Yes," she whispered.

Around the two of them, snowflakes danced through the air, notes of Tchaikovsky playing in the distance. Dimitri's other hand found Ana's waist, and he pulled her close. Instinctively, she reached up to cup his face in her gloved palms. They paused only a moment longer, then their lips touched, hers meeting the surprising softness of his.

It was unlike any other kiss Ana had experienced in her life, holding at once hesitation and urgency. His fingers dug into her back, pulling her closer. She wrapped her arms around him, removing any distance separating them. They lost themselves in each other, and as the cold of the night faded, the chills that ran up Ana's arms were of a different origin.

When they parted, they were out of breath, still entangled with one another. Dimitri swept aside a strand of hair that had fallen into Ana's face and tucked it behind her ear. They stared at each other, indulging in the strange, silent moment. Perhaps they both knew something would draw them back to reality soon enough.

They were granted a few more tranquil seconds before the doors to the terrace flew open, almost hitting them. They jumped out of its way and scattered like teenagers caught in an illicit act. From the door, Mr. Rutherford scrutinized them with narrowed eyes.

"Ms. de Winter sent me to fetch you two," he said. "Get back inside."

He departed, leaving them alone on the terrace. Ana glanced at Dimitri, unable to say anything, unsure what she would say even if she found her voice. Her body was still on edge, his kiss echoing on her lips.

"We should go back inside," Dimitri said.

Ana shook herself out of the daze and nodded. She took the lead, and they headed back inside, this time paying no more attention to the mistletoe.

They found Erica de Winter surrounded by guests of the hotel—she their sun, the guests the planets orbiting around her. She turned away from them, though, when she saw Dimitri and Ana.

"I almost thought you two had left altogether," Erica said. Her eyes pierced Ana, who had no doubt that Erica had her suspicions as to what had unfolded beyond her watchful gaze.

"Dimitri," the hotel's owner then said without even looking at him. "Get us some more drinks, will you?"

Dimitri obeyed, abandoning Ana to Erica's company. Erica started strolling through the ballroom, and Ana had no choice but to scurry along. They came to a halt by one of the windows. Next to it, a piece of art towered, taller than Ana herself. It took her a moment to realize she had seen the glass statue before; she had encountered it on the way to her audition. The opaque man looked off into the distance, toward the entrance of the ballroom, as though hoping for his beloved to step through the doors at any moment. Roses partially obscured the pedestal he stood on, but Ana could still make out his name.

Christian Dahl.

His longing features had captivated her before, and now, somehow, he seemed sadder in this light. She resisted the urge to touch his face.

"Beautiful, is he not?" Erica asked, following Ana's gaze. "He belongs to me."

A frown etched into Ana's features, but before she could say anything, Erica continued. "Are you settling in well at the hotel, Ana?"

It took Ana some effort to tear her gaze from the ice statue. "I do very much like it here."

It was true despite all that had happened. Ana abhorred the secrecy and the confusion, yet Hôtel de Neige remained the most beautiful place she had ever set foot in—and the closest thing to a home she'd had in her entire life.

"So you are planning on staying with us permanently?" As Erica scrutinized Ana, her pale blue eye seemed to hold more intensity than the plain brown one.

Permanently. The idea filled Ana with excitement and anticipation. After so many years as a vagabond, she yearned for a place to call her own, a room for which she was more than merely a passerby.

"I would love nothing more," Ana answered as the thought tingled through her.

Erica's smile stretched across her face and revealed her teeth, a predator baring its fangs. "If that is so, I would like to officially welcome you to Hôtel de Neige."

Still wearing a bestial smile, Erica leaned towards Ana as though to kiss her on the cheek. Ana found herself shivering again, frost crawling through her veins. Perhaps she stood too close to the statue of Christian Dahl, though her instincts tried to pull her away from Erica and toward the statue.

From the corner of her eye, she saw a dark figure moving towards them, but only recognized the woman once it was too late.

"Watch out!"

Ana jolted on instinct, and a moment later, she felt the red wine soaking her hair and staining her dress.

"My apologies."

Ana looked up, meeting Hedwig Sternberg's black eyes. In her hand, she held a wine glass, empty save for a few blood-like drops. A surge of heat drove away Ana's initial shock and threatened to take control. "You—"

Someone touched her arm, pulling her back into her body.

"Are you alright?" Dimitri asked, handing her a cloth napkin.

Ana blinked and nodded, though she wasn't entirely sure. "I'm afraid the dress isn't. Or my hair." The wine glass must have been filled to the brim; liquid had overtaken half of the fine gown and dripped from her curls. She shivered with embarrassment and anger.

Next to her, Erica shifted. Her face glowed with the sort of fury Ana was trying to restrain. "Hedwig," she said, any trace of kindness now gone. "I think you ought to leave. It seems you've had too much to drink."

Hedwig, who appeared utterly sober, nodded and took off.

Erica then turned to Ana. "Oh dear, what a mess. I shall lend you one of my dresses at once."

Ana almost let herself be dragged along, but she came to a stop and shook her head. "I think…I think I should go now. It's all over me. It has been a pleasure, really. Thank you very much for the invitation."

Regret tugged at Ana as Erica de Winter's smile faded. But it quickly returned, as did the honey-soaked tone. "Of course, I understand. It was a delight to have you here. We will find some other time to resume our conversation."

Ana nodded. "I'm looking forward to it. Goodbye." She turned to Dimitri and muttered a quick farewell, then stormed past the dancing couples and out of the ballroom.

Once in the hallway, Ana tried to catch some air, only to have it knocked out of her again when she saw Hedwig, standing just a few feet away from her.

At first, Ana feared she might cry. The tears had welled in her eyes, and the sight of Hedwig threatened to break them out. She was a walking monument to all the bullies who had plagued Ana throughout her life.

"What is your problem with me?" Ana asked wearily, too exhausted to yell. Their one-sided battle had stretched her thin.

Hedwig took a step in her direction, then halted again. "You don't belong here," she said, sounding equally drained.

She must be tired, Ana thought. After all, Hedwig had done most of the fighting.

"One day, you may wish you'd heeded my advice."

"Advice? Advice is not usually written in lipstick next to broken mirrors."

Hedwig shrugged, once again not bothering to deny her actions. Not even a shadow of shame or guilt crossed her face. "Maybe it should be more often. More people may listen to it then."

"I won't listen."

Something stirred in the ballerina's solemn expression. "No, I don't suppose you will," Hedwig said. She looked older than usual, with a weathered look in her eyes. "I doubt I will give you any more advice in the future."

Ana sighed; the small victory felt hollow.

"Goodnight, Ana," Hedwig said, her tone neutral. She walked past Ana and was gone a moment later, though her lily perfume lingered in the air.

Ana stayed a few moments longer before setting out on her own. The wine on her dress had sunk deep into the fabric. Behind her, the music of the ball faded away. She wagered she would remember this night for a long time to come, but for the moment, all she could think of was a quiet room and a warm bed.

CHRISTMAS AT HÔTEL DE NEIGE

When Ana returned to the ballroom, the music had nearly faded into silence. The dancing couples had departed, and the hall lay empty. Yet she had come for one last dance before the spell of the fairy godmother wore off and her fairytale melted into reality again.

"Angel."

Ana turned and smiled as she saw Dimitri approaching, his hand already outstretched. She took it and they danced, though to her it felt more like flying. The quiet music rose again as they swept through the ballroom, their gazes never letting go of each other. They wore their masks no more; Ana could see all of his beautiful face. He smiled at her.

"Let's dance until the sun rises," Ana whispered.

Dimitri lifted her into the air and spun her around. Her red skirts looked like flames dancing upon the snow. She wanted to sink deeper into his embrace and into the music, but her eyes refused to stay on him. Her gaze searched the room. Someone else was there, waiting for their turn.

"Nothing would give me greater joy than to waltz with you all night, Angel," Dimitri responded as one song was drawing to its close and they came to a halt. "But I believe there is another who would like to dance with you."

When Ana lifted her brows, Dimitri nodded behind her. She looked and saw the man coming toward her. A low gasp escaped her, for he was not made of flesh but ice. She had encountered him before, as a statue on a pedestal.

"You're here," Ana whispered. Despite his proximity, warmth kindled in her chest.

The man bowed, offering his hand. "May I have this dance?" Even as he spoke, his melancholy features barely shifted.

He must be so cold, Ana thought.

Ana searched for Dimitri, but he had vanished. So, after a moment's hesitation, she accepted the stranger's hand. As she took it, Ana realized he was truly a creature made of ice. The cold of his touch stung her, but she did not let go.

The melody began, and they commenced their waltz.

"Am I dreaming?" Ana asked. When she glanced up, she realized the ceiling had disappeared, and instead, they danced beneath the light of a silver sickle moon. Snow drifted down and covered the dance floor.

"You might be," the ice man responded. "Though I am inclined to believe it is I who is dreaming." He smiled. "I cannot express how long I have waited to dance with you."

Ana studied him. "You seem to know me, yet I don't know you."

"Don't you remember me?"

"I remember seeing you in the ballroom earlier. The pedestal you stood on said your name. But I'm afraid I don't recall."

The stranger wore a smile, though there was sadness in his translucent eyes. "I understand," he said. "It is quite alright. I believe you will remember me soon enough. Until then, I shall be content to dance with you."

They waltzed on through the ballroom where the snow began to gather. Ana observed his wistful expression, sure she ought to recognize him, but it was like seeing someone from behind a blurred glass window, never quite able to make them out.

"Have we met before tonight?" she asked.

Yet he spoke no more. The song ended, and they came to a stop at the heart of the ballroom.

A sudden pang of melancholy overcame Ana. "May I have another waltz with you?" she asked.

"I fear that will not be possible."

"Why not?"

The stranger who seemed to know her said nothing. His gaze had departed from her and traveled on. When Ana followed it, she understood.

A white fog descended upon the ballroom, and from it, Erica de Winter appeared.

"Ana," Erica said. Her tone was distorted, reminding Ana of the sound of nails scratching against a chalkboard. "Shall we continue our conversation now?"

"We need another moment," Ana responded, her voice shaking. She didn't know why she wanted the man of ice to stay.

Yet Erica granted them not a second more. She walked past Ana until she had reached the stranger. They looked upon each other for a moment, then Erica reached out and lay a finger against his chest. The moment Erica touched his frozen skin, the man burst apart, his body shattering into millions of snow crystals which floated through the air.

Ana stumbled backward. Tears filled her eyes. "What did you do?"

Erica turned to face Ana. She wore a smile, though it seemed too wide, her teeth too sharp. "Shall we continue our conversation now?" she asked once more, each word a painful screech.

Ana whipped around to flee, but the floor had frozen. She slipped, and as she fell, her eyes flew open.

The dream dissipated, and by the time Ana landed, she was wide awake. There was no more soft snow to catch her when she crashed into the hard ground, the world spinning before her eyes as it had when she had danced.

As she regained her senses, she came to a grim realization—she had forgotten to lock her door that night. She had sleepwalked again.

This time, she was not in the eerie corridor but the abandoned ballroom, as she had been in her dream. No more music played. The chandeliers glowed no longer, and everything lay in utter darkness. With achingly slow movements, Ana turned her head. A few feet away towered the pedestal where the ice statue of the strange man had stood. It was still there, but he was gone.

Ana scrambled to her feet and ran.

It felt as though Ana awoke again only moments after closing her eyes. She was torn from sleep by the sunlight shining through her curtains. For a split second, disorientation took over, and she believed herself to be back in her creaky bed in New York City. The soft pillows and blanket reminded her where she truly was—as did the aftermath of the nightmare.

Memories of the past night came back to her like the hazy remembering of a time long past. Ana wished she could forget them with equal ease. Her crumpled, wine-stained gown lay in a pile on the floor. She should be writhing with anger, but bewilderment held her still as she recalled her conversation with the ballerina. Hedwig had been different—less sharp, smoothed out by exhaustion and surrender.

Ana had no doubt she would contemplate it all morning, but there was another part of the evening clinging to her like thick, sticky syrup. Heat rose in her body as she found herself back on the terrace, back in Dimitri's arms. The spots of her body touched by him tingled still, his phantom kiss burned onto her lips.

Ana sank back into the warm sheets and decided she would sleep again with the hopes that, when she woke, the memories would be gone—or faded, at least. Just as she closed her eyes, a loud noise rang through the room.

She jolted up and looked at the door. Someone hammered against the wood. Ana held her breath, pretending not to be there, but the knocking persisted. With a sigh and aching limbs, she rose and opened the door. Outside stood the small figure of Mikkel, looking up at her with his wide eyes.

"Good morning," Ana grumbled. Despite the brightness in the hall, it might as well be midnight for all she cared. "What is it?"

The boy blinked, confused. "It's Christmas."

"Oh." Every year, the holiday took her by surprise, this time more than ever. Usually, she acknowledged it by lighting a candle if she had time to spare before heading to work.

"Merry Christmas," Ana said with some hesitancy, unsure what the holiday entailed at Hôtel de Neige. She had purchased no presents; she had nothing to give to a child.

"Merry Christmas," Mike responded and beamed at her. "The others are waiting for you."

Ana tried to remember whether they had agreed on meeting on Christmas morning, yet her thoughts remained a blur. "I'll go get dressed," she told Mike, yawning. Getting changed would grant her a few more quiet moments.

The boy giggled and shook his head so vehemently that his curls bounced through the air. "It's Christmas," he said. "You have to wear your pajamas."

Ana raised her brows. "I don't think that rule applies to adults."

"Yes, it does. Everett and Bahar are wearing their pajamas, too."

Ana was reluctant to believe him. She'd rather not take the risk of being the only one not decently dressed. Besides, her pajamas were hardly appropriate. So far, she hadn't replaced her old rags and was still wearing worn-out, gray sweatpants and a cropped shirt with the logo of some sports team she didn't know.

"I'd really prefer to change," Ana said. When Mike scowled and crossed his arms in defiance, Ana exhaled a sigh. "Fine. But let me throw on a sweater, okay?"

After some consideration, Mike allowed it, and Ana pulled on a thick sweater before heading out together with the boy, unsure what awaited her. Was this how children felt on Christmas morning?

Ana heard the chattering and bustling of the staff kitchen before they entered. As they opened the doors, the scent hit her along with the noise. The fragrances of cinnamon and hot chocolate, of toasted marshmallows and roasted chestnuts, of cloves and oranges and gingerbread lingered in the air. It filled her with nostalgia, though Ana didn't know what she would feel nostalgic for.

She felt like a child again, in awe of the holiday. Laughter rang around her, and somewhere people were caroling—a tradition she had judged mercilessly in the past but which now melded with the other merry sounds. Different cultures and traditions merged all around her. It was like a huge family gathering, loud and messy and warm. A touch of softness spread through her chest. She had hoped to find a home for herself at Hôtel de Neige, but until that moment, she hadn't known what it truly meant. She was beginning to understand.

"Angie," someone shouted.

She spotted Bahar jumping and waving to make herself seen among the crowd.

Mike grabbed Ana by the hand and steered them through the masses towards Bahar and Everett. To Ana's relief, they were both indeed dressed in their pajamas.

"You made it," Bahar said, wrapping Ana in a sudden hug. "Merry Christmas."

"Merry Christmas," Ana echoed, still somewhat overwhelmed. The others beckoned her to their table, which was as crowded as the room itself. They had laid out plates filled with colorful sugar cookies and cups of steaming hot chocolate. Yet most space was taken up by bundles wrapped in sheaths of green and white and gold. Ana had only ever seen such arrays in the movies, where she knew they were filled with empty cardboard boxes, only there for the beautiful illusion. Yet she dared to believe the packages on the table held actual gifts.

"We thought you might still be asleep when you didn't show up earlier," Bahar said. "So we sent Mike. Did he wake you up?"

"Yes, he did." Ana doubted she was fully awake yet, though the desire to crawl back into bed vanished as she soaked in the atmosphere around her.

"I can't believe you slept in on Christmas morning," Everett said.

"To be honest, I kind of forgot it was Christmas," Ana admitted, blushing.

"You forgot Christmas?" Mike gawked at her, incredulous.

"I don't even forget Christmas and I'm Muslim," Bahar said. "Though wait until you see me on Eid al-Fitr."

Ana lifted her shoulders. "I never really celebrated Christmas."

"Well, you do now. At Hôtel de Neige, there's no way around it," Everett responded with a smile. Turning to Mike, he asked, "What do you say? Breakfast or presents first?"

The boy's mouth expanded into the widest of grins. "Presents, please."

"You know, one of these times it wouldn't hurt you to choose breakfast first," Bahar said, all the while handing him a bright pink present.

With surprising patience and meticulousness, Mike unwrapped the gift, then frowned as he uncovered the little gadget.

"It's a Tamagotchi," Bahar said. "You're going to love it."

Everett snorted with laughter. "You know, there are actual good video games available."

Bahar glared at him. "It's vintage. It's trendy."

"And here I thought decent graphics were trendy."

"I like it," Mike said, thus ending the discussion, much to Bahar's triumph.

Next, it was Everett's turn. He handed Mike a large present. "I know it's not the real dog you keep asking for, but—"

Mike pulled a stuffed golden retriever from the wrapping paper, nearly as big as the boy himself. His eyes grew large.

"I love it," Mike said and squeezed the plush animal. Then, dutifully, he turned to Everett. "Thank you very much."

Everett smiled. "You're welcome."

"Alright," Bahar said and clapped her hands. "The next present is for Ana."

Ana stiffened at the sudden mention of her name. She had expected to be a silent watcher of the Christmas tradition, content with the role.

"I…I didn't know we were getting each other gifts," she said, heated with embarrassment. "I didn't get you guys anything."

"No worries," Everett said, brushing it aside. "It's not much, anyway. Consider it a welcome present."

With that, he offered Ana a soft package. She looked around, all eyes on her. "Thank you," she said, stuck between nervousness and amazement. Some of her foster families had given her small presents; others hadn't bothered. Most of the gifts she had received had been clothes and other necessities—not that Ana begrudged them. They'd done more than asked of them in the first place.

Ana cautiously unwrapped the present. Beneath the packaging, her hands touched upon a silky fabric, gliding through her fingers. She set aside the wrapping to find a beautiful pair of rich emerald green pajamas.

"Thank you," Ana whispered, her mouth open in shock.

"You mentioned that you needed a new pair," Bahar said, scanning Ana's current outfit. "And I can see why. No offense."

Ana blinked. She couldn't believe Bahar remembered some casual comment when she hardly did. Such a small thing she had said in passing without giving it much thought.

"And look," Bahar added and pointed.

Ana gazed at the pajamas and saw the two golden letters stitched on the top: A. G. Her initials. A matching pajama set with her initials. It seemed like something only someone ostentatiously wealthy would own.

"They're beautiful," Ana said. "Thank you. I'm so sorry I didn't get you anything."

Bahar waved it off. "Don't worry about it," she said. "Though I will be sharing my wish list with you next Christmas."

A smile twitched across Ana's lips. She yearned to change into her new pajamas right away, but feared missing more of Christmas morning. A novel sense of warmth and comfort gripped her.

The gift-giving now complete, it was time for breakfast. Before Ana could begin to squeeze herself through the crowd, Everett placed a hand on her arm and stopped her.

"Can I talk to you about something?"

Something shifted in his expression. Ana had caught glimpses of it throughout the morning, but now it lay barren on his face. She looked at Bahar and Mike, who headed to the kitchen with laughter upon their lips. Whatever Everett meant to discuss, she sensed it wouldn't be pleasant. She wished he had picked a different moment so this one would remain unblemished in her memory, but he seemed determined.

Ana nodded, expecting they would sit back down, but instead, he led her into the corridor, away from the buzz. Strangely, the quietness was less peaceful than the noise.

"What is it, Everett?" Ana asked.

It took him a moment to answer. "How are you feeling after last night's party?"

"Oh." Ana glanced away by impulse. She should have guessed he would know; gossip spread like a disease at Hôtel de Neige.

"I'm alright," she said. "It was no big deal. Though I don't think my dress will recover. I've yet to confess to Bahar. She will be furious."

"What? Your dress? What are you talking about?"

Ana squinted at him. "Hedwig poured red wine all over me. What are *you* talking about?"

Everett paused. "I didn't know Hedwig poured wine over you. I can't believe she did that."

Ana frowned at him, a knot tied in her stomach. Only one other noteworthy incident had occurred, the memory of which made her blush again. She'd hoped nobody had seen her and Dimitri. Mr. Rutherford might have caught a glimpse, but she hadn't taken him for a gossip.

"So, erm, what happened before that?" Everett asked. "How was the ball?"

Ana had never excelled at small talk, but his attempt was even shakier than hers. She remained nonchalant. "The ball was decadent, as to be expected," she responded as she reflected on the night. "Though not particularly interesting, to be honest."

Everett seemed unsatisfied with her answer, although he tried to conceal it. He fidgeted with the chain of his pocket watch. "Who did you spend your time with?"

Ana was tempted to tell him to just ask her about Dimitri so the awkward conversation would end, but she feared to risk it.

"Did you speak to Erica de Winter?" Everett asked.

"Yes, briefly," she responded. "Why?"

A couple of people came out of the staff kitchen and Everett tapped his foot in silence until they disappeared down the corridor before he inquired, "What did you talk about?"

"Nothing interesting, honestly. She was only making polite conversation, asking me how I was liking it at the Hôtel de Neige, whether I planned on staying permanently and—"

"Are you?" Everett looked at her, alert like a deer caught in the headlights. "Planning on staying permanently, that is?"

Despite the annoyance, Ana felt herself softening. "I am."

Everett gave a slow nod, his expression unreadable. "What happened then? After she asked you? That's my last question, I promise."

Ana sighed, hoping he would stay true to his word. "Then Hedwig spilled the wine on me. It sort of put an end to the conversation."

Everett's brows shot up. "That's when Hedwig did it?"

"Yes."

The pianist looked away, out into the empty air. His lips parted but no words came out. She could hear the thoughts rattling through his brain. He popped his pocket watch open and closed, open and closed, open and closed.

Ana moved herself into his line of sight again. "Why is it so important for you to know?"

His distant expression shifted. Through the bewilderment which had creased his features broke a hesitant smile. "We should head back to the others before the mulled wine gets cold."

"Everett." It came out so harshly that he flinched and grew still. "Why is it important?"

To her surprise, he gave in—somewhat. "It's not that important," he said. "It's just whenever someone new starts at the hotel, Erica wants to welcome them personally, to make it official."

"Isn't that what a contract is for? To make it official?"

"Yes, yes. It's more…ceremonial," he finished, as if searching for the right word.

"Ceremonial?"

"Exactly. You know…old hotel, old traditions."

Ana supposed she understood the sentiment, but not his demeanor. He looked both nervous and relieved that he'd managed to string together a functioning sentence.

"Are you alright?" she asked.

"Of course," he said and gave another shaky smile. "Why wouldn't I be?"

Before she could ask more questions, Everett left, scurrying back into the staff kitchen without waiting for Ana to tag along. She stood still for a moment, then trotted after him.

They returned to the others, who had decked the table with waffles and steaming hot drinks. Bahar gave Everett a look as they rejoined the group. In the corner of her eye, Everett gave Bahar an almost imperceptible shake of his head.

SILENT NIGHT

On Christmas night, when the world outside had long grown dark and wind and snow whipped against the windows of Hôtel de Neige, the theater was filled to the brim. No spot remained unclaimed as the guests awaited the grandest performance of the season.

Ana longed for a moment of solitude, but noise polluted the air around her. Chattering and babbling sounded on the other side of the curtain while the last preparations for the magnificent show were underway. She felt rather useless in the blur of activity. She wore her gown already, a spectacle of dark blue fabric adorned with multicolored jewels that caught the light when she moved. In the heavy dress, she could do little more than stand still, feeling more like a fragile doll than a woman.

Light footfalls sounded nearby, and Ana looked up, expecting Everett. Hedwig Sternberg came to an abrupt halt as she spotted Ana. Like her, the ballerina was already in costume, wearing a tutu in the same deep blue shade as Ana's gown, covered with shimmering stones that made her a mirror image of a clear night's sky. Ana tried in vain to interpret Hedwig's expression. All she could distinguish was the lack of malice, which struck her as a new development.

"Are you alright?" Ana asked before thinking better of it.

Hedwig blinked. Some seconds passed, and she was starting to believe she would receive no answer at all. The ballerina gave a weak shrug.

Part of Ana wanted to shake her head and turn away, for she doubted prodding further would amount to anything. Nonetheless, she took a step towards the other woman. "Listen, Hedwig, why won't you just talk to me?"

"There is no sense in it," the ballerina said. Her usually straight posture drooped as she spoke. Ana noticed the dark rings beneath her eyes despite Hedwig's attempt to cover them up with makeup.

"I disagree," Ana countered. "Everyone at this hotel seems to know more than I, but no one will say a word. You tried to get rid of me, then claimed it was for my own sake. Don't I deserve an explanation? Don't I deserve the truth after what you put me through?"

Hedwig grew still. They were surrounded, yet alone. The moment felt pivotal, though no one else took note of it.

"Ana, I—" Hedwig began, then broke off. She had to gather herself before regarding Ana again. "I'm sorry."

"What?" Some of Ana's anger ebbed away as bewilderment washed through her. She didn't know what she had expected, but she certainly didn't expect an apology. "You're sorry?"

"I am. Before you misunderstand me, though, I am not sorry for what I have done. I am sorry for what is yet to come."

Ana felt a great weight pressing down on her. The words didn't sound like a threat—more like a benevolent warning. "I don't understand."

Hedwig sighed, exasperated, then averted her eyes. When Ana followed her gaze, she saw Erica de Winter approaching.

The owner of Hôtel de Neige was clad in the most magnificent gown Ana had ever seen. While the performers of the Christmas concert wore night blue, Erica donned another gown of pure white, covered in metallic, silvery sparkles. A cape trailed behind her, and a tiara sat nestled in her elaborate hairdo. Ana felt the urge to curtsey before her, not that she'd know how to do so.

"Good evening," Erica said, her toothy smile as brilliant as her dress. "I came to wish you the best of luck for the show tonight. Though I am sure you don't need it."

Hedwig straightened like a marionette upheld by invisible strings. "Thank you," she responded.

"Thank you," Ana echoed.

"Have the two of you reconciled after the unfortunate mishap last night?" Erica asked.

Ana exchanged a look with Hedwig. The petite ballerina looked small next to Erica and Ana in their vast gowns.

"Yes," Ana said, though Hedwig remained silent.

"I'm so pleased." Erica's eyes didn't quite match the rest of her expression. Ana wondered whether her cheeks ever hurt from all the persistent smiling.

"I shall leave you now," Erica said. As she departed, her skirts rustled across the floor.

Ana stared after her, then looked back to Hedwig, but the ballerina had turned away and taken off as well.

When the clock chimed nine, Ana stepped onstage with Everett, and the spotlights set her ablaze, a galaxy with a million bright stars. She took a deep breath, as though she could inhale the moment to hold it within herself forever.

The spot by the microphone had become a safe haven for her. She felt at home on the stage, like a monarch looking upon her subjects rather than a singer upon her audience. There was a sense of beautiful power to it.

In the foremost box, Ana spotted Dimitri, all by himself. Chill and heat overcame her at the vivid memory of their passionate kiss. She could only guess whether he thought of it, too. He wore a small smile; his smiles were far more difficult to read than his smirks.

Everett took his seat by the piano. When his fingers hit the keys, music filled the room, and Ana closed her eyes, readying herself for the song. Her lips parted for the first note.

A scream shook through the hall.

Part of Ana remained so focused on the melody that she nearly started singing despite the screeching noise. The music ceased, and she looked upon the crestfallen crowd. Then the cries for help began. Her gaze scoured the audience, searching for the culprit, before she realized it was coming from backstage.

Ana looked to Everett, who had jumped to his feet. For a moment, they stared at each other with widened eyes before breaking into a run. Her dress weighed her down, but something—adrenaline, perhaps—pushed her to race ahead.

They made it backstage, where the cries were growing louder. Ana spotted their source—Palmira Fiore. She knelt on the floor, her husband by her side, trying to hold her while she writhed. Her wails were bloodcurdling, like the howl of a she-wolf upon the death of her pup. Ana defied all her instincts and moved closer until she saw the reason for the agonizing screams.

On the floor lay a figure, stiff and pale as a porcelain doll. Shining dark hair cascaded around her, sparkling with ice, and her vacant eyes were frozen, wide open. Ice crystals glinted on her cheeks and brow, dusting along her bare arms. Ana clasped a hand over her mouth to silence her own scream.

"Hedwig," Everett whispered next to her.

Hedwig Sternberg. Her arms were spread wide, one leg pulled in, as though preparing to pirouette. Even in this moment, she was the perfect ballerina.

Ana stared at Everett, praying for him to be calm and strong when she found it difficult to stand. He appeared even more horrified, staggering backwards. There was no greater force coming to the rescue, Ana realized.

"I'll call 911," she said and rushed to her purse while trying not to think of Hedwig's unnaturally still body. "Does anybody know CPR?" she called out as she scrambled to find her phone. More people arrived, most of whom stopped in their tracks when they saw the ballerina on the ground like a discarded toy. "Anybody?"

No one responded. Ana found her phone and hammered in the three digits. An eternity passed before someone answered.

"911, what's your emergency?"

Ana had spoken to 911 once before, when her foster father suffered a stroke. Back then, at eleven years old, she had cried and mumbled. Now, she found composure in the chaos. "My colleague has collapsed and isn't moving. I'm at Hôtel de Neige, 845 Andersen Drive."

"Does your colleague have a pulse?" the man on the other end of the line asked, his voice professional and level-headed.

Ana spun to Palmira and Saverio. "Does she have a pulse?" Neither spoke, but Saverio turned to her and shook his head, glossy tears in his hazel eyes. He looked even younger than usual.

"No, she doesn't," Ana responded, desperately clinging to calmness.

"Alright," the operator said, in the same unfazed tone. He didn't scream or panic, so Ana convinced herself that some hope remained. "I need you to perform CPR. Can you do that? I will give you instructions."

Ana took a sharp breath. She had only ever witnessed CPR on television in those dramatic, hectic scenes, which either ended with a gasp for breath and gleeful relief or screaming and weeping.

"Yes," she said with false confidence and put the operator on speaker as she ran over to Hedwig. Palmira and Saverio moved out of the way, gaping at her.

She fell to her knees next to the ballerina. "What do I do?" she demanded.

"Miss, could you please repeat the address?" he responded instead.

"845 Andersen Drive."

"We don't have that address in our data bank."

"It's Hôtel de Neige," Ana responded, her tone growing louder. "Please, tell me what to do now."

From the television scenes, she knew approximately where to position her hands. She laid them on Hedwig's chest. The moment she touched the unconscious woman, Ana nearly pulled away again. She was ice cold, her body stiff as though frozen. Hedwig's lips were a deep blue, and little snow crystals covered her face and body like white freckles.

"Someone get something to warm her up," Ana shouted before setting her hands down firmly. "Alright, tell me what to do," she said to the operator.

Silence.

"Hello?" She stared at the phone—connection lost.

Cold panic washed through her, driving out every last remainder of calmness she had held onto. Next to her, Palmira and Saverio clutched each other like frightened children. Screams of shock and hysteria turned into tears of pain and grief. *No, this can't be.*

Ana started pushing onto Hedwig's chest, imitating the movements and rhythm from the movies. "Come on, Hedwig, come on," she whispered.

"Someone called for a doctor?"

Ana whipped around and saw a woman, a guest of the hotel. She released a quivering breath and slumped backwards, letting go of Hedwig as the doctor knelt beside the ballerina. Ana's gaze fixated on Hedwig's face. The ballerina looked lovely as ever, her beauty quite literally frozen in time. Her skin glittered like fresh snow as frost hung in Hedwig's lashes and kissed her lips. Ana blinked—she wanted them gone, she wanted Hedwig to look alive again, as alive as she had been moments earlier.

Someone took Ana by the arm and pulled her away from Hedwig's side. She attempted to fight it, to stay there and wait until the doctor managed to bring her back to life. But she lacked the energy to protest and gave in to the strong hold on her. She glimpsed Hedwig one last time. A streak of water ran upon the ballerina's face like a tear. Or melting ice.

Ana was brought to a chair nearby, where she sank down. Only then did she look up to see who had torn her away. Dimitri's blue eyes met hers.

"Angel," he said, grasping her by the shoulder to steady her. "Look at me, Angel."

She obeyed, relieved someone was telling her what to do. Shock echoed in Dimitri's expression, mingled with concern as he eyed her.

"The ambulance should be here soon," Ana said, mumbling. "It will be here soon."

Dimitri nodded slowly, but even through her tears, Ana could see his doubts. "We should get you out of here," he said.

Ana tensed at the idea of abandoning Hedwig. Of course, Palmira and Saverio were still with her, as was the doctor. "I can't leave," she told Dimitri anyway. She craned her neck to look for Hedwig again. Surely she had been mistaken; surely no snow or ice had blanketed the ballerina.

"It's alright, Angel," he said. "There are too many people here, more than enough to take care of Hedwig."

"Am I… Am I going mad?" Ana asked. She swallowed down a sob. "Hedwig was so cold. There were ice crystals on her face. I saw them."

Tenderly, Dimitri touched her face and wiped a tear away. "You're in shock, Angel. Your mind is playing tricks on you." His brows knitted together with concern. "You did all you could. Now let me take care of you."

There was no smirk, no smugness. She found herself nodding, and he helped her to her feet. Her legs felt wobbly. Nausea hit her as she almost lost her balance.

"I can't," she whispered, her entire body shaking like twigs in the winter wind.

"Let me." In one effortless sweep, Dimitri picked her up, his strong arms wrapping themselves around her exhausted body. He carried her away from the scene, and she rested her head against his shoulder. He brought her to the staff corridor, empty and dark.

"Room 016, right?"

"Yes."

Dimitri set her down carefully when they reached her door. Ana meant to reach for her keys, then realized. "I left my purse backstage. My keys are in there." She had also left her phone next to Hedwig.

"I can go and get your purse," Dimitri said. "We could also go to my suite, but only if you want."

Normally, Ana would refuse the suggestion, but his voice was so soft and gentle. It wasn't an inappropriate proposal. In this moment, they weren't the bantering pair—they weren't the people who had kissed passionately on the snowy balcony. There was something else between them, a comforting warmth in the midst of the storm.

"Okay," Ana said.

"Do you want to walk, or do you want me to carry you?"

Ana shook her head. "I can walk." Her legs were still weak, but she had him to cling to, and he kept a hand on the small of her back to steady her. Together, they inched ahead. They had almost reached the elevators when rapid footfalls broke the silence.

"Angie!"

Ana looked over her shoulder to see the two figures that had appeared. Before Ana recognized them through the blur of her tears, Bahar had run to her side and pulled her into a tight embrace. "Are you alright?" she whispered into Ana's ear.

Ana didn't know how to answer that question. She felt squashed as she found herself surrounded by Bahar, Everett, and Dimitri. The latter had stepped back a couple of feet.

Ana managed to wrench herself from the hug and looked around. "Has the ambulance arrived?"

Silence followed. For a few moments, nobody met her eyes. "There's no ambulance coming," Bahar said finally. "Hôtel de Neige is snowed in. We're cut off."

"But...but what about Hedwig?" The name formed a lump in Ana's throat and made it difficult for her to breathe. She reminded herself that there was a doctor with Hedwig. Perhaps an ambulance was not necessary.

"Ana," Everett's voice faded into the smallest of sounds. "It's too late. Hedwig is gone."

The tightening feeling in Ana's throat spread through the rest of her body, like iron chains wrapping around her, threatening to shatter her ribs. "No."

"You did all you could, Angel," Dimitri said, reaching out for her, but Everett and Bahar shot him with dark glances. He backed away again, even though Ana craved his soothing touch.

"You need to rest," Bahar said. "We'll get you to your room."

"I don't have my keys," Ana responded mechanically.

"We got your purse and phone," Bahar said, holding them up.

Ana gave a slow nod, unsure what to do. She was caught among clashing waves, dragging her under again and again until water filled her lungs instead of air. She wanted to rest but didn't want an entourage.

Somewhere in the distance, Bahar was speaking, but none of her words reached Ana. She wished to be a child again, to clasp her hands over her ears and cry.

A soft voice rose above all the blaring noise. "Angel, what do you need?"

Ana looked at Dimitri, pained that he still didn't dare get any closer.

"How about you stay out of it, Morozov?" Everett said.

Ana flinched.

Dimitri held up his hands. "I'm just trying to help."

"Then leave. You'd do everyone a favor."

Dimitri regarded Ana. She opened her mouth to protest, but no words came out. She tried to scramble something together, to find a way of making it clear that she wanted him near. But before she could get anything out, Bahar took her by the arm and set her in motion. "Come on, Angie. We will get you settled down."

With no energy left to resist, Ana submitted. Bahar unlocked the door to her room and guided her inside. Ana then glanced back over her shoulder to see Everett throwing Dimitri one last hateful glance before following them into the room. Ana's eyes met Dimitri's, and as he looked at her, the anger vanished from his features. It melted into something else, something softer—a mixture of concern and what Ana believed to be regret.

THE AFTERMATH

For the first time since arriving at Hôtel de Neige, Ana wanted to go home. Though, of course, there was nowhere for her to go—the hotel was all she had. But Hedwig was dead, and she no longer felt sure of anything, least of all the place she had fallen in love with.

The next morning, as Ana sat with the others at breakfast, she found it difficult to fathom everything that had unfolded on Christmas Day. They were trapped in the hotel with a dead body. No police could come and examine the scene, and no coroner could tend to Hedwig. Nobody knew why the ballerina died, or if they did, they kept it a secret. Outside, the snow fell relentlessly.

"You need to eat something," Bahar said as she pushed a plate of scrambled eggs Ana's way.

"I'm not hungry."

The idea of food made her nauseated. The night before, she had washed her hands over and over again until her skin became raw and tender. She had touched a dead body. Ana had known Hedwig was dead by the time she'd called 911 and tried to revive her. All her efforts had been futile, but she still felt a terrible guilt.

Everett, too, refused to eat. He looked sick and sleep-deprived. His eyes flickered around the room like he still hoped Hedwig would walk in. Ana didn't understand their relationship, but she saw the ghost of grief in his features.

"They want to hold a memorial service for her," Bahar said in a small voice.

Ana shuddered. Since they had yet to figure out what had happened to the ballerina, it seemed wrong to plan a memorial service. A funeral was not an option since they had nowhere to bury the body.

"A lot of the guests are getting anxious," Bahar added. "They want to leave, but they can't, and—"

Ana zoned out. It quickly became clear that Bahar needed to talk to calm herself, while Ana wished to hear no more about any of it. "Where is Erica de Winter?" she asked before thinking. The hotel's owner hadn't been in the audience of the attempted Christmas concert.

Bahar shrugged and stabbed her fork into the eggs on her plate. While the stress robbed Ana of her appetite, it seemed to fuel Bahar's.

"I'm going outside for some fresh air," Ana declared. She needed a break from Bahar's incessant talking and the contorted expression on Everett's face, which reflected every painful thought shooting through his head. It suffocated her.

The others glanced at Ana with some concern, as though they feared something might happen to her while she was gone. For a moment, Ana wondered about it as well. They didn't know Hedwig's cause of death. She had been a young woman, and her body had shown no signs of illness, nor of an accident. What if it wasn't a natural death?

Despite the sickening idea, Ana headed outside. It was freezing cold, and the wind had picked up again, swirling crystals of ice into her face. Gray clouds prevented the sunlight from piercing through and threatened another storm. It seemed the hotel would be snowed in for some time yet.

For the first time in weeks, Ana craved a cigarette. She missed smoking out of the window of her shitty apartment, not caring whether the smell made its way into her room and sank into the walls and furniture. Momentarily, she considered calling one of her old roommates, but the idea was ridiculous. She'd never been close to any of them, not even when squeezed together in the same tight and dirty space. Besides, her cell service was out.

Nobody had warned Ana that a side effect of such horror would be utter boredom. Everybody had retreated into their rooms and shells, not in the mood to do anything. Rehearsals, communal dinners, parties—everything had been called off. Not that Ana would want to do any of it. But without the activities, there was nothing but the aftermath of Hedwig's death, echoing through each corner of Hôtel de Neige.

The only person she could think of, the only one she might go to, was Dimitri. Guilt weighed on her for abandoning him that night, but that, too, was far overshadowed by everything else. She could pay him a visit; perhaps it would do them both some good. She didn't know if Dimitri had been close to Hedwig or how he was taking the ballerina's sudden demise.

Behind her, the door to the terrace opened so softly that Ana almost didn't hear. When she turned around, a woman she didn't recognize waited behind her, although there was something familiar about her features.

"Ms. Greene?" The woman asked tentatively. She was around thirty years old, short, and curvy. She had a kind face, the sort one trusted easily. Ana could imagine her smile, wide and uninhibited.

"Yes?" Ana responded, scrutinizing her to pin down where they had met before.

The woman stretched out her gloved hand, and, after some hesitation, Ana shook it.

"May I ask who you are?" she asked.

"Dr. Martina Lopez. I'm the doctor who attempted to revive your friend last night."

Ana stiffened. She remembered now the blurred features of the woman who had released Ana from her hopeless attempts to save Hedwig's life.

"I see," Ana responded after a few moments, unsure what else to say. Perhaps she should thank the doctor for stepping in and trying to help, but the words wouldn't come out.

"I was looking for you," Dr. Lopez explained, easing Ana of the burden of speaking. "I wanted to tell you that you did everything right last night."

Ana dug her fingers into the snowy balustrade.

"Extreme situations show us who we are," Dr. Lopez continued. "You stepped up when no one else did, and that is admirable."

Ana swallowed hard, feeling the knot tightening in her throat. "It made no difference." She wasn't sure whether she said it to the doctor or to herself. It was the truth, either way.

"I know what it's like to lose a patient," the doctor responded. "Although that is not the same as losing a friend. I know the anger and the guilt and the thoughts that maybe you could have done more, tried harder, and then that person would still be alive."

Ana blinked away the tears. All the emotions the doctor spoke of weighed heavily on her. She didn't even know how she could begin to describe them. "We weren't really friends," she said, the words leaving a bitter taste in her mouth.

Ana had despised Hedwig for most of her time at Hôtel de Neige, but she also believed that Hedwig had known something—and that her intentions hadn't purely originated out of malice. Perhaps in a different world, they could have become friends.

Dr. Lopez remained silent for a moment. Then, in a grave tone, she said, "There's something else I want to discuss with you."

Ana lifted a brow.

The doctor sighed, clearly struggling to find the right words. "This case," she began. "It is quite odd."

Everything at this hotel is odd, Ana thought. She gave a slow nod, beckoning Dr. Lopez to continue.

"Ms. Sternberg's body...it was frozen."

Ana inhaled, the cold air stinging her lungs like needles. She remembered laying her hands on Hedwig's chest and the icy shock that rippled through her. She remembered the stiff limbs, the bluish lips, the ice crystals. Yet panic had distorted her perception and her memory—there was no other explanation. A doctor should know that; a doctor should be more rational.

"She *was* frozen, right?" Dr. Lopez said with uncertainty, as though she doubted her own mind.

"I don't know," Ana said, so quiet it was a miracle the words didn't get swallowed by the wind.

"She was so cold and stiff," the doctor said. "She must have been outside—she must have died outside."

Ana flinched. *Died.* She didn't want to say it out loud; she didn't want to hear it out loud. But the doctor was only getting started. Her next words came at a faster pace.

"She must have died outside, then somebody carried her body inside. The two other dancers said they found her lying on the floor backstage just a few minutes after they had seen her alive, but that's impossible." Dr. Lopez paused, slightly out of breath. Then she looked right at Ana. "Do you think they may have been involved in her death somehow?"

A sound of choked laughter escaped Ana's throat, which took the doctor aback. The idea was ridiculous. Ana didn't know Palmira and Saverio well, but she had rarely seen them without Hedwig. They had fawned over her.

Ana shook her head. "They would never hurt her. Besides, I saw them all backstage right before my performance. She was alive and well. There is no way she was frozen just minutes later." No matter how Ana turned it in her head, it remained impossible.

"That makes no sense," the doctor responded.

Ana repressed a sneer. None of it made sense, nothing except the decay of her own mind, the loss of her grip on reality. Though now, there was someone else. How high were the chances that the two of them succumbed to madness at the same time?

"I'm sorry. That's all I can tell you," she said to the doctor.

Bewilderment was written across the other woman's face. "I suppose," she said after some grappling, "all we can do now is wait for the police and the coroner to show up. But who knows how long that will take?"

Ana glanced skyward. It would be days before they could reconnect with the outside world.

The doctor made her way back inside while Ana lingered in the cold. She gazed upon the blanket of snow, which now seemed treacherous. The doctor had been so sure that Hedwig had died from the cold, from hypothermia. It would not be the first such death at Hôtel de Neige.

The last singer. The fate which Hedwig had held over Ana as a threat and which, in the end, had befallen her instead. Could it be a coincidence, some freak accident? As much as Ana tried to believe it, she couldn't.

Yet if there had indeed been foul play involved, what did it mean for her? She had no idea. All she knew was that she couldn't sit about and wait for the frost to thaw. By then, it might be too late.

Ana returned inside, but it felt hardly warmer than outside in the snow. An eerie silence had overtaken the entire hotel, as though its people had descended into hibernation until the long winter at last drew to a close.

She wandered through the abandoned corridors. Her room, which still held a faint trace of Hedwig's lily perfume, stifled her, so she avoided it. In the end, her winding path brought her to one of the first places she had come to love at Hôtel de Neige: the music room.

Usually, when she approached, Ana could hear the melody of Everett at the piano, drawing her in and filling her with the powerful urge to create music of her own. But he wasn't there, and without him, the music room had lost its magic. Still, something broke through its silence.

Ana came to a halt when she heard the footfalls from within. Could it be Palmira and Saverio? Ana knew they occasionally practiced there, but she doubted they would rehearse the day after Hedwig's death.

Slowly, Ana approached. She craned her neck to peek inside. A lone figure shuffled through the music room, his appearance made even smaller by the vast and vacant surroundings.

"Mike?"

The boy spun around, surprise in his large eyes. Ana spotted the ball at his feet. He was playing alone, she realized.

"Hey," the child said in a tone too somber for his age.

"Hey," Ana echoed as she stepped into the room. "What are you doing here?"

Mike bit his lower lip and avoided meeting her gaze. "I'm practicing soccer."

Ana raised her brows, and they both glanced at the mirrors covering an entire wall of the music room. It was certainly not the best playground for a child with a ball.

"Don't tell H—" Mike began before he fell quiet again.

"Don't tell who?"

"Hedwig. But she's…" He mumbled something else, which Ana didn't catch, but she understood the gist of it. The boy faced her. "She's really dead, isn't she?"

The question knocked the breath out of Ana. With Hedwig's passing still so fresh, she had no idea how much he had been told or how much he would grasp. She looked back at the empty corridor behind her, hoping someone else would appear and take over the conversation. Perhaps she could come up with some excuse to him as to why she had to leave again.

With hesitancy, Ana advanced into the music room. Mike sat down on the floor in the midst of it, and she joined him. For a moment, neither of them spoke. Then he rolled the ball her way, and she rolled it back to him, some of the distance between them fading as they continued the idle back-and-forth.

"Are you alright?" she asked after a while, although the question felt stupid. Such a young boy, and he had already experienced so much loss in his life. How could he be alright?

Mike shrugged.

"You know, it's okay to be sad," Ana said, wishing she'd had time to prepare for this.

"I'm not sad. I just miss her," Mike said, looking at the ball rather than at Ana. "Hedwig always played board games with me when I had nightmares and couldn't sleep."

Ana drew her brows together. "She did?" She found it difficult to picture Hedwig as the kindly babysitter.

Mike nodded. A weak though mischievous smile traveled across his lips. When he smiled like that, he did look like a true child.

"I didn't know Hedwig very well," Ana admitted. "Can you tell me more about her?" She hoped she hadn't said the wrong thing. Would it hurt him to speak of her?

The boy smiled. "She taught me how to play chess. I'm good at it, too. And she taught me curse words in German."

The corner of Ana's mouth twitched upwards. "That sounds nice."

The boy nodded. "Hedwig wasn't so nice to you," he then said.

Ana shook her head, a bit startled, although it was perhaps only natural that he had noticed. "No, she wasn't." She hesitated, then added, "Do you know why?"

Mike dug the tips of his fingers into the ball, creating a row of shallow dents. "No," he said. "I know she was worried about you, though."

"Was she?" Ana struggled to reconcile all the different masks Hedwig had worn.

The boy said no more, so she decided it was time to stop questioning him. She doubted it would lead anywhere. They sat there for some while, then Mike moved the ball aside and scooted closer to her.

"Ana," he said with a sudden touch of shyness. "Can you sing something to me?"

Despite the soothing effect music had on her, Ana had not sung since Hedwig's death. But when the boy asked her, she knew she couldn't deny him, nor herself.

"Of course," she told Mike. "Anything in particular?"

The boy came closer, leaning his small body against her. An unexpected feeling of protectiveness overcame Ana, and after some hesitation, she pulled him in.

"Can you sing a lullaby?" he asked.

Ana scoured her mind. None of her foster parents had ever sung lullabies to her, so she had little to choose from. She only remembered a few she had picked up from television years ago.

All else was utterly quiet in Hôtel de Neige when Ana began to sing. She had grown so used to having a crowd of people as her audience that singing for herself was a different sensation. She realized how much she had missed the intimacy of singing for just herself. Mike was there, yet the comforting feeling persisted, and she dove into it. No grand expectations, no spectacular show. Only the emotions that otherwise lay dormant within her. After her initial tentativeness around Mike, she wrapped her arms around him. He relaxed in her embrace, his warmth becoming hers and hers becoming his.

It was a quiet lullaby, but it tapped into the emotions spiraling through her. She gave herself to the melody the way she might during a performance, though in a gentler way. As she did, she discovered her desperate love for music once again.

Into the song, Ana poured the story of a little girl, troubled and unable to descend into sleep. The dark night held not comfort but terrors. The song told of sweet summer days, spent in the sun instead of the moonless night. Flowers bloomed and light won over darkness. She could almost smell the roses and hear the rustling of leaves and the lapping of the river in the distance. It brought with it a warmth not usually found at the Hôtel de Neige.

The song ended, and Mike gazed up at Ana with a strange look on his face. With too-long sleeves, he wiped a tear from his cheek, though more budded in his hazel eyes, ready to fall. Ana forced herself not to look away. He needed someone to be there for him, now more than ever. She swept the messy hair from his face and pressed a kiss to his forehead.

"Thanks for singing," Mike muttered. He pushed himself further into her embrace, and by instinct, she held him tighter.

"Is everything alright?" Ana asked.

Mike sniffed, another tear rolled down. "That's the same lullaby Hedwig used to sing to me."

A flash of cold washed through Ana as she drew back from him. She turned his body so he would face her. "Hedwig sang this lullaby to you?"

Mike gave a solemn nod. "Did she teach you, too?"

"No," Ana whispered. "No, I've known since I was a kid."

It was not so strange. Many people knew the same songs. She searched her brain, trying to figure out where the song had come from. It felt as though she had known it forever, like she had sprung into existence with it printed onto her soul.

A coincidence. Another coincidence. Another mystery she could not decipher. Another puzzle piece she could not place.

"Are you alright?" Mike asked.

Ana snapped back into her body. She attempted a smile, but the frown on his face did not vanish. "I'm alright," she said and pulled him towards her again, his back leaning against her so he couldn't see the look in her eyes.

I'm alright, she thought. *Quite alright. I promise. Ignore the madness festering within me. I am alright.*

How many more coincidences until she broke beneath their weight?

IN MEMORIAM

A sea of black stretched out before Ana, like dark waves beneath a moonless sky. The lively theater had transformed into a somber memorial service for Hedwig Sternberg, the only noises low mumbling and soft tunes from the piano. Photos of the ballerina were displayed on the stage, and even in death, her eyes seemed to follow Ana, taunting her with the secrets she had kept.

Ana stood with Everett and Bahar and looked at the stage, observing the images of Hedwig. Some of them were black-and-white portrait shots of her, giving the ballerina the distinct appearance of a haute couture model. Most of the photographs, though, depicted her dancing, caught in motion. She looked so painfully alive in them.

They found some empty seats at the back of the hall and sank down, their view largely obscured by the rows upon rows of guests before them. The sight of the guests appalled Ana. They hadn't known Hedwig. They shouldn't partake in the grief of others as though it were some sort of event. Then again, Ana hadn't known Hedwig either. Not really.

At times, she felt guilty for the sadness that had crept up on her, like she was trespassing on someone else's emotions. She wished she could shake it off and think of Hedwig as the arrogant, spiteful ballerina who had done all she could to get rid of Ana. There was, after all, no evidence that Hedwig had been more than that, except for the tightening instinct in Ana's gut.

"Hedwig would hate this," Everett said, his expression twisting as he looked about the hall.

Ana exchanged a glance with Bahar. Everett's mood and demeanor had gone through some sharp turns in the past days, shifting from grief to trance to anger. Bahar had tried to talk to him but had not gotten through.

Silence shrouded the theater like a widow's veil. Ana watched as Erica stepped onto the stage. She grimaced. Someone had died, and Erica still wore all white, setting herself apart from the crowd of black. The way she approached the stage seemed more appropriate for a performance than a eulogy.

When Erica made her way to the microphone, Ana's center contracted. She felt strangely protective of that spot. It seemed wrong for Erica to take her place there.

"Today, I welcome you with a heavy heart," Erica de Winter began. Her eyes wandered through the attendance. "It pains me greatly that we come together for such a solemn occasion. We have lost Hedwig Sternberg, a young woman with so much talent and heart. She was far more than just a gifted ballerina. She was a beautiful soul, a bright mind, and a beloved friend.

"We still do not know the exact circumstances of her death, nor do we want to draw any premature conclusions before the police have investigated the situation. For transparency, I will share with you what we know thus far."

Ana's fingers dug into the hems of her sweater. What did Erica mean to reveal? She doubted she intended to share that Hedwig's body had been inexplicably frozen.

A pregnant pause filled the hall. Erica said, "We found a letter in Ms. Sternberg's room. A goodbye letter."

The announcement barreled through the audience. Ana's stomach turned, and she felt the color draining from her face. A goodbye letter? She looked to the others, whose eyes had grown wide.

"Sometimes the people around us carry weights we do not see until it is too late," Erica went on. "All who knew Hedwig knew her strength. But sometimes strength is the best façade for pain."

Ana gazed up at Erica. Commotion next to her had her turning to see Everett jumping up from his chair and storming off. Bahar looked after him, half rising before she sank back into her seat.

Erica never acknowledged the incident. "It is an unbearably sorrowful occasion," she continued. "Yet it is also an occasion to celebrate the life of a person we greatly admired." She allowed time for a purposeful pause, then plastered on a soft smile, the perfect concoction of grief and hope.

Ana's attention drifted away when Erica introduced a guest to the stage, a man who was apparently a pastor from some prominent church. He launched into a sermon of loss and compassion and whatever else, talking on and on, never acknowledging that Hedwig wasn't Christian. It became clear that the service was intended for the guests, not those who truly grieved Hedwig. Ana had searched for Palmira and Saverio Fiore among the attendees of the service, but they were absent. She understood why.

When the memorial finally ended, most of the staff members were eager to flee. Together with Bahar, Ana found a relatively quiet spot nearby—quite the accomplishment given the outpour of people.

"That was awful," Bahar said, leaning against a frosted window.

Ana grumbled some words of agreement. She had never attended a memorial service before and did not intend to be present at another.

"If I die, at least find me an imam," Bahar said and shook her head in exasperation. "I think I need to take a nap." She looked at Ana and shifted to a gentler tone. "Will you be okay on your own?"

"Of course. Don't worry about me."

Bahar surveyed Ana before nodding and setting out for her room.

As Ana watched Bahar take off, a heaviness spread in her chest. Alone once more.

Ana got to her feet and straightened her aching back. Just as she meant to head outside for a cigarette, she heard raised voices in the theater. Even though she was a distance away from the grand hall, the noise reached her with force. Before she could chide herself for prying, she had made her way to the doors of the theater.

Erica and Dimitri stood by the foot of the stage. Ana had to take a few more steps before she recognized the other two figures. Palmira and Saverio Fiore faced off with the hotel's owner. Some guests lingered nearby, watching with wide eyes and low whispers.

Palmira looked tiny next to Erica de Winter's imposing silhouette. The ballet dancer's shoulders slouched.

"You," Palmira snarled. Tears ran down her reddened cheeks. "How are you not ashamed of the spectacle you made of her death?"

"Calm yourself, Palmira," Erica said.

"She's dead." Palmira's entire body was shaking. "My friend is dead."

"I understand your pain."

"You heartless bitch, you understand nothing."

The remaining guests who had formed a semicircle around the show gasped. Ana felt disgusted by them, even though she was eavesdropping too.

Upon the insult, Erica paused. When she spoke again, she did so with a treacherous softness, the kind that hid a sharp edge beneath. "You are upset, Palmira. I suggest you return to your room before you say something you and your husband might regret."

Palmira did not move, though she remained silent.

Erica released a dramatic sigh. "Fine. Then I shall be graceful and remove myself as a courtesy to your grief." She leaned in, her mouth close to Palmira's ear. "Never, *never* insult me again." She whirled around, her skirts flowing behind her.

It took Ana a moment to realize she was coming toward her.

Erica smiled as she approached, as though the harrowing exchange with Palmira had never occurred.

"Ana Greene," she said, and halted before her. "How did you find the memorial service?"

Ana swallowed hard. She still disliked the presence of Erica de Winter, perhaps now more than ever. The other people in the theater glanced towards them, and Ana no longer despised the guests for their watchful gazes. Instead, she felt glad to have witnesses.

"The service was beautiful," she responded after a pause.

"I take it you overheard my conversation with Mrs. Fiore," Erica said then.

The nauseating pit within Ana's stomach grew. "I did."

"Do you also think I'm heartless?"

Ana looked to the foot of the stage. Palmira and Saverio had disappeared, but Dimitri remained, observing them.

"That's not my judgment to make," Ana replied. "I do think Palmira is grieving."

Erica's smile twitched. "How diplomatic of you." She took a step closer. "Tell me, Ana, have you ever lost someone dear to you?"

Ana wanted to say yes. Yet in truth, she had lost not people but the idea of them. She grieved, but not for anyone real. She grieved the family she never had.

When Ana didn't respond, Erica exhaled a long breath. "Throughout my life, I have lost all those I loved the most," she said. "I have watched as everyone I cared about was torn away from me."

Ana stood still. Her lips parted to voice condolences, but she thought better of it. She realized no response was needed as Erica seemed distant. When the lady of Hôtel de Neige spoke again, it was impossible to tell whether she was addressing Ana or talking to herself.

"My mother died when I was just a child. I have no memories of her," Erica said. "My father passed when I was a few years older than you are now. I thought I would never feel a greater pain, nor that I could ever heal from it. Yet I did. I met the love of my life, and I recovered." She paused, and something in her expression shifted. All softness vanished from her features. "I recovered, and then I lost him, too."

Ana stared at her, first with shock, then with a sting in her chest. She had never taken a liking to Erica, the woman who seemed as cold and mysterious as the hidden part of an iceberg. Somehow, Ana had doubted that someone like her was capable of deep emotion—and more so, that she had experienced the pain which came with such emotions.

Yet as quickly as it had shown itself, the glimpse beneath the surface disappeared again. Erica's thin smile returned, and she faced Ana.

"So you see, Ana, I do have a heart, even if Palmira Fiore claims otherwise. Though you'd better not tell anyone else," Erica added and winked. "I have a reputation to uphold." She turned and walked away.

Ana looked after her white silhouette, which seemed to float rather than walk, until she left the theater. Only then did Ana notice the goosebumps on her arms.

She was about to set out as well when a voice reached her. "Angel!"

Ana straightened at the sight of Dimitri as he came towards her.

"Dimitri, hey," Ana said when he halted before her.

Dimitri surveyed her. "Are you alright?"

Ana wondered why he asked—because of the death, the memorial service, or the conversation with Erica?

"I'm fine," she replied.

A short, uncomfortable silence blanketed them. Dimitri was the first to break through it. "How about we go outside for some fresh air?"

Ana almost said she needed to go to her room and rest. Instead, she caught herself and nodded. "I'd like that. Let me grab my coat, and I'll meet you outside."

Ten minutes later, Ana stood with Dimitri out on some terrace, still searching in vain for something to say. The blizzard promised by the dark clouds had yet to descend, letting them enjoy some hours of milder weather.

"Are you sure you don't want one?" Dimitri asked, holding up his lit cigarette.

"I quit. Mostly," Ana said as she eyed the smoke drifting up into the air.

A low chuckle passed Dimitri's lips. "Why?"

She shrugged. "Cancer. Death. Wrinkles and yellow teeth. My voice. I might as well protect myself, right?" The corners of her mouth twitched upwards as she saw him smirk at her response. Somehow, though, his smirk had changed; it was no longer the same devil-may-care look he wore when she first arrived at Hôtel de Neige. How long ago it seemed.

"I wanted to thank you," Ana said. "For that night."

Dimitri shook his head. "There's no need to thank me." A touch of sadness crossed his features as he dwelt on the memories. His sharp edges softened. He looked like a watercolor painting, the shades of blue and black and gray blurring together in some grand artistic vision.

"I don't know what I would have done without you," Ana admitted.

He smiled hesitantly. "You had other people there to help you."

Ana sighed. "I also wanted to apologize. For them. They treated you unfairly."

"They don't particularly like me."

"I like you," Ana responded, and there it was again, his self-assured smirk. "I didn't mean it like that," she added.

"I like you, too," Dimitri replied. "And I'm not telling you how I mean it."

He grinned, and Ana rolled her eyes. Part of her wished they could stay out there on the terrace and continue like this, bantering and smoking and not thinking about what had happened or what lay ahead.

"Do you think she actually killed herself?" The words spilled from Ana before she could stop herself. In her mind's eye, she saw Hedwig's pale face and vacant eyes.

Dimitri's jaw clenched. She knew she was bringing him back to that night, and she felt a sting of regret. Yet she feared she might burst if she kept it all to herself.

"Hedwig had her demons," Dimitri said, his voice low and raspy from smoking and the cold wind. "She tragically lost her family shortly before she came to Hôtel de Neige, and I think she often felt guilty for being the one who survived."

"My God," Ana whispered, unsure what to make of the horrific revelation. There was so much she hadn't known about the ballerina, yet she had judged her so readily.

Ana eyed Dimitri. His gaze had grown distant, and a novel instinct tugged at her—the instinct to touch him, to comfort him. She refrained from it.

"Were you two close?" she asked instead.

"Hedwig was a difficult person to be close to," Dimitri answered. "We knew each other for a long time, and we had much in common. I'm not sure if we ever were friends, but perhaps something resembling it." He sighed and stubbed the butt of his cigarette out in the snow.

"I'm sorry for your loss," Ana said, immediately resenting herself for repeating those premade words to him.

"It's alright," he responded and gave a smile as empty as her condolences. "How are you holding up?"

"Let's just say that I am." At times, she believed she could leave it all behind and focus on her dream, on the remaining pieces of it. But far too often, the lingering shock and the bewilderment spiraled within her and left her paralyzed.

Ana studied Dimitri. How much did he know? He was the hotel manager and Erica de Winter's confidante, perhaps least likely to tell her anything at all. A sudden anger surged through her, paired with a feeling of betrayal. He owed her no loyalty, of course. They weren't allies. She doubted they could call each other friends. Still, they had shared that moment out on the terrace, the memory of which still tingled through her. Maybe it had been just a kiss, two people spurred on by attraction and lust. Nothing more.

Yet he had taken care of her the night of Hedwig's death, and she still wondered why. Decency? Pity? He didn't seem the type, and he'd appeared genuinely hurt when Everett and Bahar chased him away.

"What are you thinking about?" Dimitri asked.

Ana met his eyes, her gaze grazing his lips. She had never known a man's lips could be so beautiful and enticing. At once, she scolded herself for the thought. How could she contemplate his lips under such circumstances?

"I should go," Ana said. She was determined not to be puzzled by her own emotions, not when everything else was puzzling enough.

Dimitri gave a curt nod. Was there a sliver of disappointment in his expression? "Perhaps so," he said. He reached out and tucked a strand of wily hair behind Ana's ear. For a fragment of a moment, his fingers touched her neck, sending shivers through her. "If you ever need someone to talk to or just be around, I am there for you. Any time."

They smiled at each other. Weak, yet warm smiles. Dimitri lingered another moment as though he meant to say more, but he remained silent before walking away.

Ana was left to wonder about the words unspoken between them.

LETTERS FROM A DEAD GIRL

$\mathcal{A}$na stood before the closed door, her heart pounding as she gathered the courage to knock. Her stomach churned at the thought of it. She considered fleeing the scene; nobody would know any better. The determination that drove her to come was dwindling. She needed to act before it vanished entirely.

She rapped her fist against the door.

Silence. Perhaps no one was there, though Ana could think of nowhere else they might be. Then she heard shuffling and quiet talking. Her instincts told her to run, but she was out of time. The door opened, and she looked into the stern face of Palmira Fiore. A sliver of surprise rippled across Palmira's features, swiftly replaced by narrowed eyes and a tense jaw. Saviero stood behind Palmira, his gaze jumping between his wife and Ana. Wariness glinted in his eyes.

"What do you want?" Palmira asked, spitting the words out like venom.

"I wanted to talk to you," Ana answered.

"I can't think of anything we might talk about," the ballerina said and reached for the door, ready to slam it shut. Ana rushed forward, wedging herself in the space. Palmira stopped just in time not to squash her hand.

"I don't want to talk to you," Palmira said. "And if you don't remove your hand in the next few seconds, I will use this door to break your fingers." She gave a twisted semblance of a smile.

Ana grimaced, but she kept her hand where it was and even pushed forward a little further, positioning her body so Palmira could no longer so easily lock her out. Palmira was dainty, but Ana knew her to be strong—she had seen as much during the rehearsals. And she was determined.

"Just ten minutes," Ana argued. "Then I'll leave you alone, I promise."

Palmira exchanged a look with her husband which Ana interpreted as a good sign.

With a long sigh, Palmira stepped back and opened the door fully. Ana slipped in at once, afraid Palmira would change her mind. The room was small but inviting. Palmira and Saverio had moved into a room up on the second floor, one originally intended for guests. It was nothing ostentatious, though it was a more appropriate place for a married couple than the staff rooms. They had a small table with three chairs where they sat down.

"Do you want something to drink?" Saverio asked.

"No, she doesn't," Palmira responded before Ana could decline. "But you can set the timer for ten minutes, *cuore mio*."

Ana shifted in her seat, once more questioning the choices that had led her to their doorstep.

Palmira regarded her with an icy demeanor. "So, what would you like to talk about? Upcoming performances? New Year's festivities? The death of my dearest friend?"

Ana swallowed hard. Hedwig's death was still so fresh. Was she only causing unnecessary pain? But didn't she owe it to Hedwig to find out more about her and about the circumstances of her obscure death? Didn't she owe it to herself to unveil the secrets Hôtel de Neige hid from her?

"I do want to talk about Hedwig's death," Ana said in the softest tone she could muster. "And about what may have happened that night."

"What do you mean?" Palmira asked. "We know what happened that night. Hedwig killed herself."

Ana flinched. Before her mind's eye, images of Hedwig's dead body flared up once more, like violent lightning on a quaint night. Would she ever be rid of them? She doubted it.

"I came to ask whether you believe that she committed suicide," Ana said. "The way she—"

Palmira held up her hand to stop Ana. "If you are here to discuss your conspiracy theories, I will hear nothing of it. She killed herself. I read her letter."

Ana startled. "You did?"

Palmira sighed and turned to her husband. *"Puoi andare a prendere la lettera?"*

Saverio rose. When he returned a few moments later, he held a letter in his hands.

Ana stared at the letter, then at Palmira. "You have Hedwig's goodbye letter?"

Palmira gave Saverio a meaningful look, and he held out the letter. She reached out, but she could not bring herself to touch it. How long before her demise had Hedwig penned this?

Ana pinched the letter with her fingers. Her throat turned dry, and she wished Saverio had brought her something to drink earlier. Why had she come? She was no better than a grave robber, digging her fingers into the soil and into the rotten wood of the coffin.

"Time's ticking," Palmira said.

Ana wanted nothing more than to toss the letter aside—except answers. After all that had happened, she deserved answers. She steadied herself as best as she could and began reading.

Dearest Palmira, dearest Saverio,

I apologize for this sorry manner of farewell. I know I ought to have the courage to say my goodbyes in person, yet I am certain you'd try to stop me from my path if I did.

I have wandered this world for so long; my legs are

tired and giving in beneath the weight of it all. So I shall go. It pains me to leave you behind, but I know you will find comfort in each other as you always have. I hope it will also soothe you to know I am not fighting my demise. I welcome it. I meant to remedy some of the mistakes I made in life so I may be forgiven in death, yet I believe I have failed.

I hope to see you again one day, as I hope to reunite with my family on the other side of this journey. Shed your tears, my friends, as I know you must—but then kiss them away, as I know you will.

In love, always,
Hedwig Sternberg

Ana sank deep into her chair. Tears formed in the corners of her eyes, and she quickly blinked them away. She couldn't bear to cry in front of Palmira and Saverio—she had hardly known Hedwig. She had no right to those tears. No matter that sobs caught in her throat and choked her from the inside out.

"It is her handwriting and her style," Palmira said, as though anticipating Ana's next question. "They also found an empty pill container in her dressing room. Case closed."

"But—" Ana began, though she had no idea how to finish the sentence. *But Hedwig's body was frozen.* Had she been mistaken? If so, the doctor at the scene had been mistaken as well.

Palmira jumped in. "But what if someone forced her to write it? I would know."

"I didn't mean to suggest that."

"Then spit out what you do mean, because your ten minutes are running out, and I'm growing tired of you playing detective."

Playing detective. Ana narrowed her eyes. "Why do you even have this letter?"

"What do you mean?" Palmira asked. "It is addressed to Saverio and me. You can read, can't you?"

Ana forced herself to remain gentle, although frustration and irritation gnawed at her. "This is evidence. It should be preserved until the police can get here and examine it."

Cold laughter bubbled out of the dancer. "Alright," she said with a cold, toothy smile. "I will continue to preserve it, then." She snatched the letter out of Ana's hands, causing a small tear in the paper. "I think you should go now."

"No," Ana responded. "I'm not leaving yet. This still makes no sense. Hedwig's body was *frozen*. A farewell letter and an empty pill container don't explain that."

Palmira's smile vanished. "I think you, out of all people, should stay out of this."

"Out of this? Out of what? Nobody else is trying to figure out what actually happened to Hedwig."

"How dare you?" Palmira's voice transformed into rolling thunder. She howled with such force and volume that Ana feared the people in the neighboring rooms would hear her. Saverio hurried to his wife's side, though she paid him no attention. "How dare you? How dare you make it seem we don't care about what happened to Hedwig? I found her body. I had to look into the empty eyes of my closest friend."

As quickly as the noise had arisen, the room fell quiet again, seized by an eerie silence. "I'm sorry," Ana said. "I shouldn't have come."

The anger that held Palmira's features momentarily ebbed away, broken through by the grief. "No," she said. "You shouldn't have come. Not here. And not to Hôtel de Neige."

The last words were an echo of what Hedwig had told Ana. She almost expected a threat to follow.

"I'm sorry," she whispered again, making her way to the door. There, she looked back upon the two.

Saverio wrapped Palmira in his embrace. Tears were rolling down her cheeks. The young woman no longer looked like a hysterical girl, instead resembling a grieving crone. Ana's eyes met Saverio's. His lips parted, but he never spoke a word.

Ana yearned to say more. So many questions still weighed on her mind, but she had done enough damage. She opened the door and scurried out of the room.

She made it to the staircase before she crumpled under the weight of the terrible guilt within her. What a fool she had been. She had been chasing after secrets ever since her arrival at the hotel. The search for answers to imagined questions had mattered more to her than the people around her. It didn't much surprise her. She always had a tendency to follow her own ludicrous ideas with no regard for foster families, classmates, lovers, or friends.

Ana rubbed her temples, but the headache didn't subside. She had gone too far. She had shaken a grieving girl because she refused to believe Hedwig killed herself. A goodbye letter, an empty pill container, a troubled past.

A frozen body. Ana shook her head. Her senses had played a trick on her—no other explanation made sense. She was losing her mind from the paranoia, from all the ghosts she believed she saw. Why couldn't she find happiness at the hotel? It was all she had wanted, all she had ever dreamed of—or at least, it could be if she stopped sabotaging herself.

Her once fierce determination wilted away. It was enough. She would smother her doubts and end her quest for the truth. The police would investigate Hedwig's death, and they would rule it a suicide. A mundane tragedy, nothing more.

Ana hauled herself up again. She trudged down the stairs and returned to the solitude of her room. She wanted only to rest, to close the door on everything else.

Ana woke to utter darkness and almost utter silence. Almost. She wondered if it was the beginning of another nightmare. Her hands scoured the ground around her, but she lay in her bed, cushioned by the warm blanket and soft pillows.

Yet something shook her. She held her breath and clasped a palm over her mouth to make sure no noise escaped her. With the other hand, she checked the time on her phone. It was shortly after midnight.

Outside of her door, something shifted. In the absence of noise, the footfalls echoed, reverberating through her body like thunder. Ana reached for her drawer. When it opened with a low squeak, she flinched. The footfalls ceased for a moment. Whoever it was, they were right outside her door.

If she sat still and pressed her eyes shut, then perhaps it would be a dream after all. A dream she could wake up from.

She refused to be so helpless, not again. From her drawer, she grabbed the shard of broken glass she had clutched just weeks ago. Blood still stained its silvery surface. She had not dared get rid of it, though she had wrapped it in cloth as a makeshift hilt.

Ana watched the door with narrowed eyes. Nothing happened; all remained quiet. Then, something slipped beneath it into her room.

She shot to her feet and slammed the light switch of her bedside lamp. On the floor lay a white envelope. She swooped down and gripped it, fingers digging into paper.

Footsteps began to fade away. Whoever had left it was getting away. Ana stared at the door a moment longer. The prey animal in her told her to keep it shut, to hide under her bed and wait until the predator had disappeared. But she was no longer prey. She tore open the door.

The corridor lay in darkness, and she almost missed the silhouette dashing away.

"Stop," Ana called out. She was barefoot, dressed in the emerald pajamas she had been gifted for Christmas, but she sprinted through the cold hallway after the figure. She clutched the shard so hard that she feared it would cut through the cloth. The old wound on her palm threatened to burst open.

Ana caught the figure just as they entered the staircase. With all the strength she could amass, she took hold of their jacket and whipped them around, her weapon held high. She looked into the soft eyes of Saverio Fiore.

At once, she released her grip and lowered the shard.

"Saverio?" Ana asked as though she needed his reassurance that it truly was him. "What are you doing here?"

The boy—she could not help but think of him as a boy, for he looked so young, particularly in the low light—glanced around. He shifted from one foot to the other.

Ana held up the envelope. "What is it?"

"You were not supposed to see it until morning," he said.

"I figured as much from you slipping it into my room and then running away." She glared at him. "Tell me."

He hesitated, then responded, "Read what it says on the back."

Ana turned the envelope. The paper had a silky touch to it. All other letters she had received throughout her life had looked official, yet this one appeared as though stolen from some period drama.

Cursive letters written in black ink unfurled on the back. *To Ana, from Hedwig.*

The envelope nearly dropped out of Ana's hands. She pressed her fingers into the letter, leaving crinkles in the paper, and stared at Saverio Fiore.

"What is this?" she repeated.

"The letter Hedwig wrote for you."

Ana felt herself trembling. "Why? Why is there a letter from Hedwig to me? And why did you have it?" She had a slew of other questions burning on her tongue.

Saverio kept shuffling and fidgeting. "Hedwig entrusted Palmira and me with this letter the night before she died, after the Christmas Eve Party. She told us to give it to you in case...in case something happened."

"Why are you giving it to me now?" Ana asked. Hedwig had died several days ago. "Why like this?" Earlier, she had scorned herself for prying, for seeking answers without caring about their feelings. Now, she paid no mind to the discomfort and anxiousness in his features.

"Palmira wanted to destroy the letter altogether. She thought it would only cause more trouble—she is most certainly right. But it was Hedwig's last request. I couldn't ignore it."

A dead woman's last wish had been to deliver a message to Ana. The gravity of it compressed her chest. Part of her wanted to shove it at him. Why should she read it? Hedwig had hated her. She wanted nothing to do with those words inside.

Her gaze fell to the letter, which was sealed shut with soft pink wax. She could distinguish the minuscule symbol of a ballerina, unbroken. "Do you know what the letter says?" Ana asked Saverio nonetheless.

The boy shook his head. "No. Nor do I want to know. You should open it when you're alone in your room. And then you should probably burn it."

In a different situation, Ana would have laughed at his advice, but he was utterly serious, and somehow, it didn't surprise her, though it did alarm her. Perhaps she ought to burn it before ever breaking that seal.

She regarded Saverio again. As much as she wanted to, she could not give the letter back. She doubted he would dare to touch it again; he looked as though he had narrowly escaped some beastly thing.

"Thank you," Ana whispered.

"If there is someone to thank, it is Hedwig. Good night." With that, he darted up the stairs.

Ana looked around. Low lights lined the staircase and the corridor, but parts of the hall remained dark. She clutched the letter to her chest beneath her pajama top. She wanted to hide it from whoever would roam the hotel at night.

With steps as silent and hasty as she could manage, Ana returned to her room and locked the door behind her. She drew the curtains closed, checking for any gaps, before she sank down on her bed and stared at the envelope, wondering whether she truly wanted to know what it contained. *The worst that could happen is a papercut,* she thought, but she knew she was lying to herself.

Something creaked behind her, and she whipped around. For a second, her mind's eye supplied an image of Hedwig's pale, lifeless body. Ana blinked, then the apparition was gone.

I am alone. But she did not believe it, not fully. Not until she had knelt down and looked beneath her bed, opened every door of her closet, and looked through the keyhole to see if others circled her room at night.

I am alone, she told herself then, and still, part of her did not believe it.

With stiff fingers, she broke the seal. The world moved in slow motion as Ana pulled out the letter and unfolded it.

Dear Ana,

When you read this, I will be dead.

A wave of nausea flooded her. She had to look away and take a few steadying breaths before she could focus on the words again.

Dear Ana,

When you read this, I will be dead. I have accepted this fate of mine. It is one I ran from for years, which I now must face. While life has denied me much, I shall not cling to it like a fish to the hook. I did much wrong throughout my years, and I was a coward too many times, so I choose to be courageous now. You are in grave danger, Ana. I have tried to warn you, yet I understand my attempts were futile. As you surely noticed, nevertheless, the Hôtel de Neige is more than it seems. I wish I could tell you the truth about it all in this letter. I am already doomed, so it would not worsen my fate. However, I fear someone else may get their hands on it, and then my words would be your ruin.

My advice is to flee from this hotel as soon as you can. I understand if you first wish to uncover the secrets it holds.

All the answers you seek are hidden in Erica de Winter's suite. It is a dangerous endeavor, but a necessary one. I believe you are courageous, Ana, far more than I was for most of my days. If you want to find out the truth, you must go.

The only one with a key to Erica's suite, besides her, is Dimitri Morozov. I saw the way he looks at you, and I believe you can figure out a way to get to his key.

I am deeply sorry to leave you with little more than a mysterious death and a cryptic letter, which might never even reach you.

You knew me as an unkind, cold woman, and I will not deny those qualities, yet I hope my death will not be in vain, and I will come to be remembered for more than that. One day, someone may think of my actions as brave.

Warmest regards and best of luck,
Hedwig Sternberg

All the warmth was sucked out of Ana's body. She quivered like a small animal at the brink of death. She had received a letter from a dead woman—a woman who knew she would die, who called herself doomed. But it was no suicide note. Ana thought back to the other letter. Hedwig had never claimed she would kill herself, only that she would come to an end.

Ana drew her knees up to her chest, imitating a curled-up, fetal position. She could hear the letter spoken in Hedwig's crystal voice. *I will be dead. You are in grave danger, Ana.*

Overcome by nausea, Ana ran to the bathroom and threw up. The words beat down on her. She tried to make sense of them, to pull the thoughts out of her chaotic mind one by one, each hanging on by a brittle thread.

Hedwig had been murdered. Ana no longer doubted it, as much as she wished she could. Had she died to protect her? The idea nearly caused her to retch again. Was she responsible for the ballerina's death?

Along with it, another question, another terror arose—was she next?

CRESCENDO

$\mathcal{A}$na sat cross-legged on her bed and stared at her phone—not her cellphone, which was of no use as Hôtel de Neige remained cut off from the rest of the world. Instead, she regarded the elegant, old-fashioned telephone that was equipped in every room of the hotel.

With a deep breath, she steadied herself and dialed reception. For some while, nobody answered. Ana wasn't sure whether to be relieved or disappointed.

Then, a voice arose. "Reception at Hôtel de Neige, how may we help you?"

Ana bit back the groan, recognizing the posh accent of Mr. Rutherford. "Good morning," she said, striving to sound polite. "It's Ana Greene."

"I would hardly call this hour 'morning,'" Mr. Rutherford answered, not bothering to sound either happy or polite. "How may I help you, Ms. Greene?"

Ana was grateful he couldn't see the sour expression on her face. "I would like to be connected to Dimitri Morozov's suite."

Her request was met by silence. Ana feared he had hung up altogether. Then she heard a low sigh. "Ms. Greene, you must be aware that Mr. Morozov is the manager of this hotel. He will not want to be bothered by calls from the employees."

Ana said in her sweetest voice. "Mr. Rutherford, please, it is quite urgent. I'm sure Mr. Morozov won't mind. And if he does, I will take the blame."

"This will be the only exception," Mr. Rutherford said after some consideration.

"Of course, thank you very much," she responded, but by then, he had disconnected her. All the better for it.

It took a few moments before someone picked up. "Dimitri Morozov." His voice had a rough, raw edge to it as though he, too, had just awoken.

"Hey, Dimitri. It's Ana."

"Oh. Good morning, Angel." He sounded more awake now—and more confused. "What gives me the honor?"

Ana hesitated. "I wanted to take you up on your offer," she said. "You told me that if I ever wanted someone to talk to or just hang out with…" Only then did it occur to her that perhaps he hadn't meant it, the way people often said things when they felt sorry for others.

"I didn't think you'd accept that offer, to be honest," Dimitri responded after some pause. "I'm glad you called, though."

"When would be good for you?" she asked.

"I can always make time for you." Ana couldn't see his face, but she could picture his expression, the lopsided smile he wore so well. "I must ask, Angel, is this a date?"

Ana paused. What did she want it—need it—to be? "Would you like for it to be a date?" she asked, turning the question on him.

Dimitri sighed. "I know everything has been strange and horrible these last few days, but if you agree, then yes, I'd like for it to be a date."

A date with Dimitri Morozov. It was a terribly stupid idea. Even under different circumstances, it would be—even if the hotel was out of the picture altogether, even if they were two strangers meeting at the coffee shop or at the bar. Not that they would ever frequent the same places, were it not for Hôtel de Neige.

"Alright," Ana said. "Then it's a date. When and where do you—"

He interrupted her. "Don't you worry about that. I will take care of it and handle the details. See you tonight, Angel."

Tonight. Ana meant to protest, but she wagered it would be a lost cause. "Alright. See you tonight, Dimitri."

They hung up, and Ana let herself fall back into her pillows, burying her face in her hands. Throughout the conversation, Hedwig's words had echoed in Ana's mind—*I saw the way he looks at you, and I believe you can figure out a way to get to his keys.* Guilt stung within her chest. She owed Dimitri no loyalty, or so she tried to tell herself, although it was not quite true. He had cared for her and comforted her the night of Hedwig's death. For that alone, she owed him.

But if Dimitri knew more about the circumstances of Hedwig's death, Ana needed to know. She couldn't get someone caught in the crossfire if he himself held a smoking gun in his hand.

No matter how much she contemplated the dilemma, it was too late anyway. She would go on a date with Dimitri and find a way to steal his key to Erica's suite. Once she had her answers, she could smuggle it back, and he would never know of her betrayal.

Preparing for the date proved difficult as she had no sense of what to expect. Late in the afternoon, she received a note telling her to meet Dimitri in the Danish Pavilion, the most sophisticated and most expensive of the hotel's dining establishments, at 8 pm. The note advised her to wear something elegant.

Ana had hoped for a simple date in his suite, where nobody would see them together, and she could retrieve his keys without any witnesses. This made it more complicated, but if she wanted her plan to work, she had to play along.

A few hours after receiving the note, Ana stood before the mirror, clothed in a slip dress of shining black which somewhat resembled a negligee. Elegance was perhaps not the first attribute that came to mind, but she suspected Dimitri would appreciate it nonetheless. It fit Ana like a glove, perfectly hugging her newly-found curves, granted to her by the comforts and luxuries of the hotel. She wore a bold shade of red on her lips. She decided to straighten her curls so her hair hung down to her hips, a touch of gold against her dark dress.

As she was slipping into her heels, a knock sounded at the door. Had Dimitri come to pick her up? The note said they would meet at the Danish Pavilion.

Ana checked her reflection once more, then hurried to open the door. "Everett." All the confidence she had built up throughout the day vanished at the sight of the pianist. Her eyes scanned the corridor.

"You're dressed up," he said. "Where are you going?"

Ana gritted her teeth, scrambling to think of something to tell him. "I'm going on a date." It was not a promising start.

"A date? With whom?"

Ana saw her plan collapsing before it began.

When Everett noticed her hesitation, he granted her no privacy but instead prodded on. "Who are you going on a date with?" he repeated, more insistent.

Ana ground out the confession. "Dimitri Morozov."

Everett gaped at her. "You're going on a date with Dimitri Morozov? What the hell are you thinking?" His tone shifted from bewilderment to condemnation within the span of a few short words.

"Everett, I don't feel like justifying myself to you right now," Ana responded, annoyed by the judgment in his eyes. "I'm late."

"Late to your date with Dimitri Morozov." Everett spat out the name like poison.

"Yes." Ana lifted her chin and held his gaze while he stared at her. Part of her yearned to defend herself, and part of her yearned to defend Dimitri. She refrained from doing either.

"I know you haven't been at Hôtel de Neige for a long time, but even you should know this is a horrible idea," Everett hissed.

"Why?"

"*Why?* He's the manager of this goddamn hotel."

"I'm aware," Ana replied. "But that's not the reason you despise him, is it?"

Everett's jaw tensed. "You should just believe me that I have my reasons to dislike him."

"Then you should believe me that *I* have my reasons to like him," she shot back. Her patience hung on a thin thread, threatening to snap. "I will see you around," Ana said and slipped past him, which presented quite the challenge given the dangerous heels she was wearing. "Later, Everett."

Ana strutted off, feeling the weight of Everett's eyes on her.

TOY SOLDIER

She arrived at the Danish Pavilion fourteen minutes after the clock struck eight. Unlike the grand dining hall, the swank restaurant held only a few tables, many of which sat in secluded, dimly lit corners, which Ana appreciated. At the entrance, the hostess stopped her, regarding her with a sharp look.

"The Danish Pavilion is only for guests of the hotel," she said.

"I'm here to meet someone," Ana responded. The more she considered it, the more inappropriate it felt for her to invade such an exclusive place.

The hostess lifted a thin brow. "You're meeting with a hotel guest?"

"Not exactly." Ana scanned the restaurant, hoping to spot Dimitri, but there was no trace of him. Had he ditched her? A knot tied in her stomach. "I'm—"

"She's meeting me."

Both Ana and the hostess spun to face Dimitri, who strolled towards them. Gratitude rushed through her, swiftly replaced by a sensation tingling within her as she looked upon Dimitri. He wore a beautiful suit of the darkest shade of blue, matching his eyes. He studied Ana, and a smile twitched across his lips.

The hostess gawked at them. It took her a moment to gather

herself. "Mr. Morozov, I apologize. I did not know Ms. Greene was your date tonight," she said, forcing a smile. "Let me bring you to your table."

Dimitri offered Ana his arm, smiling as she took it. They followed the hostess to a small, rather concealed table in one of the restaurant's dark and intimate corners. Playing the perfect gentleman, Dimitri pulled up the chair for Ana before he himself got settled.

"Your server will be with you in just a moment," the hostess said, giving them one more confused look. Ana knew the gossip would spread like wildfire, but tried to push those concerns aside for the moment.

"You look beautiful, Angel," Dimitri said with a soft smile. "You always do, of course, but...that dress." His eyes glinted.

Had she left Dimitri Morozov speechless? "You look quite handsome yourself," Ana responded.

"As I always do." When Ana rolled her eyes, he only grinned. The moment hung suspended, and they gazed at each other in silence before he added, "To be honest, I was rather surprised when you called me today. Even now, it baffles me to be sitting here with you."

"Well, I'm the one who thought she got ditched when you left me waiting."

Dimitri chuckled. "Angel, darling, I was here ten minutes before eight and waited for you. When you didn't show up, I went to check on you. We must have missed each other."

Heat shot into Ana's face, staining her cheeks bright red. "Yes, certainly," she said, her voice sweet and thick as honey. "That's also what I'd say if I had been late."

Dimitri laughed and shook his head. "It's the truth. I would not dare to make you wait, Angel. Other people, yes, but never you."

Something about his tone rippled through Ana like electricity. Before she regained her ability to speak, a waiter arrived.

"Welcome to the Danish Pavilion," he said in a thick French accent. Ana had grown used to hearing many different accents at the hotel, but his was so prominent that she wondered whether it was genuine or if he donned it to sound more sophisticated.

The waiter handed them the menus and started to introduce the specials. All the while, he wore an expression similar to the hostess, a mixture of bewilderment and anticipation.

"Do you know what you would like to drink?" he then asked.

"Hôtel de Neige's best wine," Dimitri said. "Not one of the wines on the menu—I am fully aware we have better ones than that. Fetch me one saved for special occasions. Ask the chef, if you must."

The waiter gave a hasty nod. "Of course, Mr. Morozov. Would you like one glass?"

"We will have the bottle."

Ana opened her mouth to protest, but the waiter was gone before she could speak. She swallowed hard and leaned towards Dimitri. "Dimitri, I can't afford half a bottle of that wine," she said in a whisper. "Honestly, I can't afford half a bottle of most wines." She earned more at Hôtel de Neige, but there were still debts to be paid, and she had no intention of becoming wasteful.

Dimitri shrugged. "I can."

"I'd prefer to pay for myself."

"Angel, I don't want you drinking tap water while you're on a date with me. Please," he said, his voice a notch softer, "let me pay for you. You'd do me a favor if you allowed it."

Ana bit back a sigh. "Fine," she said, swallowing her pride and guilt. He treated the night like a true date, ready to spend a fortune on her. She cocked her head to the side. "So this is a special occasion?"

Dimitri smiled. "It most certainly is. I thought it would take me years to get a date with you, so I'm celebrating that we are here now."

The waiter reappeared with a bottle of red wine; when Dimitri approved, he filled their glasses. Before he could ask them what they would like to eat, Dimitri shooed him away again.

"To you, Angel," Dimitri said and lifted his glass.

Ana raised her brows. "To what do I owe the honor of being toasted?"

A smile played around his lips. "Perhaps to that dress of yours. Or maybe the lipstick."

So her tactic was working. She had to restrain herself so as not to let her self-satisfaction show. "To the dress and the lipstick then," she said. They clinked their glasses and drank the first sips of the delectable wine.

"There's something I would like to give you," Dimitri said then. He reached into the inner pocket of his jacket and produced a velvet box.

"What is that?" Ana asked. It looked like a jewelry box.

"I suppose there is but one way to find out." Dimitri winked and pushed it her way. When she hesitated, squinting at the box, he chuckled, adding, "It won't bite you. Just open it."

With gentle fingers, Ana reached out to touch the soft velvet. When she opened the box, a low gasp escaped her. On a pillow of black lay a delicate gold necklace. At its center sat a pendant: an emerald glowing in the warm light from candles on their table. The box nearly slipped from her hands, and she set it down quickly.

"Dimitri, what—"

He held up a hand to stop her. "Consider it a belated Christmas gift. I meant to give it to you during the Christmas ball, but the night ended differently than I expected." He cleared his throat. "Anyway, I know you mean to complain that this is far too expensive, and I will have none of it."

"It *is* far too expensive. I can't accept this."

Dimitri rolled his eyes.

"I'm serious," Ana said, pushing the box back to him.

"This didn't cost me anything, Angel. I handle many of the hotel's artifacts, and this is one of them."

She stared at him. "You gave me an artifact from the hotel's collection?"

"From my personal collection." Dimitri sighed.

Ana studied the necklace. She wanted to reach out and touch it; she wanted to place it around her neck. "Has…has Erica worn this?"

A humorless chuckle burst from Dimitri. "No, Erica would never wear this necklace. Why would you ask?"

Ana could not picture it either. The emerald and the shining gold would war with Erica's shades of snow and ice. "I feel like I have seen it before," she said, losing herself in the gemstone reflecting her narrowed eyes. The necklace looked like something she had seen before, in a timeless painting or some glittering period drama. Or closer still, close enough to touch.

"This particular necklace once belonged to a beautiful French socialite, Renée D'aureville," Dimitri said. "She stayed in the hotel a long time ago and left it behind. For decades, it sat on a shelf and gathered dust. I'd much prefer for you to have it—as would Renée, I am sure."

Ana gritted her teeth. She felt she had wounded him by refusing the present, but accepting it was impossible. "I'm sorry, but all my life, money has been sacred. I had to work hard to have anything at all. So all of this"—she gestured at the box and the wine and their surroundings—"is not something I'm used to."

"No, I'm sorry. I overdid it." He gave a temperate smile. "Perhaps I should let you organize the next date."

"Bold of you to assume there will be a second date," she replied with a small smile.

Dimitri chuckled, and as he did, Ana made yet another unwise decision. "Alright," she said. "I will wear the necklace—but only for tonight. I'm not keeping it."

Dimitri lit up upon her agreement, a wide grin spreading on his lips. He presented the box to her once more, and their hands grazed as Ana took it. As she picked up the necklace, Dimitri dashed to her side.

"Hold your hair up," he said and gently took the necklace from her.

Ana obeyed. Dimitri laid the necklace across her bare throat. In a mirror on the wall, she inspected her reflection. The shades of gold and emerald contrasted with her skin, but suited her blonde hair and her green eyes. It was as though the necklace had been created just for her.

As Dimitri clasped the necklace, his fingers touched her naked skin, and her chest fluttered. He stepped aside, and she let her hair descend again.

"You're stunning," he whispered.

Ana looked away, hoping to conceal the blush in her cheeks. He sat back down, and for a while, he said nothing at all.

Uneasiness grew as the silence stretched. It had been less complicated to use him when he had played the shameless flirt, a caricature of himself. But he showed her so much kindness and genuine emotion, and in turn, Ana dug into it with the hope of stealing from him. When had she become such a person? She knew the answer to that question instinctively—with each passing year, this part of her had grown. All her life, people had used and then discarded her, so why should she not do the same? She owed the world nothing. And even if she owed Dimitri something, it was not enough to outweigh her mission.

The waiter returned, and Ana let Dimitri order for both of them—salmon for her, veal for himself. "You will like it, I promise," he said once the waiter left.

"Do you often come here?" Ana asked.

"Occasionally. I usually eat in my suite unless I have company."

"Do you go out from time to time?"

Dimitri frowned at her. "Out of the hotel, you mean?" He shook his head. "Why would I? Everything I need is here."

"Doesn't it get boring after a while?"

Dimitri chuckled, though his gaze grew momentarily distant. Then the smile returned, and he looked at Ana. "Not with such interesting company."

Ana gave a slow nod. How could she suggest Hôtel de Neige could get boring? She had only lived there for a month, and already she had experienced more than her fair share of excitement. Determined not to think of Hedwig's colorless face again, she grabbed her glass of wine. "To interesting company."

If Dimitri noticed her distraction, he didn't let on. "To interesting company," he echoed.

Ana drank with greedy gulps, trying to ignore that she was swallowing bills of money.

"Easy there," Dimitri said and laughed. "If you keep on drinking like that, we'll have to get a second bottle."

Ana shrugged her shoulders. "I mean, if you're paying." She flashed him a smile.

Dimitri smirked and lifted his glass to gulp his wine.

Their growing intoxication worked wonders, melting away the awkwardness and hesitancy between them, together with the guilt and the doubts that plagued Ana.

"See those two over there?" she asked, pointing at a man and a woman who were at Erica's Christmas Eve ball.

"Oh, yes," Dimitri said. "They're staying in the honeymoon suite, though they're not actually married. Well, he is—but not to her."

Ana giggled and watched the two. The woman sat still as a statue, her face blank, while he talked animatedly, swinging his hands around wildly.

"Their bottle of wine is in serious danger," Dimitri remarked.

They both leaned forward and observed, holding their breath in anticipation, as the man continued to narrate his apparently thrilling tale. Then, in another sweeping gesture, he lurched his hand through the air, crashing into the wine bottle. The previously bored woman jerked, but her quick reflexes couldn't save the bottle from toppling to the floor. It shattered, spilling its blood-red contents.

Ana and Dimitri burst into laughter, far too boisterous for an establishment like the Danish Pavilion.

"Now there is wine on my floor," Dimitri said with a sigh of lament, though waiters hurried to clean up the mess. "And it's not even good wine." He wrinkled his nose.

Ana laughed. Some nearby guests threw them dirty glances.

"Someone's not so great at handling their alcohol," Dimitri said as he moved the bottle of wine away from her. Amusement glowed in his face—a face Ana could stare at for hours.

"I can handle my alcohol," Ana said, her words slurring, dotted with laughter—both his and her own. It used to be true. In New York, she had gotten drunk every weekend, if not more often. Though at Hôtel de Neige, despite all that had happened, she had remained mostly sober. "I haven't eaten all day," she added.

With perfect timing, their waiter returned, carrying their plates. The meals were elegantly plated, though small.

The moment the server departed, Ana turned to Dimitri. "Why are fancy meals always so tiny?"

"They're delicious," Dimitri replied, which explained nothing.

"I've never had anything this good," Ana said after they finished their meal. "Though I could eat three more plates, and I might still be hungry."

"Don't worry, there will be dessert." Ana raised her brows, making Dimitri laugh. "I mean actual dessert, Angel."

Ana stabbed her fork in the air towards him. "I hope you do," she said and regarded him with an admonishing look.

"I can't believe you choose to think the worst of me, Angel. It wounds me. I am a perfect gentleman. I will get you home at a reasonable hour and say goodbye with a mere kiss on the hand."

Ana crossed her arms. "And what do you consider a reasonable hour?"

"Ten o'clock tomorrow morning, after I have cooked you breakfast."

Ana pressed her lips together to hold back the smile. "You're lucky this wine is so good, otherwise I'd throw it in your face right now."

"That's why I chose it."

"You're exasperating."

"And you're breathtaking."

Her lips parted to reply, but nothing came out. Their gazes locked. He looked so elegant in his dark suit, so far removed from anybody else in the restaurant, in the entire hotel. His smile softened. A spark glinted in his deep blue irises, reflecting the low candlelight. His skin was smooth as marble, like a Roman sculpture—every bit perfection. And still, there was a heat that matched the fire flaring within Ana's chest.

"What are you thinking about?" Dimitri asked.

Ana blinked, realizing she had shamelessly stared at him. What was she doing? Her plan was to betray him, not to thirst for him.

"If you'll excuse me," she said and jumped up, painfully ramming her hip into the table. "I need to go to the bathroom."

Dimitri's forehead creased into a deep frown. "Are you alright?"

"Yes, of course."

Ana took off without knowing the way to the bathroom. She walked in the wrong direction twice before she found it. Once there, she headed to the closest mirror. Some of her mascara was smudged, and some of her lipstick had worn off, so she set about fixing them, praying it would distract her from the whirl of thoughts in her head.

She told herself to focus. It was not a real date, only a farce so she could get the key to Erica's suite. Her stomach contracted as she reminded herself of her plan. Would Dimitri ever forgive her if he found out? She couldn't let herself be distracted by such concerns. A woman had died—that mattered far more than this silly flirtation.

Ana took a deep breath. If not for her makeup, she would splash some cold water on her face. She did feel a bit more sober already, less affected both by the alcohol and by Dimitri.

She left the bathroom and returned to their table. Dimitri eyed her with some wariness. "Is everything alright?" he asked once more.

"Of course," Ana responded with her most convincing smile.

Dimitri looked doubtful. "I took the liberty of ordering us dessert while you were gone," he said.

"I'm full, to be honest." She was starving.

"You're full?" Skepticism was written on his face. "Earlier, you complained about the small portion sizes."

"It turns out they were more filling than expected."

Dimitri studied her, his eyes narrowed. "What's wrong, Angel?" He asked.

"Nothing," she responded, too fast, too high-pitched.

"Are you worried about what the other people at the hotel may think?"

Ana met his gaze, finding true concern there. The knot in her chest loosened. It made sense for him to assume that was her reason. He was right—she feared the consequences of their date. Everett judged her for it already, and soon, others would follow suit. It could alienate her from everyone she had come to know at Hôtel de Neige.

"Yes," Ana said. "I am."

Dimitri nodded. He took another sip of his wine. "Let's leave," he said.

Ana quickly finished her own glass, and they rose together. She meant to ask about paying the bill, but apparently, as she was with the hotel manager, it was not necessary.

By the doors, Dimitri came to a halt and regarded her, his mouth pulled into a thin smile. "I had a good time," he said.

"I didn't mean that I'm embarrassed or ashamed to be seen with you," Ana said. "It's only that—"

"A lot of people here don't particularly like me."

For the first time, she wondered what life at Hôtel de Neige was like for him. He said he never went out, yet in the hotel, he had only Erica for companionship since the staff members met him with hostility. It stung Ana as she realized that he might have hoped she would be the exception.

"I don't care what others think about you," Ana told him and gave a smile, this time genuine and soft.

Dimitri returned the smile, though it never reached his eyes.

"So," Ana said. "Where do we go next?"

RUINATION

At her sudden question, Dimitri stilled, the wavering smile steadying on his lips. "Are you sure?" he asked. "If you're not comfortable, we don't have to go anywhere else."

"I'm sure," she said, trying to convince herself as well as him. "Let's go somewhere quiet."

"What would you suggest?"

"I assume you have something to drink in your suite?"

Dimitri's eyes widened momentarily, and Ana chided herself for the content she felt upon seeing him in disbelief. "Do you think you should still drink?" he asked once he had gathered himself.

"I'm as good as sober." She was sober enough. "Besides, you said you were a gentleman, so I am sure you will take good care of me."

"Yes." His lips remained parted, and he gazed at Ana with a glow in his eyes. Ana told herself that any man taking his date home with him would wear the same expression. But then, none of the men or women she had been with in the past ever looked at her the way he did.

They headed to the elevators and were delivered to the highest floor, reserved for the most prestigious guests. Ana followed Dimitri to his suite.

He opened the door for her, and Ana entered, coming to a halt to look around. She didn't know what she had expected, but certainly not what lay before her. Like all the other parts of the hotel, its design was all white, silver, and pale blue, but dark wood furniture and colorful decorations filled the room with warmth. Modern and old blended together, antiques next to high-tech gadgets. Scattered through the entire room were books of various languages.

"I didn't think we'd head up here tonight, so I didn't tidy the place," Dimitri admitted, and Ana detected a touch of embarrassment in his tone.

"You mean the maids didn't tidy the place," she countered.

He shook his head. "I don't much like people in my personal space."

"Oh. Should we—"

"No, of course not." He smiled at her. "I don't mind having you here."

Once more, Ana wondered if these were well-choreographed pieces of flirtation or if he actually meant it. She didn't know which one she hoped for. It would be far easier to steal from him if he saw her as just another woman in his collection. Then again, it stung her to think that.

"Make yourself comfortable," Dimitri said while clearing books off the sofa. "I will be right back."

The moment he had left the room, Ana grasped her chance. She rushed over to his jacket. One quick grab in his pocket and she had the keychain in her hands. She felt a rush of triumph until she realized she was holding a single key—the one he used to unlock his suite.

Ana scoured the room with her eyes. It made sense for him not to carry Erica's key with him at all times if it guarded the secrets of the hotel. Was he hiding it somewhere in his suite? Perhaps Hedwig had been wrong, and he didn't possess it at all.

Before she could contemplate it, Ana heard footfalls. She jammed the key back into the pocket of his jacket and hurried to place herself on the couch.

"I assume you'd like something to drink," Dimitri said as he returned.

"Yes, please."

Dimitri headed to his kitchen and poured them two glasses while Ana sat on the couch, trying to formulate a new plan. The suggestion to go to his suite had served as a ruse to find the key, but that would prove more difficult if she had to comb through several rooms to locate it. She could hardly do that with him there. She considered conjuring an excuse to leave so she might try again another day, but she doubted she would ever have a better chance than now, slim as it might be. Besides, each moment that passed without her knowing the truth was precious time lost.

Dimitri joined her on the couch and handed her a glass of red wine. She dreaded the hangover she would suffer in the morning.

For a few moments, silence spread across the room. Eager to fill it, Ana spoke up. "Do you miss Russia?" she asked, nodding towards the Matryoshka doll beside the fireplace.

"Sometimes. But there's nothing for me to go back to anymore."

Ana thought of the story he had told her, of his father casting him out. Not even a lifetime could heal such a wound. "When did you last visit?" she asked.

"I don't know, honestly. Years ago." Dimitri turned to her. "You probably think I'm some whiny, rich asshole."

"Not whiny."

A smirk flickered across his lips.

"I'm sorry if I've been judgmental in the past," she said. "Just because you went through different things than I did doesn't mean you had it easy."

Dimitri laughed. "I suppose it makes us stronger."

"Perhaps. Sometimes I think I'd prefer to be weak, though."

"To weakness," he said.

"To weakness," Ana echoed, taking a sip of her wine.

Dimitri leaned toward her to tuck a wayward strand of her hair behind her ear. When his fingers brushed her cheek, a quivering breath escaped her. She could smell him when he was this close to her.

His scent was a blend of rich wine and cradling warmth—she had no other way of describing it. It was a pleasant scent.

"What are you thinking about, Angel?" he asked, his voice a whisper.

"Your scent." The words tumbled out of her mouth before she could think better of it.

Dimitri smiled. "I think about your scent, too—that flowery perfume that reminds me of spring."

Ana felt the blush coming into her cheeks and turned away.

"I also think about your eyes," Dimitri said. "And your hair. And your hands." He let his fingers run across her hand, sending chills over her body. "I think about your arms." His touch moved upwards, grazing her wrist and moving toward her shoulder. "I think about your neck." Carefully, he inched ahead, never letting go of her gaze. "And I think about your lips. I think about kissing them, if you'd allow it."

Ana sat still and stared at him. Thoughts of her scheme were growing distant in her mind. He had driven all good sense out of her. Slowly, she set down her glass on the coffee table. Each move was observed by his intense eyes, the ocean of his irises stormier than ever. If she let him kiss her, it might be her ruin. A wise woman would flee while she still could. But Ana had no desire for wisdom, only for him.

She opened her mouth to beckon him closer, but words failed her. She did the only thing she could do. She slung her arms around him and drew him into her kiss. Their collision sent waves of electricity through Ana's body. His strong arms pulled her into him, and they kissed without pause. Air was no more, only his sweet fragrance. She inhaled it.

Dimitri's lips wandered to her neck and collarbone. Flames rippled through her entire being as his mouth touched her bare skin.

Her greedy hands dug into his shirt until she had opened all those bothersome buttons. For a moment, she stared at his chiseled chest before planting her own wild kisses on his bare skin. He quaked beneath her caresses. She climbed on top of him, his hands moving toward her bottom beneath the fabric of her dress. She freed herself of the black silk and cast it aside.

Abruptly, Dimitri stopped. Ana retracted her own hands, although they yearned for the heat of his skin. He gazed up at her, his eyes wandering over her exposed body.

"You're beautiful." He looked at her the way nobody ever had before, and she no longer doubted it—this was no game he played with countless girls. His eyes had been created to see her body, his hands molded to touch her naked skin.

Ana stripped off her lace bra, and he kissed her breasts, his tongue swirling around her hardened nipples. The rest of the world fell aside; it was only Dimitri and her.

Together, with motions so hasty they turned clumsy, they tore off his pants and the rest of her clothes. Once more, Dimitri stared at her, motionless for a few moments. Then he jumped up, charging at Ana with a fervor. He backed her up to a wall, showering her with fierce kisses.

"You have no idea how long I've wanted to do this," he said, groaning the words into her ear. His hot breath burned on her neck. "You're driving me mad, Angel." The once-teasing pet name made her tremble.

Dimitri swept her into his arms effortlessly and carried her to the bedroom, throwing her onto the bed. Her entire body tensed in anticipation.

"Dimitri," she whispered.

"Angel, I forbid you to say my name until I prove myself worthy."

Dimitri's kisses traveled down her body and up her thighs. Sweet sensations thundered through her.

By the time Dimitri came to kiss her lips again, Ana was half lucid. She ran her hands across his body, longed to touch every part of him, to mark him as hers.

"Angel." He was panting. "If we do this now, there will be no going back for me. I must know if you truly want this—if you truly want me."

A wiser woman would have grasped this last chance to reverse their fates.

"I want you," Ana whispered, wrapping her arms around him.

Everything in the world faded away as they melted into each other. Her back arched beneath him as his fingers dug into her hair. Pleasure filled her so completely that there was room for nothing else. She surrendered herself to him, to the heat of his passion.

"Ruin me," she told him.

"With delight."

Dimitri lifted her and carried her to his desk. With one swooping gesture, he cleared everything off and sat her down atop it. Their eyes met, his filled with fire.

Her moans grew louder, but she no longer cared, not even if the entire hotel heard her.

"Angel." Her name was music on his lips. "Give yourself to me."

She let herself go, overcome with pleasure. "Dimitri!" His name broke from her, together with the explosion rolling through her body.

Dimitri groaned her name in turn as he finished. "Ana…"

Everything grew quiet. They were motionless, still wrapped in each other. Part of her wanted to remain like that, forever connected to him. She didn't know how much time had passed before he picked her up and carried her to the bed once again. This time, he lay her down gently before slipping in beside her.

Ana turned to her side to look at him.

"How are you feeling?" he asked.

A smile played around her lips. "I don't know. Only that I want to feel like this forever."

Dimitri laughed and wrapped his arm around her. She rested her head on his chest, listening to his rapidly beating heart. It was a song of its own.

He must never know the truth, Ana thought as she fell asleep. *He must never know I mean to betray him.*

SILVER KEY

When Ana opened her eyes, snow fell around her so thick that she could barely see. Ice crystals drifted down and landed on her face, piercing into her skin. Not ice—shards of glass. She stumbled to her feet, then realized where she had awoken. She was back in the snow-crested corridor from her first nightmare at Hôtel de Neige. This time, she knew it was a dream, but it felt so real. The cold bit into her skin, and she turned with stiff motions, like a figurine imprisoned in a music box.

The painting of the young woman hung down the hall, unveiled already. Someone had stuck a shard of glass into the woman. Her smile lost its vibrancy.

"Ana."

She whipped around, ice pulsing through her veins. She had known what she would see, but it did not lessen the blow. The corridor reeled around her. *Wake up. Wake up. Wake up.* The dream tightened its grip.

There, near enough to touch, stood Hedwig Sternberg. The ballerina was dressed in the indigo tutu she had worn the night of her death. The Hedwig in Ana's dream was alive. Frost covered her body, her skin an unnatural pale shade, her lips purplish. Any touch and she might burst into snow.

"Hedwig," Ana whispered, her voice threatening to break. "Can you tell me what happened to you?"

"You're in great danger, Ana."

Ana wanted to put distance between her and the ghastly woman, but behind her waited the portrait. She had no choice but to stay still and look into those empty eyes with irises pierced by ice crystals.

"You said so in your letter, but you never revealed why. Hedwig, can you not tell me the truth?"

"You know the truth already," Hedwig said.

Ana shook her head so hard it hurt. The pain shot through her. "Hedwig, please, I—"

A crack roared through the corridor. Ana spun around.

The portrait was gone. Erica de Winter towered in its stead. When her gaze met Ana's, her thin lips pulled into a twisted smile.

"Ana, run," Hedwig shouted.

Ana obeyed without hesitation. She burst past Hedwig and bolted through the hallway. Where to, she had no idea. As far away as possible.

Icy breath raked across her neck. Erica was chasing her, coming ever closer. Ana sprinted down a set of winding stairs and found herself in an unfamiliar corridor where she staggered ahead until she reached a door. Desperately, Ana pushed the handle down, but it refused to spring open. She hammered against the door as fog formed around her.

"Please. Please let me in." She dared not look back. She dared not look to see how much time she had left.

"You will need this."

Ana turned as a figure stepped out of the fog. Dimitri. In his hand, he held a silver key. She reached out, but he snatched it from her grasp.

"Dimitri, please," Ana whispered. How much longer until Erica caught up with her?

He shook his head. Instead of the key, he handed her a piece of jaded glass. "If you want the key, you must first get me out of the way."

Ana's body tensed up, and her hand tightened around the shard of glass so hard that it drew blood. Drops of crimson ran down her fingers, landing in the snow beneath her feet. "I can't."

Behind her, Ana heard the rustling of skirts. When she turned around, pale, thin fingers stretched towards her. Erica uttered words Ana couldn't understand. But she did not need to understand them to know they might be the last words ever spoken to her.

Run, she commanded her own body. *Run.* Her limbs were frozen in place. She could move nothing but her eyes, which grew wide as Erica charged at her.

Everything turned white.

Ana awoke in the serene darkness. Her rapid breaths calmed, as did the thumping of her heart. The dream passed, and she was safe again. It took her a few moments to realize she was in Dimitri's bed. She looked to her side, expecting to find him lying there, but she was alone. Frowning, she sat up. From the slit beneath the door, warm light crept in.

Ana spotted a black robe in his closet and wrapped herself in it before stepping out of the bedroom. The brightness of day met her, and she had to momentarily shut her eyes.

"Good morning, Angel."

Slowly, everything came back into focus, and Ana saw Dimitri standing a few feet from her near the stove.

"Someone's a bit sleepy," he said and grinned. "Or hungover?"

"No, all good," she said, surveying him. She raised her brows. "Are you—"

"Making pancakes?" Dimitri smiled. "Yes, I am. Had you slept a little longer, I would have brought them to you in bed."

"Who are you?"

Dimitri laughed and set the bowl of batter down to come to her side. Without warning, he wrapped her in his arms and pressed a passionate kiss to her lips. She reached up to cup his face with her hands. It was so easy to get lost in him.

When they parted again, he had that glint in his eyes once more. "Angel," he said, his voice raw. "Last night was incredible. And not just the sex, although…" He grinned. "I enjoyed spending time with you, talking to you."

"I very much enjoyed last night, too." The moment she said it, physical pain tore through her. What had she done? His presence filled her with warmth; he made her feel like a giddy teenager. Yet she meant to betray him.

She had used him—she was still using him. Even in this intimate moment as he regarded her with a glow in his eyes, she thought of the key to Erica's suite and the hotel's secrets. Could she still go on with her ruse after they spent the night together?

Dimitri beckoned her to take a seat. A few minutes later, he delivered the first pancakes, accompanied by maple syrup and an assortment of fresh berries. In the past, the only breakfast Ana had received after a hookup was a cup of black, bitter coffee.

"Thank you," she said and filled her plate. She had forgotten how hungry she was.

"You look good in my robe," Dimitri remarked, his gaze traveling her sparsely covered body. He wasn't wearing a shirt, only silken pajama pants.

A sudden shyness overcame her. "I couldn't find anything else. Should I change?"

"Only if you'd be wearing even less afterwards."

Ana rolled her eyes but failed to restrain her smile. It terrified her that she could get used to this. Soft, warm mornings with him by her side. Part of her desperately tried to forget her initial intentions.

"The pancakes are delicious," Ana said. She hadn't expected Dimitri to be a good cook.

"I can make them for you every morning." He said it with a smirk, but Ana knew it was more than a quip. "If you want," he added, more tentatively.

If only he knew how much she wanted it. Before she could think of how to respond, a knock sounded on the door.

Dimitri's eyes narrowed. He didn't move. Perhaps he meant to wait and see whether it was important enough to warrant another knock. When that came, he grumbled and rose.

"Sorry," he whispered to Ana.

Dimitri went to open the door, though by no more than a sliver, so whoever was bothering them wouldn't see Ana sitting there in nothing but his robe.

"Good day, Mr. Morozov." Ana winced when she recognized Mr. Rutherford's stern voice.

Dimitri did not attempt to conceal his annoyance. "How can I help you, Charles?"

"Ms. de Winter would like to speak to you."

Ana stiffened. Did Erica know she was with Dimitri? She had to know of their date—such news would reach her quickly.

"Tell her I'm busy," Dimitri responded, moving to shut the door, but Mr. Rutherford pushed his foot in between.

"Ms. de Winter said it was urgent."

"I don't care."

"Mr. Morozov, I would advise you to care. She expects you in her suite in ten minutes." With that, Mr. Rutherford retracted his foot, and Dimitri closed the door.

He returned to Ana, a dark look on his face. "I'm so sorry," he said. "It seems I have to go. Please, stay. You can take a shower here if you want. The water pressure is great." He gave her an apologetic smile.

Ana nodded and smiled, hoping to hide her disappointment—both from him and from herself. Dimitri headed back to his bedroom, and she considered getting dressed to leave, though she didn't have the energy yet. Instead, she set about cleaning the kitchen. A few minutes later, Dimitri returned from his room, dressed in one of his dapper suits.

"Do you ever wear, I don't know, sweatpants?" Ana asked.

Dimitri chuckled. "That is a question for the third date."

He swept to her side and kissed her. Ana's body went up in flames beneath his touch. She wished she could compel him to stay; she supposed there were ways to convince him, but she decided it was best not to invite Erica's anger further.

"If you grant me another date, of course," Dimitri said.

"I'll think about it," Ana responded with a small smile. It was the best answer she could muster. "But now, I think I need to let you go."

Dimitri gave her one last yearning kiss, then he left.

Ana decided to take him up on his offer of showering in his suite. It felt strange, but she was in desperate need of it and much preferred not to get caught walking through the hotel looking an utter mess.

Afterward, Ana gathered her clothes and put them back on in the random order she found them in. Part of her hoped Dimitri would return from his meeting with Erica before she left. She wondered what Erica wished to discuss with him, fearing it was the night they shared. What if it got her fired? Ana nearly laughed at the thought. Someone had died, and she was afraid of losing her job. Though with it, she would lose all she had—her home and her hopes. It would send her back to the streets, and she wasn't sure she had the willpower to fight her way through such a life again.

Ana released a deep sigh, sinking onto the sofa. Reality returned to her. She had set out on a mission given to her by a dead woman—a mission to protect her and to unveil the answers she longed for. Would she cast that pursuit aside for Dimitri? Dimitri, who worked for the woman who might well be the enemy, the reason for Hedwig's death, and for Ana's peril. All this time, she thought she was using him, but what if he had used her just the same? He was with Erica de Winter this very moment, perhaps sharing everything he had learned about her.

The way he had looked at Ana told a different story. His face had transformed upon seeing her laid bare before him, like winter thawing into spring. That had been true. Nor had Ana lied when they'd kissed, when their bodies had fallen into rhythm with one another. She wished she had; it would make it all so much simpler.

She felt him still, his presence echoing on her skin. Nevertheless, he was a man she barely knew, a man certainly keeping secrets from her. How could she trust him? She needed to think of herself first.

Ana rose and gazed around. His suite expanded before her, cluttered with all of Dimitri's keepsakes. It seemed impossible to find a small key there, and for a moment, the thought comforted her.

With slow steps, she headed to his bedroom first to check for a safe. If he had one, all was lost anyway. Yet she found no safe, neither in his bedroom nor in his study. His desk held some locked drawers, old-fashioned and easy enough to open, but they revealed no key, only notebooks and documents. Ana forced herself not to read through them. She raked through his bookshelves, which would make many a library jealous. They contained hundreds of first editions and rare copies, all meticulously maintained, but still no key. Bathroom and kitchen, long shots from the start, didn't prove fruitful either.

At last, Ana returned to the living room. Why had Hedwig not been more specific? She had known Dimitri possessed a key—could she not have figured out where he kept it?

With a long sigh, she dropped back into the plush cushions of the sofa. It was time for her to leave. Part of her had hoped all along to come out empty-handed, so maybe she should feel glad about it. She could cling to blissful ignorance—and to Dimitri.

When her eyes snapped to the Matryoshka doll standing next to the fireplace, Ana almost laughed. It was far too obvious. Nevertheless, new hope and dread grasped her. She grabbed the doll, opening it up as fast as she could, shedding each of its coats until only a minuscule one remained—too small to hold another doll inside, but big enough for a key.

Holding her breath, Ana shook the doll. Something clattered. She tore it open, and a little silver key fell into her lap. She let the doll drop aside and lifted the key. It was slim and elegant with an ornate handle, its aesthetic a perfect match to Erica de Winter. She bit her lip to suppress the squeak of victory.

The thrill of triumph passed quickly—she had to make a decision. Could she bring herself to take the key from Dimitri? Was this how she would repay his kindness? Was this the woman she wanted to be?

All her life, the world granted her little chance to be a good person. Fate forced her to be selfish first.

"I'm sorry, Dimitri," Ana whispered, pocketing the key.

FORTISSIMO

$\mathcal{A}$na despised the walk of shame. It grew far more dreadful as she trudged through Hôtel de Neige, where those who would see her were either the refined guests or her colleagues. It helped that she had showered and removed her smudged makeup, but people would nonetheless wonder why she was wearing a revealing dress and high heels at noon.

She made it to the staff corridor unseen. Relief washed through her heart as she fumbled to get her key out of her purse until the doorknob of a neighboring room turned.

Ana cursed and scrambled to grasp the key as quickly as her hands allowed. It slipped from her sweaty fingers. She dove to pick it up.

"Angie?"

With a muffled groan, Ana rose, her fist clenched tightly around the key. Bahar gawked at her with wide eyes. Everett was by her side, tensing as he faced Ana.

"Hey," Ana said, hugging herself as though it would do any good in the skimpy dress.

"What the hell are you wearing?" Bahar asked, her brows raised high.

Ana glanced at Everett. So he hadn't told Bahar about her date with Dimitri. Yet he had clearly figured out why she was still wearing her clothes from the previous night. He appeared nauseated.

"You look like you're doing the walk of shame," Bahar blabbered on before Ana could say anything. She cringed, and Bahar clasped a hand over her mouth. "Oh my God, you *are* doing the walk of shame."

"Bahar, I—" Ana began, although she had no idea what to say.

"Who did you hook up with?" Bahar asked and grinned. "Was it that Canadian girl? I heard someone saying she had a crush on you."

"It's not that big of a deal," Ana said.

"Come on, I won't judge you," Bahar protested. "We're in dire need of some fun news after what has happened."

"I don't think she has fun news," Everett said bitterly. Ana shot him a burning look.

Bahar's forehead creased into a frown. "What is that supposed to mean? You know who she hooked up with, and I don't? That's not fair."

"Yes, I know," Everett responded.

Bahar failed to pick up on his dry tone. She looked ready to hop up and down with excitement. "Someone please tell me right now, the suspense is killing me."

Upon this, Everett deigned to look at Ana, his features hardened. "It would be best if Ana told you herself."

By then, the key must have left a deep imprint in Ana's palm. "Fine," she said, her gaze fixated on Everett as she gave Bahar the answer she had begged for. "I hooked up with Dimitri Morozov."

Bahar's smile vanished. "You did *what*?"

"I thought you weren't going to judge me," Ana bit back. She didn't feel like curtailing her anger.

"Let's go, Bahar," Everett said. "This is a waste of time."

"But I don't understand," Bahar said. "Why would you do that?" She stared at Ana as though she had confessed to some horrific crime.

Ana crossed her arms. "I did it because I wanted to. I'm an adult and I don't need the blessing of others to go out and have sex." She faced Everett. "Especially not the blessing of hypocrites."

"Angie!" Bahar gaped at Ana in utter shock. "Will you calm down?"

"No, not right now." Ana looked at Everett. "You know what, let's discuss this in private." A dam had broken within her. "In my room. Now."

She unlocked the door and entered, not glancing over her shoulder to see whether he followed her. He was angry, too, and determined to defend his moral high ground. They left Bahar standing alone and bewildered in the corridor.

Once Everett was inside her room, Ana slammed the door shut behind him.

"I don't actually see a good reason to talk to you," he said.

"And, pray tell me, why?"

"You slept with Morozov," Everett accused, his entire face transfigured with anger and disgust. He no longer looked like the gentle pianist.

"And so what? Why do you hate him so much? Because he's a sellout to Erica de Winter? Why do you hate *her* so much? Will you tell me, or are you too scared to say it out loud?"

"I—" Everett seemed out of words already, but Ana was only getting started. She realized she had wanted to do this ever since her first night at Hôtel de Neige, since the first time they denied her the truth.

"Tell me, Everett, do you think I'm stupid? I'm fully aware there's something wrong with this place and the people here. Just as I am fully aware that Hedwig didn't fucking kill herself."

Everett took a step back.

Ana followed him.

"You don't know what you're talking about," he said.

"And you know so much more than you let on," she responded. "Yet you refuse to tell me, even when it may put me in danger. You're a coward, Everett. Hedwig was the only one in this place who had some courage."

Tears glistened in Everett's eyes. "And it killed her." The force in his voice faded away, leaving only a quiet softness.

"And what about me? Would you watch idly as it killed me, too?

Tell me, Everett. What happened to Hedwig? What happened to the hotel's last singer?"

"Ana, I—" All of a sudden, he fell silent. A few moments passed, then he spoke again: "Where did you get that necklace?"

Only then did Ana realize she was still wearing the necklace Dimitri had given to her. She hadn't taken it off—not when she had undressed, not when she had showered, not when she had left his suite. It felt so natural on her skin that she had all but forgotten it. Still, Everett noticing it fueled her anger.

"Are you kidding me?" she asked. "Do you want to distract me or something?"

Everett staggered back, away from her. "No." He stared into the emptiness with such intensity, she thought he glimpsed something hidden from her sight.

"What's wrong with you?" When she stepped closer, he flinched away.

Everett looked at her as though she were the headlights and he was the deer. "Oh my god," he whispered. "You..." He broke off.

Did he think she had stolen the necklace? "Dimitri lent me this," she told him, overcome by the sudden, unwelcome need to defend herself. Upon studying him, she realized something far greater than concern for a stolen necklace gripped him.

"It's impossible," he said, to himself rather than to her. "It's impossible."

"Are you alright?" Ana asked, approaching him slowly like a wounded wild animal.

Everett shook his head, then looked at her again, his intense eyes piercing through her. "Where is your bag?"

Ana was still processing the question when he burst from lethargy to action. He brushed past her and tore open her closet. He grabbed her duffel bag, nearly dropping it because of his trembling hands. "Pack your things."

"What?" Had he lost his mind? She tore the duffel bag away from him.

"Ana, I—" Everett broke off. Tears shone in his eyes.

"Snap out of it, Everett, and talk to me." Ana tossed the bag back into her closet. She felt too weak to hold onto anything. "Please, Everett, talk to me."

"I'm so sorry, Ana."

"Why? Why are you sorry?"

He shrank beneath her gaze. "Ana, you…you need to leave Hôtel de Neige. Now."

She took a step back from him. It couldn't be about the necklace, not like this. "What are you talking about?"

"I can't." His voice cracked. "I can't."

"So I am in danger. Please, Everett, tell me what you know."

When he managed to speak again, each word seemed to cause him physical pain. "Ana…you've been here before."

"What do you mean?"

Tears stood in his eyes—rare tears of fear. "You've been to Hôtel de Neige before."

The words sounded as though Ana were underwater, hearing them from beneath the surface. So distant, so unreal. "I don't understand," she said, shaking. "Do you mean I was here before the auditions?"

Something flashed through Everett's expression, and he looked around, nearly losing his balance as he whipped his head from side to side.

Ana saw she was losing him as terror overtook his features. "Everett, you need to tell me the truth."

But the pianist shook his head violently. "I've said too much already. You need to leave, Ana. You need to leave now."

The tremor in his voice shook through her. What was so frightful he couldn't speak of it, so terrible she had to abandon the hotel at once? She wanted to wring the truth from him, but he appeared fragile, as though one more word might break him.

"I should go," Everett said.

Ana considered stepping in his path and making him stay, forcing the answers out of him, but she relented and stepped aside. Everett fled the room.

The door clicked shut behind him, and she sank to the ground. She hugged her knees to her chest. She remembered the day she had first come to Hôtel de Neige and the day she moved in with vivid detail, the happiness that had set her aglow. She had found a place to call home, people to share her life with. Everett, Bahar, Mikkel, and Dimitri. She had wanted all that, and she wanted it still. Yet her entire life at Hôtel de Neige had been a beautiful lie.

Could what Everett had said be true? Had she been at the hotel before? She had no recollection of her life before social services scooped her up. Yet even if she had been to the hotel before, why did it need to be kept a secret? Something horrific must have happened back then, so drastic that it put her in danger still.

Everett had told her to leave, to flee. Maybe she should. Running away, after all, was what she did best. She would need to rebuild her life again, but it wouldn't be the first time. She could survive.

Still, all her life she had yearned for answers about her past. Without them, she felt she could never be truly rooted in the present, let alone face the future. If there was even the slimmest chance she could find those answers, she needed to take it; otherwise, she'd regret it for the rest of her days, limited as they might be with a murderer roaming through the hotel.

THE LAIR OF THE WITCH

After days of storms and blizzards, the snowfall ceased, and sunlight slipped through the clouds. Hôtel de Neige regained its connection to the outside world just in time for New Year's Eve. Beyond Ana's room, the corridors buzzed with activity as the guests prepared to leave the hotel. She wondered whether the police would arrive to investigate Hedwig's death, but she doubted it.

If Ana meant to leave, it was time for it. Amid the chaos, nobody would notice if she disappeared, not for hours at least. She glanced at the emerald necklace Dimitri had given her, which now sat on her nightstand; the shameful thought of selling it to build a new life had crossed her mind.

Yet next to the necklace lay the silver key, reminding Ana of all the hotel's secrets and tragedies—the strange dreams, the fate of the last singer, the death of the ballerina. Most of all, though, Everett's words haunted her—*you've been here before*. If Hôtel de Neige held answers to her lost, forgotten past, she could not run away without knowing first.

In the early evening, when the guests had left their suites and the bustle shifted to the lobby, Ana headed to the staircase. She didn't even know where to find Erica de Winter's chambers, though she had a strong suspicion.

Ana headed upstairs, but before she could reach the second floor, she caught movement in the corner of her eye. She spun around, expecting to see Erica there already. Instead, she spotted Mikkel peeking around a corner a few feet away from her.

"Mike? What are you doing here?" The boy looked at his shoes and shrugged his shoulders. "Are you following me?"

Mike took some cautious steps forward. "I'm sorry," he said. "Hey, Ana."

"Hey." A sigh escaped her, but she couldn't tell whether it sprang from annoyance or relief. She studied him. "You should really stop roaming around the hotel. Why don't you look for Bahar? I'm sure she would love to play with you."

"Bahar is busy," Mike replied. "I heard you and Everett argued. Why?"

Ana glanced at her watch, the seconds ticking by faster than usual. Although she had no hourglass to display how much time she had left, she knew it was limited. "Adults argue," she said. "Don't worry about it."

"Is it because Hedwig was murdered?"

Ana froze. "Mike, what makes you think Hedwig was murdered?" *Should a child so young even know what the word "murder" meant?*

Her question seemed to confuse him. Ana assumed he had picked up on the word without understanding its gravity.

"I thought everybody knew she was murdered. Why else would she be dead?"

Ana stared at him, her heart sinking. How could he know such things? And how did he dare speak them aloud when nobody else in the hotel would?

"Mike," she said, squatting down by his side.

"I miss her," Mike said.

"I know," Ana responded. She cupped his chin. "I will find out what happened to her, why she died."

The boy's eyes widened. "What do you mean?"

"I need to go now, Mike," Ana told him. Some of Everett's paranoia had rubbed off on her; she feared lingering out in the open for too long. "It would be best if you told no one about this conversation."

Mike nodded despite the glint of curiosity in his eyes. "It will be our secret." He gave her a small grin.

Ana left the boy and made her way up the stairs to the dreary corridor from her nightmares. She knew, without a doubt, that the lone door in the hallway belonged to Erica.

The moment she entered the empty hallway, chills spread across her skin. No snow fell from the ceiling, and no frost covered the walls, yet it was colder than the rest of the hotel. Ana glanced at the portrait, once more covered by the black veil. She knew it to be impossible, yet she believed she could see the woman's eyes through the fabric, watching her.

She still had no true plan. It would soon be dinnertime, and Ana wagered Erica would spend it away from her suite, which would grant her a couple of undisturbed hours. She positioned herself around the nearest corner, feeling rather ridiculous, like a child playing detective.

Almost an hour later, nothing had stirred. She started playing a game on her phone; had she known it would be so tedious, she would have brought along a book and a chair. While she should be nervous, she was rather glad for the boredom—it calmed her strained nerves.

Perhaps, she thought and chided herself for it, *I'll never get the chance to break into the suite. Perhaps it's a hopeless plan. If so, I could sneak the key back into Dimitri's room and tell myself I did all I could.*

Yet just as the treacherous idea crossed her mind, she heard footsteps. Around the corner, she spotted Mr. Rutherford making his way through the corridor. Ana watched with narrowed eyes as he knocked on the door. She inhaled sharply as Erica stepped into sight with Dimitri. He stood behind her, leaning casually against the doorframe.

"What is it, Charles?" Erica asked, one thin brow raised. "Have all the guests left at last?"

"All except one," he responded. "There is a woman, Dr. Martina Lopez, who demands to stay until the police arrive."

Erica looked unconcerned, her face rigid with boredom and annoyance. "Make her leave. We don't have much time left."

Ana's suspicion was confirmed—no police were coming to examine the mysterious circumstances of Hedwig's death. Still, she had to suppress an audible reaction. Part of her had clung to the hope that there was no conspiracy to unveil.

"I tried to send her away," Mr. Rutherford said. "She refuses to go. I believe it would be best if you spoke to her yourself."

Erica released a theatrical sigh, then gave a nod. "Fine, I shall meet with her." She glanced over her shoulder at Dimitri. "You will accompany me."

Dimitri wrinkled his nose but voiced no protest. With her heart in her throat, Ana watched as the three of them set out, at last leaving the suite. She hesitated for another minute as Dimitri's face echoed in her mind. What had prompted his visit to Erica's suite? She decided it didn't matter. She had a window of time, and she needed to use it.

Ana surveyed the corridor again to make sure she was alone, then she dashed toward the door. Her hands trembled as she retrieved the delicate silver key from her pocket. If she were discovered, she would be fired, though that prospect paled in light of what other fates she might meet.

Other doubts tugged on her. What if there was nothing sinister going on at all? What if Hedwig had killed herself, and the hotel hid nothing? What if she were losing her mind with strange suspicions that could rob her of her job and her newfound home?

She took a step back from the door, then another. How easy it would be to surrender, even though she was so close to the truth. It took all of her strength to approach the door again, to put the key in the keyhole. Turning it felt like pushing against a mountain. Then the door sprang open.

Ana stood in place, motionless, and stared into the suite.

What lay before her took Ana back to all her nightmares. Upon first glance, the suite looked to be made of ice and snow. White rugs lay scattered on the stone floor, glittering like fresh frost. Pale blue curtains framed the arched windows. Chandeliers hung from the ceiling, their crystals shining like falling snowflakes.

It was the most beautiful and eerie place she had ever laid eyes upon. She pulled her sweater tighter.

What startled her was how little furniture or décor Erica owned. Her suite mirrored a frozen tundra, an Arctic wasteland. It didn't seem like a home where anyone could truly live. It gave Ana hope—her search would be easier for it.

It took her no more than a few minutes to scour through the living area, then she moved on. She first entered a small water closet, which concealed nothing, then a large, luxurious bathroom. A giant bathtub stood by a stained glass window, which presented a stunning view of the hotel's surroundings. Much of the snow had melted already; soon it would all be gone. Ana felt some relief, and yet some melancholy, for it.

She began raking through the drawers and closets, which brimmed with beauty products, makeup, and perfumes, some of which reminded Ana of the antiques Dimitri gathered, for they were hardly what one would find in a modern store—at least not the stores Ana frequented.

In the end, Ana's guess that nobody would stash their secrets in the bathroom proved to be correct. She meant to step out again, so lost in thought that she almost didn't catch the soft sound of a door opening.

"Well, that was exhausting."

Ana clasped a hand over her mouth as she heard the honey-tinged voice and stumbled back into the bathroom, missing one of the cabinets by less than an inch. They were back. She heard Erica and Dimitri settle in the living area, mere feet away from her. The bathroom door lay open by a sliver, and a look in the wrong direction would reveal her.

Ana forced her tense body into motion and, in the lack of a better option, she clambered into the bathtub and pressed herself down into its cold curve.

"She is gone now and will not bother us anymore," Dimitri responded. His voice sent shivers through Ana. A short silence passed, then he added, "What happens once the snow has melted?"

"What do you mean, what happens? The same that always happens." Erica's tone was less soft, less staged when she spoke to him.

"There is discontent among the staff."

Erica sighed loud enough for Ana to hear it clearly as though the hotel's mistress stood right above her. "There is always discontent among the staff."

"I believe this is different. Hedwig—"

"I am sick of hearing her name all around me," Erica said while Ana perked up. "It's like the pitter-patter of the rain."

"So everything is to go on as before?"

"Of course. How else would it go on?" Although Ana couldn't see Erica, she imagined her expression, complete with that small, self-assured smile.

"What about Ana Greene?"

Ana sucked in a sharp breath as he spoke her name. She longed to leave her hideout and get closer, fearing to miss a single word.

A few excruciatingly slow moments passed until Erica replied, "Why are you asking, Dimitri?" Amusement danced through her words.

"You know why."

Ana heard Erica rise, her heels clicking against the marble floor. "To be honest, Dimitri, I don't know. What would you have me do about her?"

No response. Ana wished she could see his face.

Erica chuckled, a deep sound compared to her usual high-pitched, pearly laughter. "Is she to stay or to be sent off?" she asked. "I shall leave it up to you."

Ana's entire body clenched up. Were these the consequences of their night together? All the power in his hands, the power to throw her back out on the streets. The thought made her nauseated, but worst of all was his hesitation.

"Come on, Dimitri," Erica said, not concealing how she enjoyed his predicament. "Here is the opportunity to be selfless for once in your life. Do you care for the girl?"

Ana held her breath in anticipation of his response.

"I do," Dimitri finally said.

The two words washed through her, overtaking her with both warmth and regret. He cared for her—and she could not deny that she cared for him too. As much as she wished it was not true, she was falling in love with Dimitri Morozov.

"Shouldn't your decision be obvious then?" Erica asked.

"It's not so simple."

"Oh, but it is," Erica countered. "Just not for someone like you."

Ana pressed her hands against the cool surface of the bathtub to combat some of the heat rising within her. She was foolish to care so much about staying in this secretive, murderous hotel—and for caring so much about a man she had betrayed. It would be poetic justice if he exiled her.

Nothing happened for a few moments. It was as though Erica and Dimitri had disappeared altogether. Then he spoke. "She stays."

Ana reined in the sigh of relief while Erica's laughter rang through her suite, taking her aback.

"Of course," she said. "I will see it done. Shall we go to dinner now? Oh, don't look at me like that, Dimitri. I'm not judging you. You and I, we are alike. I appreciate that."

"I'm not like you." It sounded as though he forced out the response through gritted teeth.

"Are you not? What would the others in this hotel say to that? What will your darling *Angel* say in a few years to come?"

The pet name had a bitter touch, a wrongness to it, when Erica spoke it. Ana wanted Dimitri to tell her to take it out of her mouth. Yet he remained silent. In her mind's eye, Ana saw Erica's large, white silhouette towering over him.

When he raised his voice again, there was no more defiance. "Alright," he said. "Let us go to dinner."

It was so anti-climactic. Up until Ana heard the door closing, she still believed something would follow, but nothing did. The suite fell quiet again.

She remained crouched in the bathtub for several more minutes, then she gathered herself. Her limbs ached from keeping still and silent, and she had to stretch them before she could climb out of the tub.

If Erica and Dimitri were out for dinner, they should be gone for a while. She could waste no more time, take no more risks.

MEMORIES

Ana hurried into the next room and found Erica's bedchamber. Before her expanded yet another desolate space, containing little more than a bed and a wardrobe.

And a vast pianoforte which stood nearly as large as the bed itself.

She stopped in her tracks. Was Erica de Winter a musician? The thought of it startled Ana; she could not imagine the composed woman sinking into song.

Ana could have marveled at the beautiful, classic piano for a long time, but she forced herself to look away and set out to continue her search. She tore open the wardrobe, which nearly burst with all of Erica's glittering gowns in shades of white, blue, and silver. Yet in their midst hung one exception—a soft pink dress, its color faded. It was the same dress worn by the girl in the portrait behind the veil. Ana wondered why it was among Erica's private collection instead of the storage room with the other historical garments. She doubted Erica would ever show herself in such a color.

The wardrobe revealed nothing more. Ana meant to tackle the nightstand or the bookshelves when her eyes fell to the room's second door. She had planned to move from room to room in an orderly fashion, but it demanded her attention.

Forgetting all her intentions of being methodical and quick, she slowly approached the door. The handle was metallic, but somehow cold and warm at once, as though alternating in waves. She took a deep breath, then pushed it down.

The small room was clearly intended to be a walk-in closet. Instead of clothing, it contained a large, old-fashioned, dark wooden chest and a broken mirror. The pieces of it still hung within its frame, threatening to fall at even the most careful touch. A couple of shards were missing in the middle. *Why would anyone keep a broken mirror?*

Her reflection in the fractured mirror didn't look distorted. Rather, it showed her as she perceived herself—torn apart and in the painstaking process of piecing herself back together. She watched as her reflection shifted with each movement, caught by the shards.

The wooden chest drew her attention. Ana stepped towards it, afraid to touch it as though she feared it hosted some demon that would lash out the moment she opened it. She knelt and lifted the lid. It was old, though well-maintained.

Ana didn't know what to expect. Hôtel de Neige had enamored her. Finding answers could mean losing the new life she had built there. But something else terrified her even more, and she released the lid, letting it fall closed. All her life, she had yearned for answers about her past. She had so often dreamed of her family, of reuniting with them, of being welcomed home like the prodigal daughter. What if she learned that they were gone, that there was no one left to reunite with? Or—perhaps worse—what if she learned they had willingly abandoned her and didn't want her back?

Everything she'd hoped for was crammed into this one choice.

She opened the chest again. It was filled to the brim with letters, pictures, and journals. Ana blinked, surprised. She pulled out the first letter, white paper grown yellow over time. With dismay, Ana realized the letter wasn't written in English. Erica had come from Denmark, so the letter must be in her native Danish. Ana pulled out her phone, but it was disconnected from the internet again. And so she resorted to skimming the words, hoping to decipher at least some of them.

The letter was addressed to Christian Dahl. Ana understood nothing of the letter itself, so her eyes dropped to the signature.

Erica de Winter, December 21, 1844.

Ana narrowed her eyes and read the signature and date a few times over. It had to be a different Erica de Winter, one who lived over 150 years ago. Perhaps the Erica Ana knew was her descendant; it would make sense. The portrait in the hallway had to be of this woman. Ana scoured through the other letters, all exchanged between Erica and Christian, dated in the mid-1840s. Perhaps they had been in love.

After realizing they would grant her no answers, she carefully put the letters back, tucking them into the chest neatly—not merely for fear of discovery but rather because she wished to honor these keepsakes. She moved on and found a journal, bound in black leather. It was old and more worn than the letters.

Ana opened it gently and discovered neat, handwritten tables which appeared to be old records. The columns were not in English, but she could guess some words—name and date were among them, so she assumed it was a record of people, perhaps a guest book. The handwriting was the same as in the letters. Doubting it would be of any help, Ana was about to close the journal again when her gaze fell onto the first entry, and she saw a familiar name.

Charles Benedict Rutherford. November 1832. London, England.

Ana stared at the entry and read it again to make sure she was not confusing the dates.

She skipped to the next one. She didn't recognize the name, though it sounded vaguely familiar. A couple more followed, then one caught her attention.

Hedwig Sternberg. December 1939. München, Tyskland.

Hedwig. It was her name and her origin, but yet again, the date made no sense. December 1939, nearly a hundred years ago.

Ana started flipping through the pages, seeking an explanation. Instead, she found more familiar names.

Dmitriy Alexei Morozov. December, 1877. Sankt Petersborg, Rusland.

Everett Michael Shaw. February, 1925. New York City, USA.

Mikkel Kai Dahl. December, 1855. København, Danmark.
Palmira Romano. January, 1913. Venedig, Italien.
Saverio Fiore. January, 1913. Venedig, Italien.
Bahar Yilmaz. February, 2007. Innsbruck, Østrig.

Names upon names filled the lines, many of which Ana recognized from hearing them around the hotel and seeing them on her colleagues' name tags. The origins matched, yet the dates made no sense. They spread across eras, from the early 18th century to the 21st.

Ana's mind returned to the letters, to the woman with the same name as the hotel's mistress and almost the same face. Could it be? She choked out a sound of laughter. She must be going mad.

She knew there was something strange about the inhabitants of the hotel. Palmira and Saverio, who were married but looked like teenagers. Everett, always dressed in a suit, carrying an antiquated pocket watch with him. Hedwig, who had written in her goodbye letter that she had walked the world for too long, even though she still had the face of a young woman. Surely those were coincidences, odd details and habits which meant nothing.

Ana put aside the journal. Reaching into the chest again, she found a large bundle of photographs. She untied the string holding them together and studied the first picture. It showed Hôtel de Neige, faded and blurry, from more than a hundred years ago. Even then, it held an air of magnitude, towering over its surroundings. Ana narrowed her eyes. The world around the hotel looked different. The forest was farther from the building, which lay in the midst of lush gardens. She grabbed the next photograph, which seemed no younger, but the gardens were gone. The background appeared different, too; there was a lake in the distance.

Ana placed the two pictures side by side to figure out whether they showed different buildings, but they were identical to each other and to the Hôtel de Neige she knew. She sifted through the other photographs, laying them out next to one another. Some showed the hotel within pine forests, others in glittering cities, some had the wild ocean in the background, others nothing but ice and snow. The quality of the photos alternated: many were black and white, others sepia, and some clear and colorful. Ana flipped around a few of them and found captions.

Danmark, 1845. Japan, 1962. Schweiz, 1998. Rusland, 1877.

With trembling hands, Ana grabbed the journal again and flipped through its stiff pages. So many of the photographs had a matching entry.

It had to be a joke, some beautifully orchestrated lie to make Ana question her own sanity. Or was she truly going mad? She had spent so long chasing ghosts; perhaps she had lost her grip on reality.

Ana was about to slam the lid of the chest shut when something caught her eye, another photograph. Unlike the other ones, it was kept in a frame, thus standing out from the rest.

Reaching for it, Ana found it was, like many others, black-and-white. Five figures, their bodies rigid and their expressions somber, gazed at the camera.

The first of them Ana recognized was Erica de Winter—or her lookalike from the 19th century—who stood in the center of the picture. A shiver crawled upon Ana's spine, the same sensation she always experienced upon the hotel owner's presence.

Another woman stood to Erica's left. If Erica was winter, this woman was spring. Even in black and white, warmth radiated from her. She was beautiful, extraordinarily beautiful, yet her eyes looked unreal. They were empty, filled with a sadness as painful as electricity as it hit Ana. Something was so familiar about her. It took Ana a moment to spot it. The necklace. The woman wore the emerald necklace Dimitri had given to Ana. By instinct, she touched her collar, finding a chill on her bare skin.

Dimitri's words echoed in some faraway corner of her mind. *It once belonged to a beautiful French socialite, Renée D'aureville, who stayed in the hotel a long time ago and left it behind.* It had to be her. Ana traced her index finger across the woman's blank features. What had happened to her? What had caused her such anguish? Ana wished she could reach through the frame and speak to her, take her hand.

To Erica's right—Ana couldn't prevent the two women from

melting together in her mind, they were so identical in appearance and expression—stood a man. Ana sucked in a breath through her teeth. She had seen him before, she had touched him before, and she had spoken to him before. Ana blinked—she had to make sure it was him.

The ice statue who had danced with her in her dream.

He had asked whether she remembered him, but she still couldn't recall his name. *I'm sorry,* she thought by some aching instinct. *I should have remembered you.*

Who was he, that he appeared around every corner of the hotel? He had crept into her dreams, and still, she could not remember.

It was like a wall of ice had arisen in her mind. She hammered against it but could not break through. It was hopeless. How could she expect a chest of Erica's keepsakes to get her to the other side?

Ana's gaze drifted to the next figure and gasped. The photograph threatened to slip from her grasp.

Before the man stood a young boy, staring intensely at the lens with eyes Ana knew all too well. *Mikkel.* She clasped a palm over her mouth. Everything in the world stilled. As much as the central woman in the photograph resembled Erica de Winter, the boy resembled Mike, not a day younger than she knew him now.

And yet, Ana couldn't focus on him. Her attention shifted to the girl by his side. She looked to be the same age as Mikkel, with wide eyes, wild curls, and sharp features. And, much to her dismay, she knew that face.

It was as though looking into a mirror. Ana stared at the girl through her own tears. She had seen pictures of her younger self, taken after social services had gathered her up.

It was her face.

The picture dropped from her shaking hands, chipping a corner of the wooden frame.

Those were her eyes, her curls, her features.

It was her. Impossibly. Unmistakably.

And at last, Ana remembered.

HEART OF ICE

*H*er body writhed as the memories crashed down in waves and buried her beneath their force, driving the air out of her lungs. She jumped up and staggered away from the chest. Her hands stretched out in a desperate search for support, but found only emptiness. Just in time, she caught herself and kept from colliding with the broken mirror.

She leaned over, afraid she might throw up. Her heart hammered against her ribs.

She remembered. All her life, she hungered for her lost memories, but now they threatened to suffocate her. A lump filled her throat. She collapsed into the closest wall, surrendering herself fully to its hold.

On quivering legs, she inched towards the door, pulling herself along the wall to keep from crumbling. Her fingernails scratched across the beautiful tapestry with such vigor that they left marks. She didn't care. She didn't care that she was leaving behind evidence; she only wanted to escape.

She stumbled back into Erica's bedroom. Gazing at the bed, rage filled her, making her want to rip apart the white pillows. She imagined what it would look like, feathers drifting through the air like snow.

Fueled by violent anger, Ana found the strength to break into a run. It was a dragging, slow run, the kind one did in a dream. She made it out of the suite without falling apart and slammed the door shut behind her. She reached the elevators and pressed the button over and over like that would accelerate it. When the elevator didn't arrive within a few seconds, Ana turned to the staircase and she sprinted downwards. Again and again, her feet got tangled, and she dug her fingers into the railing to keep herself from falling.

Somehow, she made it to the ground floor without breaking a bone. Panting heavily, she rested for a moment before continuing on. She didn't know exactly what she meant to do, but she couldn't stay. People had died so she could be free.

Ana ran to the staff corridor and burst into her room. It was quiet and cold. She looked around, not bothering to turn on the light. The wind whipped against her window.

How she had fallen in love with this place, with the entire Hôtel de Neige, when she had first arrived…it was because she had been here before.

She had imagined the hotel as a home, its people as her family. What a cruel irony to realize it was the reason she had neither. Hatred and rage coursed through her body, and she feared it might rip her into pieces.

And grief. So much grief. Through the years, she had clung to hope, never allowing herself to surrender to it or to mourn what she believed could be recovered. Now, she mourned. She trembled beneath the weight of her grief. The long ago loss hit her as though it had happened mere moments ago.

Ana tore open her wardrobe and grabbed her old duffel bag, throwing clothes inside, whatever her shaking hands found first. She took hold of the silk pajamas she had received for Christmas, and another sting of pain pierced her chest. She cast them aside. In their stead, she grabbed the emerald necklace on her nightstand. It was not stealing—she was only taking back what rightfully belonged to her.

Once the duffel bag was full, she dressed in her warmest clothes and pulled on her boots. The weather outside was better, but the night would be freezing cold. The thought of it sent shivers through Ana's bones already. She had survived it before.

She left the room, quivering like she was already outside. Her clumsy feet carried her through the halls. The guests were gone, and the employees had retreated to their rooms. It was like she was alone in the vast hotel.

Hurrying to the lobby, Ana passed the dimly lit bar and nearly missed the silhouette sitting there, only spotting him when he rose.

Momentarily, a feeling of warmth washed through her. "Dimitri," she whispered, a touch of relief in her tone. Then she realized her mistake. He had never been the man she had thought him to be. He could not—would not—protect her from anything.

Dimitri stood before her, his eyes narrowed. He set aside the glass of whiskey in his hand. "What are you doing, Angel?" he asked. A hint of lightness still lay in his words. Ana didn't doubt it would wilt soon enough.

Ana glanced at her duffel bag. "What does it look like to you?"

Dimitri stepped closer when she backed away. His brows knitted together. "Honestly, I'm not sure," he responded.

"I'm leaving." So much anger boiled within her, she couldn't contain the truth—not towards him. She wanted this confrontation, in all its ugliness.

Dimitri's eyes widened. "You're leaving? Why?"

"Why?" Ana echoed, releasing a humorless laugh. She let the duffel bag drop to her side. She could only imagine what he was seeing—her reddened eyes, blotched face, and the unrestrained fury which had befallen her. "I want to leave while I still can."

"I don't understand what you're saying," Dimitri responded, though a glint in his eyes betrayed him. Ana believed it was dawning on him.

From her pocket, Ana pulled out the little silver key and tossed it to his feet. "I know the truth, Dimitri. You can stop the charade."

Dimitri stared at her, his face crestfallen. Despite everything, Ana enjoyed the moment of spite and satisfaction.

"Is that my key?" Dimitri made no effort to pick it up. "Where did you get that? Did you steal it from me?" He paused and paled. "Is that why—"

Ana interrupted him with cold laughter. "Do you really want to throw accusations at me, Dimitri? You have no right. I heard your conversation with Erica earlier. Do you remember? When she asked you whether I was to stay at the hotel."

"How? You—"

Ana only nodded at the key lying on the floor. "She gave you the choice, and you decided to condemn me to a life at Hôtel de Neige like I'm some toy to keep at your pleasure."

"Angel, stop." He lifted his hand like he meant to reach out to her, but he thought better of it. Ana would have slapped it away.

"Don't call me that," she snarled. Hot tears ran down her cheeks. "Erica was right. You're selfish. You're just like her. Worse, she may have let me go, but you wanted to keep me here, as miserable as all her other prisoners."

Ana thought of all those she had come to know—Everett, Bahar, Hedwig, Palmira, Saverio. It pained her to think of them, people who stumbled upon the hotel, who had let themselves be ensnared by its beauty until it was too late. Condemned to a life of eternal winter.

"I never meant to make you a prisoner," Dimitri said, his tone softening, though she could sense his irritation. "What I wanted was to be with you. We wouldn't have been miserable, not together."

"What gave you the right to make that decision for me?" She was louder than she should be. If someone overheard, it could be her demise. "You only thought of yourself, never of what I might want."

"Do I need to remind you that you did want this? You made the decision to stay, remember? The night of the masquerade ball. It was your choice, and it was to be sealed, if not for Hedwig's interference."

The glass of wine. Ana finally understood. It was Hedwig's last desperate attempt to rescue her before a cursed kiss bound her to the hotel forever. That night was meant to seal Ana's fate; instead, it brought about Hedwig's. That last act of bravery had cost the ballerina her life.

Ana glared at Dimitri. "I wanted to stay, but under what pretenses?

Nobody would agree to remain here if they knew they'd never leave again, if they knew it meant an eternity spent traveling from winter to winter, never stepping beyond the grounds of the hotel again."

"I did."

His declaration took Ana aback. He had agreed to stay, knowing the truth. Yet after her initial astonishment, more anger followed. "This place and this woman you pledged your loyalty to—they killed Hedwig. How could I stay here? How could I stay with a man like *you?*"

Dimitri flinched but didn't back away. "Hedwig knew what she was doing. She knew the consequences."

"And what was she doing? She tried to warn me, to protect me from this cursed hotel."

"You were never in any danger, Ana. You could have walked out at any time, and nobody would have stopped you. And if you wish to leave right now, you may go." He took a step back into the semi-darkness near the bar, opening up the path for her to go.

"So everyone who is not yet bound to the hotel and wishes to leave gets to do so?"

"Of course."

"What about Christian Dahl, Renée D'aureville, and their children?" Speaking the names aloud sent another wave of nausea and agony through her.

Dimitri's lips parted. "How do you know about them?"

Ana should walk away and leave the Hôtel de Neige for good. If he knew the truth, her chance might be gone. But she needed to say it out loud; she needed that part of her life to exist beyond her memories.

"Don't you recognize me, Dimitri?" She asked. "I believe Hedwig realized who I was the very first day, when I auditioned. That's why she never wanted me here. She knew how dangerous it would be for Christian Dahl's daughter."

Dimitri froze, turning still as a statue, yet breathing hard as though he had a battle behind him. "Christian Dahl's daughter? What are you saying, Ana?"

"I don't know how much time has passed for you, for this place, but for me, it's been fifteen years. Fifteen years since my family went to stay at Hôtel de Neige at Erica de Winter's invitation. Fifteen years since she killed my parents." She shook with the force of her own voice.

"Ana, that's impossible."

"Is it? What about the girl, the daughter, who ran out into the snowstorm? Did no one wonder what became of her?"

Her eyes met Dimitri's, though he tried to look away. "We thought she was dead," he whispered, trembling. "We thought nobody could survive such a blizzard, let alone a small child."

"She survived. *I* survived."

All color had drained from his face. "It can't be you." Ana watched him as he considered it and realized it all fit together. The ages, the appearances, even the voices.

"Thank you for giving me back my mother's necklace, by the way," Ana said bitterly. "I will keep it."

"That's why Hedwig tried to protect you," Dimitri said, his voice shaking.

"And she died trying." All the death and destruction Ana had left in her wake. What would happen when she left Hôtel de Neige this time, what would be her legacy, her path of ruin? But she couldn't think of that. She needed to get herself to safety.

"Goodbye, Dimitri," Ana said, unable to contain the tinge of regret in her words. Their gazes locked one last time; she felt something within her shatter. His eyes shone and, for a moment, he looked as though he meant to say more. But nothing could crack the wall of ice between them.

Dimitri let her go, and Ana never glanced back. She had no idea whether he would run straight to Erica de Winter or not.

What would the hotel's mistress do when she knew the truth? Ana tried not to imagine it, not to liken it to the frightful memories of that night sixteen years ago—or rather, 171 years ago—which orphaned her.

Ana made it to the lobby. The chandelier filled it with light, though not a soul was there. She looked to the windows and out at the world beyond. All had fallen silent, and a clear night sky blanketed the world. No more snowflakes drifted through the air.

There were no porters now, so she pulled the doors open herself. A gush of cold wind met her, and she nearly staggered back. Freedom was so close, but she feared those would be the hardest steps of her life.

"Wait."

Ana almost ignored the shout, lost in her determination. With great pain, she recognized the voice and could not ignore it. She turned around.

Mikkel stood in the midst of the lobby beneath the glowing chandelier. Everett and Bahar were with him, staring at Ana with emotions ranging from blank shock to utter bewilderment.

"What are you doing?" Bahar asked, her hand on Mike's shoulder.

"I'm leaving." Ana's throat was sore and her voice raw from the encounter with Dimitri.

"You're leaving? Where are you going in the middle of the night on New Year's Eve? Do you even have a cab?"

"I know the truth," Ana said. All the raging emotions faded from her, replaced by exhaustion and surrender.

Bahar failed to grasp what Ana meant, but realization washed over Everett's features. When Bahar glanced at him, she saw it, too.

"Everett, what is she talking about?"

"I'm leaving before I meet the same fate as my parents," Ana responded in his stead.

Bahar gaped at her. "*Bitte was?*"

Ana caught the gist of her words. "I was once a guest of Hôtel de Neige, in the winter of 1855, before your time here." She glanced at Everett. He had been there; he had witnessed her tragedy. "My parents were Renée D'aureville and Christian Dahl—the hotel's last singer." A cruel lie to claim he had died of hypothermia, though it was not entirely untrue. "My name is Gerda Dahl."

"Oh my god," Bahar whispered, clasping a hand over her mouth. Her gaze jumped to the boy standing before her.

Ana looked at him, too. He hadn't moved since she'd begun speaking. Did he understand? Did he remember his sister? For all she knew, decades—if not centuries—had passed for him.

They were twins who had shared a womb and nearly every second of their first years together. It hurt her to think he might not remember her, even though she had forgotten him, too.

Their eyes met, and Ana felt pain she had never endured before. Her insides contracted, and each bone seemed to break into pieces, making her no more than a sorrowful heap of herself.

Mikkel blinked and cocked his head to the side. "You used to steal my dessert."

Ana pressed a hand to her mouth, muffling the cry that escaped her. He remembered her. Her brother remembered her.

Her brother, who had teased her that he was older, born a few minutes before her. Her brother, who had always wanted to play hide-and-seek and chose the same hiding place every time. Her brother, who had not aged a day in all the years he had spent as a prisoner, while she had grown up and lived a life apart from him.

Ana should fall to her knees and beg his forgiveness for abandoning him that night, for not holding on to his hand more tightly when she ran out into the storm. Except, she was trying to do just the same once again.

Ana broke the tense silence. "Dimitri knows," she said, a knot in her throat. "Which means Erica will likely find out soon."

Everett and Bahar understood immediately. Everett met Ana's gaze. The last time they had spoken was in the midst of an argument. Now, instead of anger, tears glinted in his dark eyes.

"You need to leave now," he said. He attempted to conceal it, but Ana sensed the rising panic in his voice.

She gave a slow nod. Leaving Hôtel de Neige. A month ago, she would have thought it impossible, no force could have moved her. Once more, Ana wished she had never stolen that silver key, never stepped into Erica's suite. Part of her regretted not becoming her victim—the bond to the hotel was a curse, but what awaited her beyond its borders? The loneliness she had endured was now tinged with the guilt of leaving behind the only people she had ever cared about.

Ana picked up her duffel bag; it felt heavier than before. A silent tear ran down her cheek as she looked at the others for the last time. She was sure their faces would be branded in her mind forever. She would not have the grace of forgetting once again.

"Angie," Bahar whispered, taking a step forward before growing still again.

How to say goodbye to them? Ana wished she had slipped into the night without them knowing, not until the next morning, not until Hôtel de Neige had traveled again and they were separated by time and place once more.

"I'm so sorry to leave you here," Ana said. "I wish you could—" She stopped, unable to speak the words aloud.

"Don't be," Everett responded. "We will be alright. We will take care of each other as we always have."

Would Erica hurt them? Would she take out her rage on them? The image of Hedwig on the cold floor rose once more before her mind's eye. She told herself it was not her responsibility to protect them, not even her own brother. She couldn't help them anyway—she would only come to share their fate.

Ana opened the doors, her muscles straining with the effort.

"We will remember you, Angie—Gerda," Bahar said. Her eyes glistened.

"I will remember you, too," Ana responded, holding back her tears. She turned her back on them, her makeshift family.

Outside, Ana hardly felt the cold as she stomped through the snow. It reminded her of the nightmares where Erica chased her through frozen corridors. She now realized those were not strange figments of imagination—they were distorted memories of that horrible night.

The world stretched out before her, illuminated only by the bright lights of the hotel behind her. The distance to the nearest road was not so far. Once she was there, perhaps she would have enough of a connection to call a taxi. It promised to be a far more pleasant escape than her last one.

Ana trudged ahead, each step a battle. Cold winds blew toward her. Their whistling filled the darkness with sound and drowned out all other noise. When a voice called out her name, Ana didn't hear it. A shiver ran through her bones.

Perhaps it was coincidence, or perhaps it was the bond between twins. Whatever the force, Ana felt compelled to look back to Hôtel de Neige and spotted the small figure coming her way.

Her heart stopped. "Mike, don't," she yelled.

Her brother came to a stop, and for a moment Ana thought no harm had been done.

Then he collapsed in the snow.

ALL IS LOST

When Ana screamed, it held such force that it split the night like lightning and thunder. Frost and fire shot through her at the same time, together with adrenaline. She let her duffel bag fall aside and broke into a sprint. All she could do was look at the crumpled body of her twin brother until she finally reached him.

Ana dropped to her knees by his side, her hands stretching out. The moment she touched him, it transported her back to the night of Hedwig's death. The boy was nearly as cold as the snow itself. She picked him up, startled by the ease of it. Her older brother was light as a feather in her arms.

Ana ran back to the hotel. Mikkel had made it no more than a few feet before the curse descended upon him. Everett and Bahar held the doors open, and Ana stormed inside. She carried her brother to the nearest sofa, where she lay him down.

"He just bolted… I couldn't—" Bahar broke off. She shook like branches in a storm. Tears of black mascara stained her reddened cheeks.

Ana sank down, and Everett joined her. Mike's face had grown white and purple and blue, ice hanging in his dark lashes. So this was the brutal fate that met those who attempted to flee the hotel.

"He's still breathing," Everett whispered, and Ana noticed the painfully slow heaving and falling of her brother's chest. Could the curse be reversed and prevented from unleashing its full might? Mike had broken the cardinal rule of the hotel. Which step had been too far, which moment out in the cold too long? If Ana had acted faster, could she have saved him?

"We need to get him out of his clothes and into something warm," Everett said. "Let's take him away from here."

He picked up Mike gently, and the child looked even smaller in his arms. The boy seemed to be slowly diminishing.

"We will take care of him, Ana," Everett then said, and the look he gave her pulled Ana back into her body.

She ignored the pianist; all her attention remained fixated on her brother. "What do you mean?" she asked.

"You need to go, Ana. Erica may appear at any moment. We cannot…not again."

He was right, Ana had to leave. Each minute at the hotel put her life in peril. It was a miracle Erica had not shown up and devoured her.

Ana's gaze traveled to her brother. Was there anything she could do for the boy? They knew him far better than she did. They were his family far more than she was. It broke her heart into a million sharp pieces.

She rose slowly, her legs trembling beneath her. It all came down to this. All her memories passed by in her mind's eye, all that she had lost. She knew she couldn't survive another lifetime of longing and regret and guilt.

"I'm not leaving," she said, overcome by a sudden calm.

The others stilled. "Angie, you can't—" Bahar began, but her voice failed her once again. Their eyes met, and after a moment, she gave a nod. She understood why Ana could no longer run, not when her brother lay dying.

Everett shook his head. "Ana, you're throwing your life away."

"What life? I had nothing before I came to the hotel." She swallowed hard. "You are my family. All of you, not just Mikkel." Saying his name aloud hurt her. She needed a few seconds to steady herself, then she took a deep breath and regarded them again. "Take care of him. I will confront Erica."

Ana didn't know whether she expected protests, but the silence seemed right. The looks on their faces spoke for themselves. All of a sudden, Bahar launched forward and wrapped Ana in her arms. She responded slowly, then returned the tight hug.

"Be careful," Bahar whispered.

Caution wouldn't save Ana. She wasn't sure whether anything or anyone could save her anymore. She knew this was the only choice, the only path to follow, even though it might be her last. It had to end, one way or the other.

Ana gazed at Everett and Bahar. "I love you," she said. The words felt strange, unfamiliar on her tongue. She wished she had said it sooner, had gotten more accustomed to it.

"We love you, too," Everett responded.

They stood suspended in time, the moment stretched out. "Goodbye," Ana said. "Take good care of him." She ruffled the boy's hair, and ice crystals fell like snow from his curls.

Ana tore herself away from them, continuing on. By the time she made it to the stairs, she had dried her tears. She could feel the cold no more, although that might change when she came face to face with Erica de Winter.

Time was meaningless until Ana reached the colorless corridor. It seemed fitting to end it there—perhaps she had seen the future in her dreams.

Ana made her way through the abandoned hallway, the hairs on her neck rising. She found herself glancing over her shoulder, fearing Erica was behind her already. Nobody was there, so she had to muster the courage to seek out the hotel's mistress herself.

The air around her cooled, seeming to grow colder the closer Ana got to Erica's suite. She came to a halt a few feet away from the door and leaned against the nearest wall. She had burst through it hours ago after learning the truth about her past. Now she might lose her future.

What was her plan? How would it end when Ana knocked and confronted the mistress of Hôtel de Neige? She didn't know the full extent of Erica's gifts, only that they could be lethal, sucking all the warmth from her victims, as she had done with Hedwig—and with Ana's parents.

Ana dared another step forward, her mind void of clear thoughts.

"What do you think you are doing, Ms. Greene?"

Ana whipped around, expecting to see Erica de Winter. Instead, she looked down the barrel of a gun.

Everything blurred before snapping back into focus, clearer than ever. Ana stared at the man before her, holding the weapon steady as he pointed it at her.

"Mr. Rutherford," she whispered.

"Ms. Greene," he responded, his tone even as ever. "Or should I say Ms. Dahl?"

He knew the truth.

Mr. Rutherford came closer, and Ana backed away from him, her heart hammering against her ribcage. The air grew thin.

"Does Erica know?" Ana asked, unsure why she chose this concern rather than the immediate one pointed at her.

He shook his head. "No, I do not believe she does. Not yet, that is to say. I overheard the lot of you down in the lobby. You ought to have left, Ms. Dahl, while you still had the chance." Ana wished she could read his tone—it was as robotic as his motions.

"Why are you doing this?" The words somehow came out steady even though Ana was shaking. One twitch of his index finger and that would be the end of it.

"I am an employee of Hôtel de Neige, and I intend to be loyal to it," he responded.

"Why would you be loyal to a place like this?"

Mr. Rutherford scowled at her the way an irritated teacher might. "Hôtel de Neige is my home."

It was a familiar sensation, but Ana could no longer relate to it.

Not after what happened to her brother. "This place is a prison." Ana prayed it was not an exceptionally stupid idea to argue with the man holding a gun.

His expression darkened. "Ms. Dahl, do not presume to make judgments about this hotel or my connection to it. You were foolish to stay."

Ana took a deep breath. If she angered him too much, he might shoot her. "I read your entry in Erica's records," she said. The tension grew in his jaw. "You were the first one. How long have you been here? One hundred years? Two hundred?"

"Approximately 144 years—over five hundred winters," he responded, his teeth grinding. "What is your point, Ms. Dahl?"

"What about the people from the life you had before you came to the hotel? You must have had a family, perhaps a wife and children."

His rigid features grew blank, utterly transforming him. Immediately, Ana understood the truth to her guesses. She honed in on them. "How old were your children when you were forced to leave them?"

"I know what you are intending, Ms. Dahl, and I advise you to stop it."

One mistake and he would pull the trigger. He still held the gun high, though she could see his hand trembling; she couldn't tell whether it was a good or bad sign. There was no time to dwell on it, though. It was not the moment for doubts. She decided it was the moment to be brave.

"Is it painful to remember them?" Ana asked, softening her tone. "You must miss them dearly? Did you ever get to see them again?"

Mr. Rutherford fell silent, but the distant look in his eyes served as answer enough: he had never reunited with his family. Perhaps he hoped for it still, yet with each passing year, he came to realize they were forever out of his reach.

"Why would you protect the place that took your family from you?" Ana asked.

The gun lowered the slightest bit. Mr. Rutherford faced her, his eyes glassy. "This place is my home," he said, echoing his earlier words. "Without it, I have nowhere and nobody."

His pain reverberated through Ana. She had suffered it for sixteen years, but he had endured it for more than a century. "You know I lost my family when I was a child," she said. He had been there that night, a silent bystander. "Ever since, I have never had a true home. It was torture. And then I came here, and for the first time in years, something felt like home. But it wasn't the place. It was the people." She looked him straight in the eyes. "I lost my family once. I refuse to lose them again."

Ana dared to take a step towards him. He turned his face aside, avoiding her intent gaze. "You can find a new home," Ana said. "One where you are free."

Mr. Rutherford looked at her, the gun dangling by his side. Ana's fear was suddenly overshadowed by compassion for the man who had lost as she had. When she reached for the pistol, he allowed her to take the weapon from his slack hand. It was heavier than she expected.

"Thank you," Ana said, setting out for Erica's suite.

Ana held her breath in those time-warped moments as she approached the door. The white wood eerily reminded her of the wall of ice in her nightmares. She no longer had the silver key to unlock it, so she was left with but one option.

She knocked.

THE SNOW QUEEN

$\mathcal{A}$na took a step back from the door and clutched the gun. It felt strange in her hand. Should she raise it and pull the trigger the moment Erica opened the door? Could it be so simple? Ana didn't know whether she had it in herself to kill someone—even someone like Erica de Winter. Nevertheless, she lifted the gun.

Footsteps sounded on the other side of the door. Ana stiffened, her hands sweaty despite the cold. The doorknob turned and she readied herself to confront Erica.

Instead, Ana was met by Dimitri Morozov.

If she had held onto the gun less firmly, it might have slipped from her grasp as she looked into his widened eyes. For a moment, they stared at each other, everything else around them forgotten.

"Ana," he whispered.

Ana almost lowered the gun at the sight of him but caught herself. "Where is Erica?"

Dimitri stood frozen like the hotel's curse had suddenly befallen him. Then, he breathed out the words. "What are you doing?"

"What should have been done a long time ago," Ana responded and glanced at the gun. "Is Erica here?"

"Ana, you cannot confront her. She will kill you."

She winced when he spoke her name. He had no more right to it—and even less so to the reaction of warmth which instinctively pulsed through her chest. "Why do you care?" she responded.

Dimitri looked at her for a moment, then reached out to touch her. Before his hand could meet her face, Ana raised the gun and placed the barrel against the sharp line of his jaw.

"Whatever you mean to do," she said, her voice nearly failing her, "I've had enough of it. You lied to me."

"I did," he responded. Were those genuine tears that glowed in his dark blue eyes? "I lied to you, and I condemned you. I was selfish. All I wanted was for you to stay here. To stay with me."

Ana struggled to keep the gun held high. "Stop it," she whispered.

"You can shoot me when I am done telling you the truth," he said. "With you, Angel, I felt something true and warm for the first time in decades. I thought, after such a long and empty life, I would not experience deep emotion again. So when I realized I was still capable of it, I desperately wanted to hold on to it. I understand you hate me for my decision to keep you here, but know it was not out of spite or boredom—it was out of love."

Ana's vision blurred with her own tears. She shook her head. "It's too late."

"I know," Dimitri responded and took a step closer, ignoring the gun. He touched her face. "I know it's too late for us. But, Angel, you *must* leave before it's too late for you."

"I won't leave this time," Ana said. "I can't run away again."

His jawbone tensed against the barrel. "If you stay, you will die."

"So be it." Before Dimitri could say another word, Ana pushed past him into the suite. "Erica," she shouted. "Erica de Winter, where are you?"

Dimitri gripped her by the arm but she pointed the gun at his head, forcing him to back away.

The clicking of heels echoed through the suite, and Ana held her breath.

Erica de Winter stepped into the room, a gush of cold wind preceding her.

"What is—" The lady of Hôtel de Neige began but then she broke off the moment she saw the scene unfolding before her.

Ana whipped around and aimed the gun at her heart. The shock in Erica's features felt like a triumph to Ana, albeit a small one.

Erica's eyes reduced to slits. "What is the meaning of this?" she asked, calmer than Ana expected her to be.

So Dimitri hadn't told Erica yet. Ana glanced at him and saw he had retreated. He stood hunched over, his lips lay parted.

Ana looked at Erica again. "I remember you now," she said, shaking. She put her other hand on the gun's grip to make sure it remained in place. "Don't you remember me?"

"Ana, don't—" Dimitri began but Erica silenced him with a sharp look.

In her eyes, Ana recognized a shine, an expression she had seen only a few times on the hotel's mistress, only during the concerts when the music had risen and reached its crescendo.

"Enlighten me, Ana," Erica said, her head cocked to the side. "Have we met before?"

Ana gave a rigid nod. "You have a picture of me among your keepsakes."

Cold anger flashed in Erica's features, though it paled compared to Ana's hot rage. "You broke into my room? How dare you." It seemed to upset her more than the gun pointed at her.

"You still don't know me," Ana responded and nearly laughed at the bitter irony. This woman had murdered her parents but didn't recognize her face—even more ironic, she had never recognized her voice.

"I'm losing my patience, Ana," Erica said and took a step closer.

"Gerda. It's Gerda Dahl."

Time came to a halt after she spoke. It was the moment before the wave hit land, before the bomb touched ground, before the guillotine met flesh. Ana had sealed her fate.

Slow, achingly slow, realization rippled over Erica's features. Her face contorted, the icy beauty cracked. A vein bulged on her forehead. "That's impossible."

Erica knew. Ana could tell from the crazed look in her eyes. "Now you remember me," Ana said while a tear rolled down her cheek. "And I remember what you did."

"Gerda Dahl is dead," Erica said.

Ana shook her head even though perhaps it was partly so. That girl she had once been was dead. The girl who spoke Danish and sang in French, who had crept into her parents' bed when nightmares plagued her, who had lived in a grand manor near the stormy ocean.

"Gerda Dahl ran out into the blizzard," Ana said and shivered as she recalled the iciness biting into her skin. "The hotel was in a forest by the mountains then. After it had left behind the winter in Copenhagen, it traveled to Montana, to December 2010." The town where Ana had been brought after a couple had found her on the side of the road had glowed with colorful Christmas lights.

For a moment, Erica de Winter didn't look like the formidable queen of Hôtel de Neige. She appeared old and young at once, her true face bared from shock. Her irises swam in the whites of her wide eyes.

"You are a monster," Ana whispered. She wanted to say more but feared her words would turn into sobs.

Erica had grown still as a statue. Dimitri had backed away into a corner of the suite, watching with an expression of horror as their showdown played out before him. Ana felt a momentary rush of sympathy for him.

"Look at me," she told Erica.

When the lady of Hôtel de Neige obeyed, the initial shock had vanished and something else had taken hold of her features. "*Lille Gerda*, little Gerda. What a strange surprise indeed," she hissed. Erica had used to call her that all the time, patting her cheeks with cold hands and pinching them with sharp nails. "So you are here to exact revenge for your parents."

Was she? Ana felt the curve of the trigger beneath her finger. How much strength would it take to pull it?

"No, I'm not," Ana said, even though Erica deserved all the bullets the gun held. "I want you to release the people of Hôtel de Neige." If she broke her curse on them, Mikkel would live, she was sure of it.

Erica broke into cold laughter, shrill like nails scratching ice. "You think you can march in here with a gun and that will be it? You are as naïve as your parents."

Erica took a step forward, and Ana almost backed away but forced herself to remain unyielding.

"What now, *lille Gerda?*" Erica asked. "I refuse to let them go. What will you do now?"

Ana gritted her teeth. She had never had the time to think her rage-fueled plan through. "Let them go," she said, "or I will pull the trigger."

A glint flared up in Erica's eyes. "You think you have it in you, *lille Gerda?*" Her smile widened, no longer looking natural.

The weapon was loaded. All Ana needed to do was press down her fingertip—it would take no more than a simple motion. Erica came closer. What would happen if she laid her cursed hands on Ana? Would she meet the same fate as Hedwig and Mikkel, as her parents?

"You look scared." Erica's blue eye seemed to be turning ever paler, like water freezing. "My god, I never realized how much you look like your father. That expression of terror, though—that is all your mother, dear Renée. Are you sure you don't want to run away again?"

Erica's white hand reached out, her fingers like the claws of a beast. In the corner of her eye, Ana saw Dimitri, frozen in terror. Erica's face twisted as she drew closer and the ugliness of decades shone through. Her nails were about to dig in.

Ana pulled the trigger.

The air in the suite split with deafening noise. Ana stared as Erica staggered back, surprised. Ana's eyes flew across her body, searching for the wound, for the spilling blood, red unfurling on white.

Yet there was none. A hole was torn into Erica's glittering dress, just over her hip. Yet there was no wound. The bullet had ricocheted and fallen to the ground between them. What remained looked like cracked ice.

Erica straightened and faced Ana with her coldest smile. "Did you truly think it would be so easy?"

Ana sucked in a sharp breath. Erica approached her again and this time, Ana didn't hesitate to shoot. She pressed the trigger, again and again. Like thunder, it trembled through Hôtel de Neige. Each time, Erica stumbled backwards and each time, she regained her balance and composure with ease.

Panic washed through Ana, tightening around her insides. She pulled the trigger once again, yet no roar sounded. The magazine was empty. It dropped to her side and Ana shuffled backwards, her limbs stiff.

Erica smiled with triumph. "I never believed in destiny until today," she said. "It must be destiny, though, for you to have found Hôtel de Neige again. Your voice," Erica mused on, "now I realize why it made me so nostalgic. It reminded me of Christian."

Ana tensed. "You have no right to speak my father's name."

"I have every right." Her voice roared through the suite.

With that, Erica took hold of Ana's face, clutching her hand around her chin and resting the long nail of her index finger against her temple. Erica pulled Ana closer until they were but a breath apart.

The light in the room changed. Despite the tight grip on her face, Ana managed to glance at the doors to the terrace. Outside, the quaint night had gone. Instead, bright white shone beyond while strong wind whipped ice against the window.

"Oh my god," Ana whispered.

Hôtel de Neige had traveled. For all Ana knew, they could have slipped a century or two into the past or the future, to some place across the world. Snow crystals landed on the glass.

"Your parents deserved what happened to them," Erica said and pulled Ana's gaze back to her. The vein on her forehead pulsed. "Your father deserved what happened to him and his whore of a wife."

Ana writhed in Erica's hold. She reached out for the other woman's face and went for the eyes. Erica snarled and pushed her away from her with a strength she hadn't anticipated. She lost her footing and toppled to the cold stone ground, staring up at Erica.

Dimitri had dared a step closer, but Erica gave him a look and he retreated again. Still, his gaze met Ana's and he opened his mouth. She could tell words lay on his tongue, ready to be spoken, but he never made a sound.

"Did your father ever tell you that we once loved each other?" Erica looked out into the distance and upon it, the world beyond altered again. For a moment, the lights of a city arose alongside the smoke from hundreds of chimneys. Ana squinted. Could it be Copenhagen?

Yet even more rapidly, the hotel departed again, headed to another winter. Great mountains arose and even inside, the air seemed to grow thinner.

"We were meant to be wed," Erica said, and Ana looked up at her.

When Ana had come to the hotel in the winter of 1855, her father had told them it was to visit an old friend of his. How they had known each other, she had never inquired.

"Christian Dahl first came to Hôtel de Neige a nobody, a poor boy with grand dreams," Erica continued. "Back then, I had just inherited the hotel from my late father, though others controlled it, as it would have been unseemly for a woman to do so.

"They took him on as one of the lesser performers, little more than a faint voice in the background. I, however, saw his true potential. My parents had avidly loved music and taught me a great deal about it. I was determined to pass the knowledge on. What I coaxed out of him was magnificent, angelic even. And as I taught him, we fell in love." She tilted her head to the side. "He never told you that, did he, *lille Gerda?*"

Could Ana believe a word of what Erica said? She didn't seem to be lying. The other woman had grown still and hardly looked at Ana anymore. For her, decades had passed since then, yet she had flinched when speaking of falling in love with Ana's father.

"Christian's voice filled the hotel with a new light, and he became the main act, a famous man in his own right. I told him I wanted us to be married, and he kissed me and promised we would be. Our engagement was to last through the winter and our wedding to be celebrated on the first day of spring. That was, until Renée D'aureville came to stay at the hotel." Bitterness seeped into Erica's tone.

"She came all the way from Paris, some claiming she was the most beautiful girl in all of France, and with a great fortune behind her. Your treacherous father took one look at that French whore and forgot all his loyalties and promises. When the first snowdrops sprouted from the earth, they left together." A single tear shone in her brown eye. That half of her face looked almost human.

"He left. He left, and I was alone again in this cold hotel which belonged to me in theory but not in truth, now void of beauty and music as the dust gathered on my piano." Ana had seen the grand pianoforte in Erica's bedroom. The last time its keys had sounded, her father had been there, singing. For a moment, the echoes of his music seemed to ring through the suite.

"I swore to take revenge on Christian and his bride. In the attic of the hotel, we had many artifacts, including a mirror my father had long ago purchased from a merchant, a mirror allegedly forged by the devil himself. In it, I saw myself, ugly and unloved, but with the power to punish those who had wronged me. As I shattered the mirror, I spoke my wish. Two of its shards pierced me: one in the eye—" she pointed at her pale blue eye, "—and one in the heart." The hand that had clutched Ana's face rested now on Erica's chest.

"I wished to be the hotel's true ruler, not those men who had taken over my legacy. I wished that the first snowdrops would never blossom, that winter would never end. And I wished that those who promised to stay at Hôtel de Neige would never be able to break their promises."

All warmth left the suite. Ice crawled over the ground, and frost covered the walls and windows. Ana scrambled to her feet. Her rapid breaths clouded the air. Could anything still save her? She doubted it, but she vowed to be courageous, now more than ever.

"All this because a man broke your heart?" Ana asked once she stood upright.

"Your father was a traitor," Erica responded. Snow began to fall in the room. The flakes covered the ground but melted on Ana's hot skin.

"Christian and Renée left Denmark and moved to France while I remained in the hotel. He became a renowned singer as I traveled from winter to winter." As she spoke, Erica looked outside. Despite the fog and ice blurring the glass of the windows, Ana could see the landscapes beyond the hotel changing more and more rapidly. Every few seconds, a new world, a new time blurred past.

"Years after our broken engagement, I wrote a letter to Christian. I invited him and his family to stay at Hôtel de Neige again, for old time's sake." Erica smiled a crooked smile and a heaviness befell Ana. This part, she remembered.

"Christian brought his wife and two little children." Erica grimaced. "You were such a happy family, always laughing and singing and dancing."

Ana wanted to cover her ears. The memories tore through her, sharp as daggers. She'd had a family, warm and loving, and then gone within a single night. She looked around. There had to be something that could hurt Erica, that could counter her cruel curse. Ana glanced again towards Dimitri as though he would give her the answers she needed.

Atop a cupboard, Ana spotted a silver candelabra. Her gaze darted around but she found no better option.

"I offered your father a position at Hôtel de Neige, and when he agreed to stay this time, he found he had no choice but to keep his promise."

Ana dared a step towards the cupboard. Erica was distracted by her own words. "Both he and his foolish wife came under my spell." Her mouth widened into a thin smile. "By the time they figured it out, it was too late."

Ana reached the cupboard and positioned herself in front of it. Behind her back, she began to remove the candles, laying bare the sharp stems beneath.

"Christian and Renée desperately tried to get their children out."

Erica's gaze landed on Ana again. "Though I am sure you remember that."

She wrapped her hand around the candelabra. It was cold to the touch, almost painfully so. "I remember," she responded.

Looking back, she realized her parents had known they'd stood no chance of escaping. They'd only wanted to get their children to safety, no matter the cost. Erica had killed a father and mother, but death was never what they had feared.

"They were such—" Erica began, but Ana wanted to hear nothing more from her.

"You know what?" Ana asked, breaking her off.

Erica stared at her with narrowed eyes, indignant that her speech had been interrupted. "What, *lille Gerda?*"

"I changed my mind," Ana said and gripped the candelabra more tightly. "I do want to exact revenge for my parents."

Ana bared the candelabra, holding it high like a spear as she charged at Erica. Like an echo in the distance, she heard shouting, but it faded, drowned out by the beating of her own heart. Erica's eyes widened and she raised her hands, but Ana was faster. She reached her, and with all the strength her body could amass, she drove the stems of the candelabra into the woman.

The moment the metal pierced through Erica's skin, Ana stumbled back and stared. She realized only then what she had done. Erica hadn't flinched even though one of the stems stuck in her cheek and another in her neck. Without looking away from Ana, she grabbed the candelabra, pulling it away and tossing it aside.

"Enough of this." As Erica shouted, the hotel shook. The ice beneath Ana's feet cracked, as did the walls.

Erica moved toward Ana slowly, like a beast knowing its prey had nowhere left to run. The air was sucked from her body. This was what Hedwig had seen before her demise, what her father and mother had seen in their final moments.

"You are a fool, like your parents," Erica said. "Do you have any last words, *lille Gerda?*"

Ana ground her teeth together so hard that pain shot through her face. "Fuck you."

When Erica set off the blizzard, Ana didn't run or cower. She decided to meet her death with courage.

She braced herself for the cold, but it never came.

A dull sound echoed through the suite. Moments passed before Ana understood what had happened. On the frozen ground before her lay a crumpled figure.

"Dimitri."

Ana fell to her knees by his side. He had curled up into a fetal position and Ana could hear the chattering of his teeth—he was still alive. She turned his face up gently. Within a matter of seconds, he had grown pale as fresh snow. His sapphire eyes gazed up at her.

"What have you done?" Ana whispered, holding him even though it stung the skin of her palms like needles.

"Angel," he responded, giving her a weak smile. He tried to reach up to touch her cheek, but his strength failed him.

EVER AFTER

Tears blurred her vision. She wanted to shake Dimitri for his foolishness. This was the man who stayed loyal to Erica for decades. He had been there the night of her parents' deaths, and she should hate him just as much as she hated Erica. "You idiot," she whispered. "You idiot. Why? Why did you do this?"

"Your mother wore just that expression when she held your dying father." Ana looked up. Erica towered over them, looking down with her lips curled. She shook her head. "I should have known not to trust him when he fell in love with you."

"Undo it," Ana said. First it was a whisper, then she strengthened her voice. "Undo it."

Erica laughed. "Why would I?"

"It's me you want," Ana responded. "Not him, not even my brother. Take your rage out on me. Don't let them suffer." In her arms, Dimitri shivered. How much longer did he have before the cold consumed him?

"Don't worry, you shall feel my rage," Erica said.

"Dimitri," she said again and met his glazed eyes.

"I'm sorry, Angel," he replied, the strength in his voice fading. Life was draining from his body.

"Don't be." Her tears dripped down and fell onto his face, onto his cheeks as though they were his. They mingled with the snowflakes drifting down from the ceiling.

"How poetic," Erica said. "The lovers shall die together. Again."

Ana met Erica's eyes again. "And when you have finished it, then what? It won't change anything. I will die here in the cold, but you're the one who must live with it for eternity." She clutched Dimitri's cold, weak hand.

Erica's lip curled and when it did, a thought struck Ana. "Erica," she said, although she feared speaking it aloud. "I want to propose a deal."

Erica cocked her head to the side as a moment of curiosity intercepted her rage. "What could you offer me, *lille Gerda?*"

"I offer you my life instead of my death."

"What is it you're suggesting?"

Ana's lower lip quivered as she spoke. "I am the legacy of Christian Dahl. I am his voice, I am his daughter, and I am your vengeance. If you kill me now, it's over. You don't want that."

Erica narrowed her eyes. "And what do you believe I want?"

"You want to torture me. You want to live out your pain and your anger every day for the rest of your existence." Ana swallowed hard before she braved the next words. "And I am prepared to offer you your ever after. Release all prisoners of Hôtel de Neige. In turn, I promise you my voice and my torture. Forever more."

In her arms, Ana felt Dimitri stir, but he no longer possessed the strength to speak or protest.

A moment passed, then a smile twitched across Erica's lips. "Do you understand what this entails, *lille Gerda?*"

"I understand perhaps only a fraction of what it entails. But I won't let the people I love die or remain prisoners."

"How honorable you are," Erica said and chuckled.

Ana looked at Dimitri again. She could still feel his shallow breaths, each one growing slower. She pressed a painful kiss on his temple. "I promise it will be alright," she said. "I promise spring waits beyond this winter."

"If you mean it, stand up," Erica demanded.

Ana gently lowered Dimitri's head from her lap to the floor and rose. Wobbly on the icy ground, she made her way to Erica until inches separated them.

"Do we have a deal?" Ana asked.

Erica smiled at her. "We have a deal."

The lady of the Hôtel de Neige leaned in, and Ana felt a cold she had not experienced since that fateful night in the blizzard. Still, she didn't back away nor did she close her eyes. She stared down her fate.

Erica's lips brushed against Ana's, just for the faintest of moments. She expected to feel some great and terrible sensation, but all that overcame her was a shiver. Then, Erica drew back again, still smiling.

"It is done."

Ana spun around and ran back to Dimitri. He still lay on the ground, motionless. A lump formed in her throat. "Please, wake up," she whispered. "Please, Dimitri, wake up."

Time stretched out as the tears rolled down Ana's face. It could not end like this, she had sacrificed herself so that he would live. She shook him but he didn't stir.

Ana whipped around to face Erica. "Why isn't he waking up?"

Erica gave a nonchalant shrug. "Perhaps it was too late for him, *lille Gerda.*"

Ana jumped to her feet. "It can't be. We had a deal. *Save* him."

"Yes, our deal was that I release the hotel's prisoners. Not that I bring back to life someone already dead when we sealed it. Such miracles are not within my power."

Ana charged at Erica, driven by a rage reborn and more forceful than ever before. Yet before she could reach the woman of ice and snow, something peculiar happened.

Erica's eyes widened and her body contorted. Ana gaped at her with utter bewilderment.

Then blood started flowing.

Upon Erica's unblemished white dress, crimson unfurled, springing from the spots where the bullets had hit and the stems had entered. Erica reached to her neck and abdomen and gaped at her fingers which came back dripping with blood. A choked gasp escaped her, then the lady of Hôtel de Neige collapsed.

Heat and nausea shot through Ana's body as Erica hit the frozen ground where she stained the ice red with her blood. She was fighting for air.

Ana refused to trust her own eyes. She inched ahead towards Erica's slumped figure. Just as Ana reached her, Erica's head turned and their faces came so close they almost touched once more.

"What is happening?" Erica whispered. Each of her breaths was accompanied by the low whimper of pain.

Ana scanned Erica's body. There were suddenly so many wounds, all those which had earlier shown no effect on the woman of ice now spilled blood.

"You're dying," Ana told her—and herself, for she couldn't quite fathom it yet. She expected her tone to drip with malice, but found it to be neutral, soft even.

"Dying," Erica echoed. "How is that possible?"

Ana looked at Erica de Winter, afraid and suddenly human, and she realized what she'd done. "We struck a deal that would release the prisoners of Hôtel de Neige," she said. "All of them. That includes you, Erica."

Erica groaned, feeling physical pain for the first time in over a hundred years. "I cannot be dying," she whispered.

A tear formed in her pale blue eye and rolled down her cheek. In it swam the tiniest shard of glass. With it gone, the iris returned to chestnut brown. Erica looked around. "I forgot what it was like to see," she whispered.

Ana should despise the hotel's mistress with every fiber of her being. She should feel glad of the excruciating pain Erica must be experiencing. Yet before her lay the snow queen, and she was just a woman on the brink of death. Warmth glowed in her glassy, chestnut brown eyes as she regarded Ana.

"I must uphold my end of the bargain now," Ana said, her words so small they almost faded away. "I promised you my song, and while you shall not have it for eternity, you shall hear it in your last moments."

At this, Erica de Winter smiled, and for the first time, her smile seemed genuine. "I'd like that very much."

Ana chose to sing a lullaby—the same one Hedwig had hummed for Mikkel, the same one Christian Dahl composed on a cloudless summer day long ago and devoted to his beloved children. For the first time, Ana truly paid attention to its words. It told of a meadow on a warm night, covered in soft grass and encircled by tall oak trees. It beckoned the listener to fall asleep embraced by red roses.

As Ana sang, Erica's gaze grew distant. On her lips rested a faint smile. Was she feeling the touch of summer at last after the long winter? When she finished the lullaby, the last breath departed from the lady of ice and snow. She stared down at her, still not utterly certain that it was truly over.

Then, a warm, croaking voice arose. "Angel."

Ana whipped around and saw as Dimitri sat up. His motions were slow, his expression tense, yet he wore a soft smile.

"Dimitri." All else faded away. "Dimitri." Could it be?

She jumped up and dashed towards him, nearly losing her balance on the frozen ground. She broke down, hot tears streaming down her cheeks as she pulled him to her. He was still cold, but the color was returning to his face.

Dimitri's hands dug into her hair and he held her close.

"What happened?" he asked once they parted again. She could tell that each word was a struggle. Ana glanced towards Erica's lifeless body, and he followed her gaze. "How is that possible?"

"It doesn't matter," Ana said. "It's over." She smiled at him. "You saved my life, Dimitri."

"And I believe you saved mine," he responded. A short silence prevailed, then he spoke again. His eyes shone like a night sky filled with millions of brilliant stars. "I love you, Angel."

If any coldness had still clung to her body, his words would have driven it out entirely. "I love you too, Dimitri."

When they kissed, it was a kiss like the first blossom after winter, the first ray of sunshine after a blizzard, the first day of a new life.

Yet they were torn from each other once more as a tremor shook through the hotel. Instinctively, Ana spun around to see if Erica had risen from the dead, but her body remained motionless.

A cracking sound rang through the suite. A great rift tore through the ice on the ground. The snowfall ceased, and the frost covering the room was melting at the edges. Drops of cold water ran down the walls.

Ana grabbed Dimitri's hand. "We need to go."

The ice subsided rapidly as the foundation of the hotel beneath crumbled. Tears snaked through the tapestry as more water spilled from them. The icy curse which had held the hotel together for decades loosened its grip.

Hôtel de Neige rattled as though a sudden earthquake had arrived. Furniture toppled and clattered onto the floor, breaking the remaining ice beneath. The soft dripping of water was turning into a river.

Holding each other, Ana and Dimitri got to their feet and tumbled out of the suite. The entire hotel churned around them. In the hallway, the artworks came crashing to the floor. The portrait of Erica fell as lights above them flickered violently.

Together, they made it to the stairs and sprinted down. On the second floor, two familiar faces joined them: Palmira and Saverio Fiore entered the staircase, clinging to one another. Their eyes widened when they spotted Ana and Dimitri.

"What is happening?" Palmira yelled out as they all kept on running.

"Erica is dead." There was no time for elaborations.

Ana had no chance to watch their reactions, though she heard sharp gasps among the thundering noise.

They reached the ground floor as the lobby filled up with people. Ana scanned the crowd. At the other end, she spotted Everett and Bahar. Ana looked for her brother in their arms but didn't see him.

She froze. It couldn't be—the curse was ending. He had to be alright. Where was he?

"Everett!" Ana called out.

His head whipped around, and he faced her. He reached down and scooped Mikkel into his arms. Relief flooded into her at the sight of her brother. He looked as weakened as Dimitri, but he was alive. Her twin brother was alive.

Before Ana could rejoice, another quake rippled through the hotel. "Get out," Ana yelled. "Everybody get out."

People looked at her; they huddled together like terrified birds in a flock.

"Angel," Dimitri said. "If there is even a chance that the curse is still intact, stepping outside could kill us."

Ana glanced around. She had no idea whether the hotel would stop or if it would crumble until the ceiling fell in on itself. Looking up, she saw the giant crystal chandelier swaying above their heads, threatening to crash down at any moment.

"Staying will likely kill us just the same." Somewhere, windows shattered and screams sounded.

Dimitri hesitated as he looked towards the doors. So much time had passed since he last left the grounds of the hotel. All that time, nothing but death had awaited him outside.

He took Ana's hand and squeezed it. "Alright, let's go."

"Dimitri, you don't—"

He understood what she so selfishly meant to say. "Someone has to go first. Might as well be me."

With that, he set out and pulled her along through the crowd. They made it to the doors. Darkness lay beyond, and Ana could see little of the scenery beyond the doors. Where were they? *When* were they?

Dimitri gazed at Ana, then drew her in for a passionate, albeit brief, kiss. Then, no longer faltering, they stepped out together. Ana held her breath as Dimitri walked ahead until he was several feet away from the hotel.

He looked around and then at himself, at his hands, checking whether they were turning blue. He stood straight, and Ana could feel his warmth. As he realized it too, Dimitri released the most beautiful sound in the world—he laughed with true, unbridled joy.

"I'm free," he roared. "I'm free."

He spun around and swept Ana into his arms, whirling her around. Her chest exploded with joy.

"We need to get the others," she said as he set her down again. There was no victory unless everyone made it out.

Dimitri sobered, though the smile still echoed on his lips. Together, they ran back to the collapsing hotel and burst through the doors.

"Get out," Ana screamed. "The curse is broken."

For a moment, nothing happened. Then everything erupted into motion all at once. People started running, pushing towards the exit. Ana scrambled aside to let them through while her eyes scoured the crowd.

"Mike," she called out as loud as her lungs allowed. At the end of the lobby, the marble staircase broke apart. Water splashed down the fractured steps. "Mike!"

Ana was ready to storm back inside, but Dimitri was faster. He pushed himself into the masses and disappeared like a boat swallowed whole by the waves. Ana meant to follow, but couldn't make it through the stream of refugees. All she could do was stare and hold her breath.

Then, among the blur of faces, he appeared again with Mikkel in his arms. Behind him, Everett and Bahar followed. They reached the doors where Ana reunited with them, and they fell into one another.

"I thought I'd lost you," Ana whispered, not sure whom she was speaking to, embracing them all at once.

She then looked back into the lobby to see whether all had made it out of the deathtrap.

By the reception, as on her first day at the Hôtel de Neige, stood Charles Rutherford, observing the chaos unfolding before him.

"Mr. Rutherford," Ana called out, and, by some miracle, he heard her and turned. She shouted and waved him towards them. Large pieces of stone rained down from the ceiling.

Yet he stayed still and gave Ana a small nod. A gasp escaped her as she realized his intentions. "No."

But there was no time for arguing. Dimitri grasped her by the arm and pulled her ahead to put distance between them and the disintegrating palace. She gave Mr. Rutherford one last look and hoped he would see his family again at last.

They ran ahead, along with the other people of the hotel, until they were far enough from it. Out of breath, they came to a halt and looked back. Hôtel de Neige glowed in all its beauty, even in those final moments. A strange sense of melancholy, coupled with a beautiful sense of hope, overcame her as she faced what had been her home not once but twice.

Silence fell around them, and Ana saw the tears glinting in the eyes of many around her. There were tears of joy and grief. Even if it had held them prisoners, they had known nothing but the hotel for so long.

Ana reached for Dimitri, and he drew her towards him and Mike, who was still in his arms. Everett and Bahar stepped closer, and together they watched Hôtel de Neige fall.

As it did, Ana noticed the snowdrops by their feet. She tapped Dimitri and nodded at them. "It's spring," she said.

A smile spread on his lips. "So it is," he responded.

Spring, a new life—where and when, it hardly mattered to her. For the first time in so many years, Ana didn't feel alone. She had lost her family once, yet she had found—built—one again. This time, she would not let them go.

Her fairytale had just begun.

ACKNOWLEDGMENTS

Publishing a book has been a dream of mine ever since I was a child, and there were so many wonderful people who helped and uplifted me on this journey. From readers who left kind words to other authors who inspired me, I could fill an entire book with the names of those I'm thankful for, but for the sake of time and page space, I will focus on those who were most important to Once Upon A Song's creation.

First of all, I would like to thank Quill & Crow and Cassandra for taking a chance on this story and giving it the perfect home. I will always remember sitting on my kitchen floor and staring at that life-changing e-mail.

A huge thank-you goes out to my editing team, Tiffany Putenis, Lisa Morris, and Cassandra L. Thompson. They took this story to the next level and helped me tease out its potential.

I also want to thank Alma Garcia, Quill & Crow's Marketing Director, for getting the word out there, as well as Fay Lane for creating the cover of my dreams and capturing the heart of the story.

A big milestone in my writing journey was the #WriteHive mentorship program, which made me feel like I could actually become an author. I want to thank Lauren T. Davila for being my mentor and for offering her advice and guidance. I'm also immensely grateful for my co-mentee, Kimberly Lynn Hanson, who celebrated every success with me. Being a debut author can be a scary experience, and so I need to thank my debut groups for keeping me sane and for all the support.

Lots of love and gratitude go out to my partner and first reader,

Simon, who pushed me to pursue this passion and who was with me during the highs and lows of this adventure.

Most of all, I want to thank my parents for always believing in me and supporting me. Thank you to my mom, Sylvia, for fostering my love for reading as well as my love for musicals, which were a huge inspiration for this story. Thank you to my dad, Rolf, for encouraging me to dream big and to never give up. Without you, this wouldn't have been possible.

ABOUT THE AUTHOR

Nadine Bells is a Gothic fantasy & horror author from Germany, currently living in Cyprus with her partner and their cats. She graduated from the University of Mannheim with a degree in English & American Studies and a minor in Business Administration. When she's not writing, she can be found snorkeling, gaming, or worshipping Aphrodite.

THANK YOU FOR READING

Thank you for reading *Once Upon A Song.* We deeply appreciate our readers, and are grateful for everyone who takes the time to leave us a review. If you're interested, please visit our website to find review links. Your reviews help small presses and indie authors thrive, and we appreciate your support.

Other Fantasy Titles by Quill & Crow

Her Dark Enchantments, Rosalyn Briar

Brides in the Dark, Jacob Steven Mohr

The Bone Key, Mary Rajotte